RICK PARTLOW

DROP TROOPER BOOK TWO

KINETIC STRIKE

www.aethonbooks.com

KINETIC STRIKE

©2020 RICK PARTLOW

Aethon Books
PO Box 121515
Fort Worth TX, 76108
www.aethonbooks.com

Print and eBook formatting, and cover design by Steve Beaulieu.

Published by Aethon Books LLC.

Aethon Books is not responsible for websites (or their content) that are not owned by the publisher.

WHAT'S NEXT IN THE SERIES?

CONTACT FRONT
KINETIC STRIKE
DANGER CLOSE
DIRECT FIRE

[1]

I was a Titan, my footsteps hammer-blows against the dirt trail, echoing off the hillside at my right shoulder and down through the twisted, gnarled trees on my left. Billows of dust rose at my passage, remnants of a dry season nearly gone with the advance of Inferno's orbital precession, and the afternoon glare of 82 Eridani sliced through the clouds in one last hurrah of brutal punishment, a reminder of who was in charge.

The star's wrath meant little to me, encased in two tons of BiPhase Carbide, wrapped in the cold embrace of the WF4100 Vigilante battlesuit. Chill air washed across my face and even the heat of a star too close for this world to truly be called hospitable couldn't penetrate my armor. I could just as well have been floating in the saltwater weightlessness of a full-immersion virtual reality tank, watching someone else's life play across the display inside the suit's helmet. Nothing stirred on the overgrown dirt road ahead, not as far as I could see, two full kilometers to the next curve. I could have been alone on this whole imagined world.

Lt. Ackley's voice in the headphones of my helmet reminded me I wasn't.

"Alvarez," she admonished, just a hint of dry humor in her tone to let me know she wasn't seriously angry. "You're a squad leader, let someone else run point."

Spoilsport.

"Aye, ma'am." I toggled to a private channel with a flick of my forefinger on the controls inside the suit's left glove. "Henckel," I transmitted to the man behind me in the extended file formation, "get your ass up front."

"Roger that, Sergeant," PFC Thomas Henckel said. He was trying to sound cool and unaffected, but he still retained the excitement of the unblooded, the thrill of battle, even a make-believe training battle, undiluted by the reality of the death and loss it represented.

Jesus, I sound old.

I wasn't even twenty-one yet, and sometimes I thought I had no right being an E-5 staff sergeant or a squad leader, but that's what happens when half the NCOs in the company get themselves killed in one giant cluster-fuck of a battle. I suppose the question wasn't whether I was prematurely old, but whether I had ever really been young.

Henckel passed by me with long, bounding strides, his Vigilante armor a mirror image of my own; broad-shouldered and barrel-chested, matte grey and faceless and three meters tall, a hunched-over giant burdened down with an angular, boxy back-pack. The backpack wasn't a hindrance to our armored infantry, though, it was what kept us going. Shielded isotope reactor, jump-jets, ammunition stores, it was all in there, everything that kept the Vigilante from being an obscenely expensive piece of lawn art.

"We're coming out into the open in another three klicks," I warned Henckel. "The objective is another two klicks after the road opens up. I know Fourth Platoon is supposed to be treating this like they don't know we're coming or what our target is, but let's get real."

"They'll be set up and waiting for us."

Henckel didn't seem at all upset about the prospect. And I suppose I wasn't, either. Fourth was full of themselves after taking the top score in the virtual reality pods two months running. We'd all been looking forward to showing them the differences between reality and a computer game.

And of course, the fact this would be our last training mission on Inferno made it all that much more significant.

"They will," I confirmed Henckel's assumption. "Or at least, I would be."

Something moved just off the road, and I nearly swiveled around with a gunfighter's instincts, ready to put a plasma charge—or, in this case, a harmless targeting laser—through it, before I saw the analysis from the suit's tactical computer. Biological, non-humanoid. Inferno had some nasty megafauna, most of it cold-blooded and scaly, nothing I'd want to encounter outside my suit.

"You think the lizards are scouting for Fourth Platoon, boss?" Henckel teased. I'd barely moved, but he'd noticed it, even on the very edge of his suit's visual display. I should have been surprised, but I wasn't. Henckel didn't miss anything.

"What I think," I told him, "is that the Skipper doesn't want us to act like we know they know we're coming because he wants to see how well we react to an unavoidable ambush. So, we can't count on Lt. Ackley letting us deviate from the route or change the travel formation."

"Which leaves just trying to shoot faster than the other guy." Now Henckel did sound disgruntled. It may have been practice war, but it was the only kind he'd had so far, and I knew he didn't like to lose. His stride changed ever so slightly, pounding his feet into the dirt with just a bit of extra force, the armor responding to his tension.

"Not quite," I said. I stared at the faded outline of the map overlay and it sharpened under my gaze, the lines brightening, the labels becoming clearer. The dirt road curved through the hills until it flattened out onto the river valley. Our target was a mock-up of a deflector dish on the other side of the river, in the lee of a notional fusion reactor that piped the river water in for cooling.

The easiest place for an ambush, the one where Fourth Platoon probably thought we'd be on the lookout, was just the other side of the river. They could take cover behind the pre-dug bunkers and hit us as we came down. I was confident they wouldn't set up there, though maybe they'd leave a couple decoys for our long-range sensors. They'd want to hit us just as the road widened, where they'd still have plenty of concealment.

If I was in charge of Fourth Platoon, I'd split my force to either side of the road and try to catch us in a crossfire while our attention was on the river. The plan wasn't without risk, but after months of going against Fourth, I had Lt. Costas, their platoon leader, pegged as a gambler. The ground on the right would be higher, with more cover among the rocks, and I figured he'd have three squads up there, the fourth in the low ground to the left in the copse of trees the map showed.

I highlighted the spot on the map with a piercing glance and a flick of my thumb, then cast it over to Henckel's suit via our line-of-sight comms.

"You seeing what I'm seeing?" I asked.

"You want me to go right or left?" he responded, and I grinned.

We were moving pretty fast and we only had a couple

minutes before we came off this hill. *Beg forgiveness or ask permission?*

"Scotty," I said, targeting Gunner Sergeant Scott Hayes with a private transmission, "do you trust me?"

Scotty didn't object to the nickname as long as there was no brass listening in, or at least he hadn't when he'd been squad leader and nothing seemed to have changed since he took over the platoon. We were still friends, despite the difference in rank.

"You're about to do something that's going to get us yelled at by Top, aren't you, Cam?" The words sounded ominous, but their tone was playful. Scotty was wary of Master Gunnery Sergeant Campbell, our Top, or company first sergeant, but he knew as well as I did, she never came down hard on troops showing initiative.

"Probably," I admitted. "You gonna let me do it anyway?"

"If it means kicking Fourth's ass, I am." He snorted derision. "I lost forty bucks to Gunny Surio on the last round of simulator pod scores."

I could see blue sky ahead, through the gap in the hills. We were almost there.

"Pick up the pace, Henckel," I told the point man. "Make 'em think we're just running in blind and eager, like a private on his first leave after Basic."

He put on a burst of speed, the legs of his suit swinging like pendulums, ripping up huge clods of dirt and collapsing craters into the desiccated dirt, and I followed, closing the gap between us. The blue icons on my helmet's Identification Friend-or-Foe display that represented the rest of the squad accordioned backward before they caught back up with us, then the rest of the platoon did the same.

"Alvarez," Lt. Ackley's mild, unflappable voice said into my ear, "you'd better know what the hell you're doing."

"Your lips to God's ears, ma'am."

She said nothing else, and I felt a warmth spreading in my chest at the realization that she had as much confidence in me as Scotty Hayes.

"Graciano, Linebarger," I told my team leaders, "we're going to break right and hit the jets on my signal. Suspected enemy ambush ahead. Charge right into them, get inside missile range and cut them off from mutual fire support. Got me?"

"Yes, Sergeant," came the antiphonal chorus from the two Lance Corporals. They were both older than me, but there was an unmistakable respect in the words, either for the Bronze Star I'd reluctantly accepted after Brigantia or the combat experience it represented.

The road was softening up, less clay, more mud, and I knew we were getting close to the river. I pushed the map overlay down and concentrated on the tactical display. Two hundred meters. Henckel and I would be vulnerable before then, but Fourth would want to wait until they had at least a couple squads of us out in the open before they hit. I drew a phase line in the dirt with my mind, intending to tell the point man to jump when he hit it.

Henckel's backpack jets ignited the second my mouth opened, the screaming whine of the turbines reaching even through the armor of my suit. Air was sucked into the isotope reactor and superheated, then expelled out through the bottom of the backpack jets in a wavering heat-mirage haze and a spray of baked dirt. Henckel launched like a missile straight into the hillside and I followed him before I'd even registered the flashing red of the alarms from the suit's sensors, warning me of the threat from both sides of the path.

Details emerged, probably realized in hindsight and filtered through my memories with a false sense of having perceived them in real time when in fact, they were microsecond-old ghosts of perception. I was acting on instinct before my brain knew what it was facing. Fourth Platoon's Vigilante battlesuits were identical to ours, but the tactical display identified them as Tahni High Guard armor, going so far as to alter the images coming over the helmet cameras to match the alien gear.

The appearance of the armor might be Tahni, but the tactics were standard Marine Drop-troop training. Costas had deployed his troops in a pair of half-circle arcs, one above the other as the hill sloped upwards, stadium seating for our firing squad. They opened up immediately, but even the targeting suite in the Vigilante's helmet hadn't expected the ballistic trajectory First squad descended right into the midst of them.

Targeting lasers weren't nearly as impressive as plasma guns, but their effect on this battle was just as disruptive. Not one of the opposing force had the time or the distance to deploy their backpack missile launchers, so this was all in beam range, a knife fight in a storage closet as Captain Covington liked to call it. I didn't give orders and heard none given to me, either because of the auditory exclusion of the adrenaline dump or perhaps because Ackley was smart enough to know my squad had its hands full.

The simulated grimacing golem of a Tahni High Guard battlesuit was only ten meters away when I slammed into the hillside, barely getting the Vigilante's legs beneath me. We fired simultaneously, but his was a hurried, panicked shot while mine was premeditated. He missed. I used his wreckage as cover, giving me the few seconds that the training program told my systems they needed to wait for the capacitors to recharge, then ducked around the paralyzed bulk of his armor and began shooting again.

One of them had been trying to hop off the hillside, probably on his own initiative because I didn't envision Lt. Costas sending his people out into a possible crossfire with his forces spread on both sides of the trail. I nailed him with the laser designator and felt an immediate surge of annoyance as the helmet's computer-enhanced training display insisted on showing a big, splashy plasma blast and the battlesuit tumbling backward to the ground, bathed in sunfire. In reality, the Vigilante just touched down safely and automatically before the systems totally froze up, and besides distracting me from the actual fight, all the computer-generated fireworks did was make things seem *less* realistic and more like the simulator pods.

The rest of the squad was swarming in around us, filling in the gaps, and I knew it was my job to keep track of them, but things were too tight and my sensors were overwhelmed by static discharge and thermal blooms. It was all I could do to keep my people behind me and the enemy in front of me and hope I didn't get shot in the back by accident. And either by dumb luck or by virtue of the training we'd been running through incessantly, I didn't.

I fired and moved, feet scraping metal over dry stone, bursts of jump-jets keeping me upright and moving forward, and the only one in my squad I could manage to keep track of was Henckel, because he was keeping even with me and only ten meters away. Jump-jets screamed and more and more of the enemy tried to escape the hill they'd picked for their trap, but laser designators disguised as plasma blasts picked them out of the air and I knew that meant the rest of the platoon had arrived to back us up.

One of Fourth Platoon's troopers was distracted enough by the mid-air explosions that he didn't notice me until I was bounding over the rock outcropping just in front of him, and by the time he did, I'd already shot him straight in the face. Unfortunately, that left me only a few steps away from the very last of the platoon formation, the oversized rifle shape of his plasma gun aimed right at my Vigilante's chest and my weapon's capacitor still needing three seconds to recharge before I could fire again.

A reflexive curse was forming on my lips, but before I could spit it out, Henckel slammed into the side of the Fourth Platoon trooper with the dull, metallic clunk of a sledgehammer pounding home a steel spike. The computer might have tried to dress the Fourth Platoon Vigilante up as a Tahni High Guard suit, but I knew who it was. Lt. Costas always stayed at the hindmost spot whenever his platoon was arrayed in a fixed position. I'd heard him arguing about it once with Lt. Ackley, insisting it was the best place to direct fire. I didn't like the guy. I got the impression he thought he was a future general, God's gift to the Marine Corps, so there was some satisfaction from seeing Henckel swing a backhand punch into Costas' chest, driving him back a step. He'd given me the time I needed for my capacitors to recharge and I took advantage of the opening to put Lt. Costas out of his misery. I knew it was impossible, but I could have sworn I heard the junior officer cursing from inside his armor.

"Index, index, index."

I let out a relieved breath. That was the signal for the end of the exercise, usually from the range master but in this case straight from our company commander, Captain Covington, known respectfully but affectionately as the Skipper.

The Tahni High Guard battlesuits changed back into Commonwealth Marine Corps Vigilantes, and the raging plasma fires and scorched metal battle damage disappeared as the simulated dead regained the use of their servomotors and byomer muscles. Lt. Costas still had a dent in the chest plastron of his suit and I couldn't keep down a snort of laughter.

"All right, Third and Fourth," Covington said, the hint of a sigh of annoyance in his tone, "police up your people and head to the collection point for our company AAR. And maybe while you're heading there, I'll think about whether or not I have to explain again why it's a good idea to treat every training exercise like you *don't* know where the enemy might be waiting for you or in what strength."

"Damn it, Alvarez," Lt. Ackley said, though the smile in her voice belied her words, "I just knew you were going to get me in trouble."

Fourth Platoon was filtering out from our ranks, sullen and silent, and I could almost see Henckel's grin as we stood and watched them go.

"Thanks for covering my back," I told him. "It would have been embarrassing to let Costas take me out."

"We'll be in the real shit soon enough, Sergeant," he said, waving the thought away with a casual motion of his suit's left hand. "I know you'd do the same for me, right?"

"Come on, Third Platoon," Ackley urged, still standing at the foot of the hill. "This is our last After-Action Review on this miserable swamp of a world. Let's get it over with and get to work packing our shit for the move." I saw a flicker of changing colors in the communications corner of my Heads-Up Display as she changed from the general net to the NCOs only. "Except for the lucky one who gets to go with me to the operational brief from Brigade Command, of course. I'm going but Scotty has to oversee the gear prep, so I guess I'll have to choose a squad leader to stand in for him. I don't know...maybe the one who pissed off the Skipper, Sergeant Alvarez?"

"Aye, ma'am," I said, trying to sound dutiful and obedient but cursing inwardly.

Damn. I hate briefings...

[2]

"Our plans, ladies and gentlemen, have changed."

Lt. Colonel Connelly had what I recognized as an Australian accent, and it seemed at odds with the sense of momentous self-importance in his tone and the purposefully stoic set of his square jaw. He paced across the stage of the auditorium, hands clasped behind his back, the creases in his dress uniform sharp enough to shave with. I hated him already. We were all in our field utilities, which meant he should have been too, but he wanted to stress how much more important he was than us. Brigade staff was like that, a bunch of dead-ender colonels who'd never be promoted any higher unless every other senior officer in the fucking Marine Corps died.

Connelly peered down at us, chin against his chest, feet planted wide, chest puffed out. The whole brigade was present, though General McCauley, the brigade commander, had decided his time was more important than ours.

"I'm sure I don't need to remind all of you just how great a blow to our war effort it was when we lost four cruisers during the Battle for Mars. Our offensive and defensive strategies were

13

built around those cruisers, and now that our fleet has been cut in half, those strategies have had to change."

I turned to Lt. Ackley and rolled my eyes. She frowned at me and nodded back towards Connelly, the unspoken command to pay attention.

Aye, ma'am.

"As those of you who've paid attention to the monthly threat memoranda from General McCauley should already know, the new commander of our military forces, Fleet Admiral Sato, has moved away from the capital ship strategy towards something more versatile and agile."

Connelly touched his datalink and a hologram sprang to life above the stage, an image of a delta-winged spacecraft with a human shape displayed next to it for size comparison. From the scale, I estimated it at around a hundred meters long and about half that wide across the broadest section of the wings. It was thick and massive and obviously not built primarily for atmospheric flight but just as obviously capable of it.

"This is a VRT-221 missile cutter, the building block of the Fleet's new Attack Command. They're the smallest Transition Drive spacecraft in the Fleet, but they're relatively cheap and quick to build, and they offer the ability to project military force on multiple fronts. The cruisers we have and the ones soon to come out of the new shipyards will be reserved for defense of the Solar System and a few of the core colony systems, such as this one."

"Shit," Ackley muttered under her breath, barely loud enough for me to hear right next to her.

She wasn't the only one. I could hear an undertone of troubled murmurs rolling out over the gathered Marines like a wave, and I knew why they were concerned. Connelly did too, of course. It was why he was trying to sound so momentous.

"I don't have to tell you how this will affect the Fleet Marine Corps and our utilization in the war effort."

Well, yeah, dumbass, you kind of do. That's why we're fucking here, after all.

I had so wanted to say that out loud.

"Up until now, our tactics for assaulting enemy bases has been to overwhelm their orbital defenses and send drop ships in under the cover of the proton bombardment, but this will no longer be an option."

And there it was, the other shoe we'd been expecting. As if the admission had flipped a switch, the low murmur turned into a gabble of protest, like this stuffed shirt desk jockey could do anything to change Space Fleet policy. Lt. Ackley wasn't saying anything, but she'd slumped down in her seat, shoulders sagging as if she was suddenly very tired.

And she probably was, after spending all day out in the field and then coming straight to this dog and pony show. I knew I was.

"I don't like this any more than any of you do," Connelly assured us. Which was a fucking lie, since he wouldn't be on any of the drop ships heading into the teeth of the Tahni without orbital bombardment. "We're just going to have to improvise, adapt and overcome, like Marines always have since well before the Commonwealth."

He straightened his jacket, like the statement of faith in the Corps had made his chest swell and ruined the lines.

"That is one of the reasons for the relocation of elements of the brigade to Hachiman."

Hachiman sounded like a planet, and I figured it was where we were headed. No one had mentioned a name yet, ostensibly for operational security reasons.

"Lacking the cover of Fleet cruisers, we're going to need to move our base of operations out into the old Neutral Zone in order to launch raids on Tahni worlds in their space. Hachiman is one of the former squatter colonies the Tahni destroyed at the start of the war." He frowned as if he wanted to convey the gravity of the decision. "We know some may consider it disrespectful to base our operations on what is essentially their graveyard, but I like to think of it as the first step toward avenging their deaths."

"Colonel, question." The voice was unmistakable, as was the rigid stance and the stern, commanding expression on the lined, weathered face. It was Captain Covington, seated three rows up from us in the auditorium, beside Top.

"Yes, Captain?" Connelly acknowledged, his tone clipped with irritation at the interruption. But if he was irritated, he didn't take it out on the Skipper. Captain or no, the Skipper was one of the most feared and decorated Marines in the Corps. He'd been in for decades, and maybe God knew why he was still just a captain, but I didn't.

"You said we're going to be attacking Tahni worlds inside the Imperium," Covington said. "But what about the human colonies inside the Commonwealth already occupied by the Tahni? Surely freeing those worlds would take priority?"

Connelly seemed uncomfortable with the question, wincing as if the words hurt.

"Captain, let me first say I do not make policy and I am not here to debate it with you or anyone else." He was very determined to appear sincere and slightly pissed off, as if what he was about to say made him angry, but he wasn't allowed to say so. "I also frown upon spreading rumors. But enough people at every level know this so I don't feel I am betraying any secrets to say an attempt has been made to liberate the Demeter colony from Tahni occupation."

More murmurs and general ruckus that I had to assume

most people here *didn't* know about this particular operation. Me, I wasn't totally clear where Demeter was. I had a vague memory it had some sort of wildlife preserve, but that was it. I made a mental note to look it up later and kept my attention focused on Colonel Drama.

"The operation involved a Force Recon platoon and some intelligence assets," he went on, "and, as I understand it, was intended to work in conjunction with the civilian resistance on the planet."

His expression became bleak, and I believed this part was sincere.

"It was a disaster and has led to thousands of civilian deaths and has become a huge boost for enemy morale. Rather than risk something like this happening again, President Jameson himself has decided to pursue a different strategy. He intends for the new Attack Command, working in conjunction with the Marine Corps, to strike as far as possible into the heart of the Imperium, to hurt the enemy where they consider themselves the strongest, until it becomes impossible for them to extend themselves far enough to maintain their occupation of our colonies."

"That's a fucking horrible idea!" someone shouted from behind us. "They'll fusion bomb those worlds behind them as they leave!"

"That's a risk," Connelly admitted, "and perhaps not one I'd take if I were in President Jameson's position, but as I said, I am not here to argue policy. The decision has been made and it's our job to carry it out."

"Why weren't the Armored Infantry involved in this mission?" someone else asked. I think it was Alpha Company's commander, a tall, rail-thin woman who kept her head completely shaven. "Why just one platoon of Force Recon?"

"You heard the keywords already, Zoe," Covington

answered the question before Connelly had the chance. "Intelligence assets. This was some spook bullshit, probably dreamed up by the brass hats back on Earth. Some admiral thought he could have victory cheap, fast and good and forgot you only get two out of those at once, maximum."

"Be that as it may," Connelly said, raising his voice and maybe turning up the volume on his microphone as well, "our targets for the time being are Tahni staging bases and industrial facilities. The Attack Command will handle the targets on uninhabitable worlds, moons, and asteroids, but we're going to be pulled in when the objective is on a living planet."

"Why don't we just nuke them," an NCO behind me wondered, his voice pitched low enough to not interrupt Connelly, intended more for the Marines sitting around him, "or hit them with a big rock from orbit?"

I turned back to him. He was a bullet-headed man with a thick chest, and he struck me as a gym rat. You saw a lot of those in Force Recon, not so many in the drop-troopers, and sure enough, he had a Recon badge on his collar across from his E-6 stripes.

"Because if we start ruining their habitables," I told him, "they'll do the same to ours. So far, we've each maintained an unofficial policy of preserving living worlds and if one of us breaks it, well...I hope you like living on space stations, because that's all that'll be left."

"Your first target will be one of the newer Tahni colonies just the other side of the Neutral Zone," Connelly told us, ignoring the cross-chatter, if he even heard it. "The name is something long and unpronounceable, but our intelligence analysts have designated it Oasis."

Connelly manipulated his 'link and brought up the image of a gas giant, with a green and blue moon passing across its face.

"Oasis is the largest moon of the system's inner gas giant, and the only habitable world in the system." His thumb stroked the screen of his 'link and the view zoomed into the face of the giant, zooming in on something artificial floating high in its orange and yellow atmosphere. "The Tahni have a gas mining operation in orbit around the gas giant, automated mostly. They also have a refining plant in orbit around the moon and use the surface as a place to house workers who aren't on duty turning hydrogen into metallic hydrogen fuel, as well as the military base that defends the whole thing."

The image soared down through the atmosphere of Oasis, past the smudge marks of active volcanoes and over fields of geysers and thermals erupting from yellow-tinged rock. In the river valleys, the bare rock gave way to greener pastures, the trees the same sort of twisted, hardy growth most of the Tahni worlds were home to. And beyond the forests lay the Tahni base, familiar in its efficient, practical ugliness and only notable for the landing fields jammed with stiletto-shaped dual-environment fighters and the boxy, three-story buildings arrayed in a half circle around a small retention pond west of the landing fields. They looked like some sort of housing units to me, possibly for the civilian workers.

"This won't be too terribly different from the targets you've serviced previously," Connelly said, my dislike for him growing immensely at the words. No one who wasn't a rear-echelon poseur used the phrase "servicing targets" as a euphemism for killing the enemy. "The only difference here is, rather than relying on orbital bombardment from our cruisers to distract the enemy defenses, you'll be covered by the missile cutters. They'll be striking at the gas mines and the orbital refineries simultaneously and that should be enough to distract the enemy defenses."

"Should is a fucking slippery word," Ackley opined, just loud enough for me to hear, and I grunted agreement.

"You'll receive more details when you arrive at Hachiman, but I'm afraid there won't be much time for unpacking before you head on this mission. It's considered vital by the President and the High Command, a proof of concept of their new strategy, and they want it carried out immediately."

"Great. Nothing like heading out on a mission half-assed."

That was Lieutenant Costas, and he hadn't even tried to keep his voice down. I winced in anticipation and the Skipper didn't let me down.

"Lt. Costas," he said, his voice cutting through the noise, "you will maintain a respectful tone when speaking to a superior officer or I'll have you relieved. Am I understood?"

"Sir, yes, sir!" Costas barked, a slight tremble in his tone.

He was sitting at attention as he said it, and it was all I could do to keep from barking a laugh. It must have been as embarrassing as shit for the poor guy, but I couldn't find it in my NCO's heart to feel bad for a butterbar. Except maybe Ackley, but she was a *good* butterbar who listened to her NCOs.

"Well, then," Connelly said, stuttering at the interruption, as if he'd neither expected the outburst nor Captain Covington's reaction, "if there are no further question, I know you all have a lot of work to do to prepare for the move to Hachiman and I don't want to keep you any longer than necessary." He smiled ingratiatingly. "I know everyone hates long briefings where the questions never end and everyone else just wants to go home, so good news, no more questions tonight."

Yeah, I was so sure he was doing that out of the goodness of his heart and not because he didn't want us asking any more questions that he didn't have the answers to. Connelly nodded to the side where a major braced to attention before calling out an order.

"Battalion!"

We were already coming to our feet, the bottoms of our chairs bouncing upwards without our weight to hold them down.

"Attention!"

Dozens of boot heels thumped together, mine included, and if I didn't keep my eyes straight ahead, it was only because no one could have seen them.

"Dismissed!"

Boot soles scuffled on the concrete floor and I saw a couple of senior NCOs rubbing at their back from sitting down for too long.

"Delta," Covington said, and I fought to keep from jerking back to attention. I have never been able to hear him sneaking up. He should have been Force Recon. "The shuttles lift at ten-hundred hours and I don't want my leaders being careless because of lack of sleep. Get back to the barracks and rack out. Four hours, minimum, and that means you too, Ackley."

"Aye, sir," she said, nodding. It wasn't an idle order. More than once I'd seen her office light burning well after one in the morning.

"This may be a poor military strategy," Covington said, sparing Costas a meaningful glare, "and we may disagree with the political policy behind it, but this is our mission and we are going to carry it out to the best of our ability." He let his glare carry over the rest of us, making sure we got the message. "And I expect all of you to convey that same sentiment to the rest of the troops. Am I clear?"

"Aye, sir!" we all replied in antiphonal chorus.

He nodded to us and headed out, Top at his shoulder. The rest began filtering out and Ackley and I brought up the rear. I leaned in close to her, not wanting to be overheard.

"I'll toe the party line and be a cheerleader for the High

Command in front of the troops, ma'am," I assured her, "but that don't change the fact this is some fucked-up shit."

"Ours is not to reason why, Sergeant Alvarez," she said, smiling thinly, "ours is but to do and die."

"I don't know who said that, ma'am," I said, snorting with skepticism, "but that fucker was never a Marine."

[3]

"Jesus, it's cold here," Henckel said, cupping his hands around his mouth and blowing into them, then rubbing them together as if he were trying to bring feeling back to them.

I nodded, acting as if the two-degree temperatures and the remnants of snow on the ground didn't bother me, pretending to be paying attention to the power loaders hauling our gear off the cargo shuttles. Not our suits. Those were still up on the *Iwo Jima*, orbiting silently above Hachiman, waiting for us to return in forty hours for our mission...after spending just about every minute of it stowing our gear and getting everything settled into the prefab buildfoam domes that would be our new homes for the foreseeable future.

Fuck it, we can sleep on the ship.

And I was fooling myself if I thought that would happen. The flight was a week long, but everyone would be keyed up, training constantly whether or not they'd been assigned to. I was already so wrapped up in the mission I hadn't even bothered to look around until Henckel mentioned the weather.

Hachiman was a colder world than Inferno, which wasn't saying much because Inferno was about as hot as a world can get and still be habitable. The short, single-column data packet I'd read on the way here had said Hachiman was at the outer edge of the Goldilocks Zone and that only the equator was ice-free year-round. Only a few hundred kilometers north of us, glaciers edged closer and closer every year, and someday they'd win the fight and the whole planet's surface would be frozen and lifeless, but for now, vegetation clung to the hillsides raising off the lakeshore and the whole thing was kind of picturesque.

Henckel was right, though. It was damned cold, especially for a kid from Mexico who'd spent most of his life indoors, and the field jacket I wore seemed inadequate. My ears and nose were stinging and I thought I was losing feeling in my fingertips. While I felt the cold, what I *didn't* feel was the agoraphobia, and I realized with a bit of a start that I hadn't felt it as more than a slight background buzz since I got back from Brigantia.

"Henckel, go make sure the maintenance racks get set up right in the shop," I told him.

"What?" he asked, laughing sharply. "You think the cargo crew ain't never moved an Armored Infantry Battalion before?"

I cocked an eyebrow at him, trying to decide if I was going to chew him out or explain patiently. I decided for somewhere in-between.

"Sure," I said, lip curling in half a sneer. "You can just stand out here and watch me watching them unload until Top sees you...and she *will*, because she just loves to wander around looking for privates who don't have anything to do and finding some really unpleasant shit to teach them that there is *always* something to do. Then we can both be in the shit with Top and I'll take it out on you after she's done taking it out on you."

"Roger that, Sergeant," he said, a little cowed, nodding. "I'll make sure they do it right."

I watched him follow two of the power loaders into the hangar, the twin forks at the ends of their massive arms each carrying a pallet of maintenance racks for the Vigilantes. The loaders were big, each twice as broad as a battlesuit but unarmored, their cabs skeletal things designed to protect the operator from falling debris rather than enemy gunfire. Their feet were upside-down flower petals digging into the rocky soil with each step, a regular drumbeat rhythm that nearly lulled me to sleep.

"Didn't take you too long to master the art of supervision, *Sergeant* Alvarez."

I grinned at the voice even before I felt Vicky Sandoval's hand brush against my arm, just the slightest touch, barely enough for me to feel it through my jacket. Vicky was tall and slender, with a gentle curve to her jaw and the barest wisp of blond hair sticking out from the edges of her watch cap.

"You'll learn these things, too, after you have more time in grade, Sergeant Sandoval," I assured her, trying to keep the grin from turning into a blithering-idiot smile and giving everything away.

"You're just not going to let me forget you got promoted to squad leader first, are you?" She shook her head. "You know I've been in the Corps longer than you, Hood Rat."

"A whole six months," I acknowledged, "yet now I have rank on you..."

"You keep that attitude going, that's the only damned thing you're going to have on me."

"You really think we'll be able to sneak away with all the shit everyone will be doing before we ship out?" I asked, half dubious, half hopeful. Vicky and I had kind of a thing. What kind of a thing, I had no idea and I was afraid to ask, but it involved full-time friendship and occasional sex, and I wasn't big enough of an idiot to be looking gift horses in the mouth.

"Improvise, adapt and overcome," she said, the corner of her mouth turning up in a way that drove me crazy. "That's what Marines do. Besides, it's a new planet. Gotta break it in."

"I wonder how long we'll be spending here." I eyed the barracks domes and gave a dismissive sniff. "The setup doesn't look too permanent to me."

"They'll keep us here until the brass decides this new strategy you told us about isn't going to work," she guessed. "Or maybe three or four months after they realize it's not going to work. It's the government, Cam. You know how that shit works."

Another of the power-loaders cleared the ramp and I caught a glimpse of Scotty Hayes walking down behind it, hopping off the end to the dirt half a meter below. I took a strategic step away from Vicky. I wasn't sure what the regs were about two squad leaders in the same platoon...well, doing whatever we were doing, and I didn't want to find out the hard way.

"Glad I caught you two," Scotty said, and I stiffened involuntarily before I realized what he meant. "I just found out from Top there's been a change to the schedule?"

"They move back the mission?" I asked, hopeful. Shit like that happened all the time and, normally, I found it annoying as all hell. In this case, though, I had a reason to hope they'd pushed it back a couple days.

"The opposite," Scotty told me, the scowl passing across his face seeming unnatural there. Scotty was a cheerful guy by disposition, which had almost made me not like him on first acquaintance. "We're basically dumping everything here and boarding the shuttles in twenty-four hours. Don't bother making everything nice and neat, just get the shit in the right building and we'll sort it out once we get back, Top's orders."

"Damn," Vicky murmured. "That doesn't sound like Top... or the Skipper."

"I think we're getting a lot of pressure from Fleet on this," Scotty said, hooking his thumbs in his belt and cocking his head to the side, the look he got when he was deep in thought. "You told me about that shit that went down with Demeter, Cam...

well, I think the Tahni got themselves all hot and bothered and thinking their shit don't stink, and now the Fleet wants us to teach them a little humility."

"That's one way of looking at it," I said. "The other is that someone got their ass reamed and needs a quick win."

"You're too young to be this cynical, dude," Scotty bemoaned. "Go find Chen and Abrams and all of you pass the word down to your squads. Tell them to get their shit together by evening chow so we can get some actual sleep before the birds take off."

"Roger that," Sandoval said. She waited until we were halfway across the landing field and a hundred meters away from Scotty before she aimed a frustrated sigh my way. "No sneaking away for us, I guess." She flashed me a sly smile. "But you know, it's a long flight..."

———

The *Iwo Jima* stretched out across the field of stars, boxy and pragmatic, an interstellar delivery truck. And we were its cargo. It felt odd riding up without the suit, even odder sitting in a passenger shuttle like I was a tourist. I didn't care for it, didn't like being herded out of the bird by the crew, wayward children on a field trip, then being chased down to our berths and told to strap in immediately, without even the chance to inspect our suits.

We weren't crew, so we were required to strap into our bunks for the boost out of orbit, which was ridiculous. It was a one-gee burn, which meant I lay there in normal gravity with a strap across my chest for three hours like an idiot and tried to fall asleep but couldn't because Scotty insisted on regaling me with tales of growing up a country boy on Hermes.

"Is this one of the perks of being a squad leader?" I finally asked him. "Getting to share a compartment with your platoon sergeant?"

"Well, someone had to do it," he said, as cheerful as always. "What? You'd rather sleep?"

"Now that you mention it..."

"Fine, then," he said, sounding hurt, though his face was hidden from view in the bunk above me. "I'll shut up."

I had just closed my eyes when the drives cut off and the Transition alarms began to sound.

"All hands prepare for Transition in two minutes," the stern voice from the bridge announced.

"You ever seen a Transition from the Bridge?" I asked Scotty as we waited out the countdown.

"Oh, now you want to hear my stories..."

"Jesus, Scotty." I rolled my eyes, though he couldn't see it.

"No, I haven't," he admitted. "But I hear it's nothing much. Transition Space isn't really *there*, isn't part of our universe, so you couldn't even see it if you looked at it. The screens just go black and you see about as much as you do lying here in the compartment."

"It'd still be better," I grumbled. "How the hell did they ever figure this shit out if we can't even see T-space?"

"Math, I guess. I mean, I did watch a documentary about the Transition drive once, when I was at the NCO course. You never read about it?" He seemed surprised. "I mean, you're the one who's always watching educational shit."

"I'm not big into physics," I said, shrugging.

"It's pretty cool, had to do with them discovering some natural wormholes way back a century ago and studying them until they found out how to manufacture artificial holes in space with gravimetic energy. Whatever that is."

"Transitioning now," the compartment's intercom speakers told us.

Some people didn't experience anything during a Transition. Others got violently ill or disoriented. I was somewhere in the middle. It felt as if the universe had turned inside out and taken me with it, a rubber band stretched too far, right at the edge of breaking, until it snapped back.

Reality settled down into its groove again and with it came the return of gravity. The all-clear sounded and I pulled the straps loose from across my chest, hips and thighs, swinging my legs off the bunk.

"That's the one thing I can't understand, even after watching the documentary," Scotty admitted, dropping down off the top bunk, the soles of his boots thumping solidly off the deck. "Why artificial gravity only works when we're in Transition Space."

"I guess the rules are different here," I said, following him out into the passageway. The rest of the battalion was emerging as well, some slower than others, some still wiping puke off their chins.

"Yeah, but some rules are the same everywhere. Get your squad together, Cam. There's work to do."

The work I didn't mind.

I'd spent enough time in a Vigilante, had the thing save my life more than once, that there was something comforting about going over the systems, making sure every connection was clean and operational, every power lead intact. Propped up on the maintenance rack, running diagnostic scans while I scrubbed down fittings with a wire brush had a sort of calming effect. I could shut out the banter between the other squads up and down the compartment and just be.

Of course, not everyone felt that way.

"Didn't we just run these checks before we left Inferno?" Henckel asked from beside me.

I'd been watching him in my peripheral vision while I

worked on my own suit, making sure he did a competent job, and he had. But griping was as old as the notion of a foot soldier and a vital part of staying sane and I didn't begrudge him the privilege.

"We did," I acknowledged. "And we'll probably run them one more time before we drop on Oasis."

Linebarger was on my other side, but he was a Lance Corporal, one of my team leaders, and he'd heard this speech before so he just grinned and kept polishing the connection port for his Vigilante's power feed to the main gun.

"Is there a why in there somewhere, Sergeant Alvarez?" Henckel wondered. "Or is this one of those Marine things where we just do it that way and that's it?"

He was pushing it. It came with the territory. You could take the kid out of the Underground, but you couldn't take the Underground out of the kid. I didn't take it personally, though I noted it in a special mental file where I would store the instances up and decide when the best time was to exercise a bit of authority and keep him humble. I'd learned about that in NCO school, and it was one of the few things they'd taught me that I'd found immediately useful.

I'd bring him back to ground level later. Right now, I'd tell him the truth, the same truth a Master Gunnery Sergeant had shared with me at NCO school.

"There's a lot of reasons, Henckel," I said, wondering if I could have exercised this sort of restraint if he'd been some farmboy from Aphrodite. "There's the officer reason, which is that it keeps us familiarized with our equipment so that we don't lose our ability to diagnose breakage and do competent PMCS because we're always operational and never breaking our shit down and seeing what makes it work.

"Then there's the NCO reason, that leaving Marines sitting around with nothing to do on a ship heading into combat is just asking for trouble. When you're tense and bored and waiting to go get shot, you get fights, you get depression, you get some poor son of a bitch who can't stop thinking about his own impending death getting so scared he cycles himself out of an airlock because it seems like an easier way to go."

Or so I'd heard. I'd never actually seen it myself in the two whole years I'd been in the Marine Corps. But Henckel looked suitably impressed, so I went on.

"Then there's the real reason, the Marine reason, the one that'll keep you alive in combat. There's something called Murphy's Law, a saying older than the Commonwealth, older than the first human being into space. It says, 'whatever can go wrong, will go wrong.' You can't change that, but you can damn well do your best to make sure your shit's in order and you kept up your end." I waved a hand at Henckel's Vigilante. "These suits are complicated. The Force Recon pukes are constantly going on about how we drop-troopers can't operate for more than a day or so without a logistics train running all the way up to orbit, and they're not wrong for all that they're worthless straight-leg lightweights. Anything breaks in the field, you're done. Maybe you can get back to the LZ and wait for help to come or more likely, you're dead right there."

I raised the brush in my hand, using it like a pointer.

"So maybe we did these PMCS checks before, and maybe we'll do them again, because maybe shit can't break while the suits are just sitting here in the maintenance racks...or maybe it can. You read me, Private Henckel?"

"Five by five, Sergeant," he confirmed, what might have been a sigh of resignation in his voice as he turned back to working on his suit.

His eyes off me, I allowed myself a frown. Everything I'd told him had been correct. It had even been true. But it felt like someone else had said it, or more accurately like I'd been leader, pretending to be something I wasn't?

I could ask Scotty about it, but he never seemed to be pretending to be anything he wasn't, at least not to me. I'd known him as a squad leader and he didn't seem much different as a platoon leader. He'd probably tell me something like I was just finding my way and eventually, I'd develop my own leadership style and wouldn't have to copy anyone else's. And he'd probably be right, because he would have been repeating what Top had told him.

I checked the time on my 'link. It was easy to lose track of it in here, where the lights were always on and someone was always working, just like the Underground.

"All right, First," I said, trying to sound more cheerful than I felt, "it's half an hour until chow which means Gunny Hayes is going to be coming through the hatch in five, four, three..."

I counted the last two seconds off silently, folding down the fingers of my right hand, and on the last, boot soles tapped a jaunty rhythm in the passage outside the storage bay and Scotty Hayes stepped through, hands spread wide.

"Okay, Third Platoon!" he said, smiling broadly, "it's a half hour until chow! Put your suits back together and go clean up. Your day is over and you have a marvelous three hours of free time until lights-out, so make the most of it."

"Regular as clockwork," Vicky said from the next row of suits over. "Come on boys and girls, wrap it up."

I was slapping the dust covers back on the joints of my Vigilante and didn't notice Vicky walking up to me until she was brushing against my right shoulder.

"We have three hours," she said next to my ear. "Meet me in Drop-Ship C3 in two."

Improvise, adapt and overcome.

[4]

"Where the hell you going this time of night, jack-head?"

I knew who it was before I even turned around. No one else used the term jack-head to describe drop-troopers except straight-legs, Force Recon. What I didn't know was why the hell any of them would be down in the docking bay.

It was sort of night down here, or the closest it came to night anywhere on the ship. The docking bay was pretty much deserted during Transition since the shuttles were nestled into covered niches in the hull while they were docked with the *Iwo Jima* and not only were they not going any distance away from the ship in Transition Space, but they couldn't even be accessed from the outside. The docking crews doubled as engineering techs during Transition and no one came to the bays except the occasional cleaning bot.

And Marines looking for a place to be alone.

The Force Recon troops weren't here for the same reason I was, unless they were into something way kinkier than I had in mind, as there were three of them and they were all male. They were in utility fatigues, but one of them was carrying a field jacket wrapped around something.

"I was just taking a walk," I told the one who'd asked, a lean, dark man a bit older than me, "hoping I'd run into some straight-legs trying to find a dark, quiet place to get drunk."

The three men exchanged guilty glances and the bigger one carrying the jacket clutched it tighter.

"Hey man," the leader, a lance corporal named Rhodes, if his uniform's name tape was to be believed, said, raising a hand. His eyes went to my rank. "Uh, I mean, Sergeant, we aren't looking for any trouble..."

I laughed softly and waved it off.

"Neither am I, Lance." I thought about it for a moment, then offered him a hand. "I'm Cam."

He hesitated just a beat before shaking with me, his grip firm and dry.

"Tony," he said. "This is Andre and Terry."

The other two nodded, their eyes cautious, as if they thought I was trying to lure them out so I could get them busted for whatever illicit alcohol they had concealed under the jacket.

"You guys going to be part of the raid on Oasis?"

"Yeah," Tony confirmed. "We're supposed to plant the demo charges to destroy the base after you and your crew finish off their air defenses." He laughed. "So, good luck to both of us, I guess, huh?"

"You said it." I grinned lopsidedly. "I'd drink to it, but..."

Tony shot a look at the one he'd called Andre, the big guy, and the PFC rolled his eyes but unwrapped a plastic jug from inside the jacket and handed it to me.

"Have a drink on us, Cam." He cocked an eyebrow. "A small one, though. This shit is rough and home-made."

I popped the cap and took a whiff, making a face at the rubbing-alcohol smell.

"Just like old times," I reflected, holding my breath and taking a long swig of the stuff.

It burned its way down my throat and chest and into my stomach, a reverse lava flow heading back into the depths of the earth and smoldering. I let out the breath and it was thick enough I could have set fire to it. Tony seemed impressed by the fact I hadn't gagged at the taste.

"Where you from, Cam?" he wondered.

"Trans-Angeles," I told him. "Earth," I added, just in case. Some of these Force Recon types were real backwoods hicks from small colonies, so I couldn't take it for granted they'd even know.

"That's the big fucking city, man," Tony said, taking the jug back from me. "I'm from Earth, too...way up in the Anchorage preserve.'"

Now it was my turn to look like a hick, because I had no idea what he was talking about and it must have showed on my face.

"That's up in Alaska," he supplied, grinning as if he'd read my mind.

"People live in Alaska?" I asked, dredging up a dim memory of seeing it on a map. "Isn't it awful close to old Russia? Is it still radioactive up there?"

Tony guffawed, the liquor shaking in the bottle as his shoulders shuddered from laughter.

"Jesus man, the Sino-Russian War was like two hundred years ago. But no, not a lot of people live up there. There's like a huge nature preserve though, so there's some tourism and my family works at one of the resorts where the Corporate Council types come to get closer to nature when they're tired of looking down on it from their towers in the big cities."

"Only time I ever got to see a Corporate Council tower," I told him, "was on the shuttle up to McAuliffe Station to catch the bus to Inferno when I joined the Marines. My home was about a kilometer straight down from there, if you know what I mean."

"Yeah," the one he'd called Terry said, nodding. "I went through Basic with a bunch of guys from the Trans-Angeles Underground. They get a lot of recruits from the Undergrounds in the mega-cities, I guess."

"Sure, we're all volunteers," I said, laughing with a bit of stored-up cynicism. "I'm sure it don't have anything to do with the fact that we usually got the choice of punitive hibernation or the Corps."

"I just figured you guys were all really patriotic." Terry grabbed the home-brew and took a gulp, turning a little green when he made the mistake of tasting it.

The other two drank from the jug before handing it to me one more time. I took a longer hit this time but handed it back firmly, already feeling a bit light-headed.

"Thanks guys, but that's it for me." I jerked a thumb at the docking umbilical off to my right. "Gotta meet someone and if I have any more of that rot-gut, I'll pass right out."

"Sure thing," Tony said. "You know, you seem pretty okay for a jack-head."

"And you guys aren't the huge, self-important pricks I usually expect from Force Recon," I returned, grinning. "But don't worry," I assured them. "I won't tell anyone."

"See you on the ground, Cam." Tony saluted me with the jug.

"Maybe." I waved behind me as I headed for the docking collar. "I hear in the armor, we all look alike."

The airlock to the dropship was supposed to be kept locked, but it never was. Just like the whole compartment was supposed to be under video surveillance by ship's security, but that never happened either. Ship's security, like everything else in the military, was run at its base by junior NCOs and enlisted, and they wanted to use the place for the same thing as the rest of us, so there was a sort of unofficial understanding that the docking bay during Transition was neutral territory for all the illicit things everyone knew went on in a ship but no one really cared about stopping.

The interior of the dropship was blanketed in shadow, the only light coming from an airlock control panel just inside the lock, and I hesitated beside it, trying to let my eyes adjust before I moved farther in.

"You scared of the dark, Cam?" Vicky asked from somewhere deeper inside the lander. The darkness clarified with the passing seconds and the steps down into the passenger compartment took shape.

"There are a lot of things I'm scared of," I admitted, "but the dark isn't one of them."

I scraped the soles of my boots along the metal grating of the stairs, feeling for the edges since I couldn't see well enough to be sure of catching the next step. I half-expected Vicky to be in one of the acceleration couches, but instead she was past all the empty rows of seats, back by the utility lockers where the vacuum suits were stored. She was sitting cross-legged on an olive-drab blanket she'd laid on the metal floor, looking up at me with eyes lost to the shadow.

"You always take me to the nicest places," I said, lowering myself down beside her. The blanket wasn't thick enough to make the floor comfortable, but I figured I'd survive.

"What took you so long?" she demanded, thumping me on the shoulder.

"I ran into some straight-legs looking to get drunk."

"Yeah, I can smell it," she said, leaning in and kissing me. "And taste it. That's some nasty shit. You didn't bring me any?"

"I doubt they would have let me borrow their home-brew," I pointed out, folding her into my arms. She was solid and muscular with very little body fat, so different from the girls I'd been with in the Underground. She was a predator on the hunt and I was the prey. "And I didn't think you wanted me to bring friends along to the party."

"Since when do you have straight-leg friends?" Vicky wondered, working at my clothes, not wanting to waste any time, I supposed.

"They aren't so bad," I protested, helping her pull my shirt off. "They're heading down to Oasis to plant demo charges and take out the base."

Vicky paused in her systematic undressing, her frown more visible now that my eyes had fully adjusted.

"They're planting demo charges? *Nuclear* demo charges?"

"I guess so." I shook my head, confused as to why she'd be upset. "I mean, the base will be mostly underground, so the blast won't cause much contamination or affect the civilian population."

She settled back, arms hugging her knees to her, dark eyes staring down at the deck.

"Why the hell are we nuking anything instead of just occupying it?" she demanded, though I figured she wasn't actually asking me. "This is supposed to draw the Tahni off our occupied colonies, right? Why should they pull troops off Demeter or wherever if we just blow their base up and leave? That doesn't make any sense."

I grinned, wondering if she could see it. It would probably be better if she couldn't, I decided. It would just make her angry.

"You always say you've been in the Corps longer than I have," I reminded her, "but you still think anything the High Command does is supposed to make sense?"

"It really doesn't bother you?" she asked, and it sounded more like an accusation.

"I guess if I sat around and thought about it, it might," I allowed. "But it's happening whether I like it or not, right? Honest, girl, growing up on the streets of the Underground might qualify me for a lot of things, up to and including killing Tahni, but it didn't make me an expert on politics or military strategy."

"It bothers me that people are going to get killed basically just fucking around to see what dumbass idea works. What if *you* get killed?"

"Then I'm going to wish I hadn't spent whatever time I had left arguing about politics on a blanket with a hot, half-naked girl when there's so many better things we could be doing."

It wasn't the smoothest line I'd ever delivered, and I'm not known for being a particularly smooth operator, but it got a smile.

"Fair enough, Hood Rat," she said. She grabbed me around the neck and pulled me into a kiss, kept pulling, bringing me down to the blanket on top of her.

She tasted like soap and sweat and just the faintest hint of strawberries, and two hours passed like five minutes.

———

"Where the hell have *you* been?" Scotty asked when I slammed through the door to our compartment about one minute before lights out, breathing hard from running the last couple hundred meters after climbing up the ship's central access hub, which was usually only used in microgravity except in emergencies.

Getting back from a bootie-call before lights-out was close enough to an emergency to suit me. The look on Scotty's face as he sat on the edge of his bunk, tossing an issue datalink up and down in his palm made me very glad I hadn't stopped to use the head, like I'd originally planned.

"I was hanging out with some dudes from the Force Recon company I ran into," I told him, which, while not totally the truth, wasn't an outright lie. "Just lost track of time."

"Lost track of your 'link, too, huh?" he said, tossing the device to me underhanded, the set to his face skeptical enough to be the dictionary definition's illustration. "That was pretty fucking convenient."

"I left it here while I took a shower," I explained, though it sounded a bit weak even to my ears. "I must have forgot it when I took off again. Why? Did you need me for something?"

"Nothing too important." He seemed to find the admission distasteful, like he'd wanted to be angry with me but couldn't keep himself from being fair about it. "I just thought we could go over the op order for the mission and see if we were down on the responsibilities up to two command levels above us."

Which was standard. It meant I had to know his responsibilities and Lt. Ackley's, and he had to know Lt. Ackley's and Captain Covington's just in case everything went to shit. Not an idle exercise, either, since I knew from painful experience just how badly everything *could* go to shit. I had a Bronze Star with a V for valor on my record and the dress blues I never wore to remind me of it.

"We can still do it," I said, shrugging as I pulled off my fatigues and tossed them over my bunk.

I popped open a storage cabinet and retrieved a fresher strip, letting it dissolve in my mouth to get rid of bacteria and plaque on my teeth...which would also get rid of the smell of the booze on my breath as well as other smells I might have picked up.

"I looked the op order over on the flight to Hachiman. I think I got it straight."

I climbed into my bunk and laid down just seconds before the lights switched off automatically. It wasn't totally dark. There was a pale glow from the security screen at the compartment's hatch, just enough to see by if one of us had to get up and hit the head during the notional night.

"All right," Scotty acceded, feet disappearing as he stretched out on the top bunk, his voice distant and disembodied. "What's the mission? First yours, then mine, then the LT's?"

"Well, Fourth Platoon is going in first, then First, then Second, and we're going to be held in reserve. When Fourth launches, we..."

I have a pretty good memory. A psychologist told me once it was because I was born and raised to mid-childhood out away from the cities, without the constant connection to the data net and the instant access to information and I had to actually retain information instead of just looking it up again. I didn't know about that. I thought it might be the constant moving around, having to learn new names, new social pecking orders, new safe routes to get to my room with every new group home. Or it just could have been genetic. Whatever the reason, I could look at something a couple times and have it memorized, and I was able to spout off the parts of the operations order to Scotty's satisfaction.

He took a bit longer and needed some guidance through Captain Covington's duties, but maybe forty-five minutes after we'd laid down, he was satisfied that neither of us would forget what to do when the real bullets started flying. He fell silent and I yawned, drained and ready to get some sleep.

"You know it's not a good idea, right?" he said, maybe a minute after I'd decided he must have finally nodded off.

"What?" I wondered. "This mission?"

"No." He paused. "Well, maybe that, too. But I mean you and Sandoval."

I swallowed hard and said nothing. *Damn it. I thought we'd been more careful than that.*

"What?" he asked, amusement in his tone. "You thought I wouldn't know? How stupid do you think I am?"

To be fair, I'd never thought Scotty was stupid, just a bit naïve. Provincial, I think was the fancy word for it. A farmboy raised on one of the colonies, sure. But not stupid.

"Is it against regs?" I asked him. It wasn't a challenge. I honestly hadn't wanted to know.

"Well, yeah," he said, like it was obvious. And maybe it was. "But that's just details. Lots of shit is against the regs, but no one cares. People make booze, people have sex, the shit happens and if we tried to stop it all, morale would go into the shitter. But yeah, she's in your platoon. Not your chain of command, but you could be asked to step into my position in an emergency and then you'd be her direct superior. So, it's a no-go, but that's not why it's a bad idea."

"I don't understand," I admitted. "Why is it a bad idea?"

"Because you two want different things."

I frowned, wishing he could see it because I wasn't sure if words alone could communicate how confused and slightly pissed-off I was.

"Scotty, how the hell do you know what we both want?"

"I've known Sandoval longer than you, but I think I know you pretty good by now, too. Sandoval is a good Marine, and a hell of a good person, but she's not looking for anything more serious than friends with benefits. You know that phrase? I'm not sure if they still use it on Earth, but my grandpa told me about it and I always liked it."

"I've heard it," I grumbled, getting even more pissed off. "But so what? What makes you think I want any more than that?"

Scotty blew out a breath and went silent for a second, and I sensed he was trying to think of a way to say what he wanted to say without making me even angrier. Which made me even angrier.

"When you first got here," he finally went on, "I think you would have been fine with that, but you're not that person anymore. You haven't been that guy since Brigantia."

Shit. I hadn't thought about Brigantia, about Maria, in weeks. What Maria and I had shared wasn't love, not in the sense that my mother and father had loved each other. We hadn't known each other long enough for that. But she'd offered me a place to call home, a reason to live through this war, even if she hadn't survived.

"You're afraid I'm gonna get hurt?" I asked him. I wanted to laugh at the idea, but I wasn't in a laughing mood. "You think she's going to break my heart or something? I hate to break it to you, farmboy, but getting my balls busted by a girl isn't anywhere near the worst thing that's ever happened to me." I thought about Henckel and realized I was doing the same thing he'd done earlier. I was pushing things, making it hard for Scotty. He was my friend but also my platoon sergeant, and I was being intentionally disrespectful to force him to choose which one he wanted to be.

"I suppose it isn't," he said so quietly I could barely hear it.

I wanted to tell him it didn't matter, that whether it was just sex or something more, it was enough right now to just prove to myself that I was alive, that in a few days, we'd be throwing ourselves into the fire again and I was scared enough that just feeling anything was enough. I wanted to tell him I was sorry, but darkness closed in and I surrendered to it.

[5]

I bit down on the mouthpiece inside my Vigilante's helmet, clenching my jaw against the boost as our dropship accelerated away from the *Iwo Jima* at a hair over eight gravities.

Everything about this felt wrong. I watched the external camera views from the ship's nose and saw nothing ahead of us but the gas giant, the queen of this system, the fusion drives of the assault shuttles thousands of kilometers in the distance, and the missile cutters a hundred thousand beyond that lost in the bright oranges and yellows swimming across the giant planet's upper atmosphere. I'd grown used to the familiar comfort of the cruisers, massive obelisks floating ahead of us, guardians soaking up attention and enemy fire while we slipped past in their wake, unnoticed, cockroaches scuttling in the dark behind a rampaging bull.

This time, we were ants crawling through a well-lit kitchen, and the extermination 'bots were on their way.

The gas giant was too far away, Oasis barely visible at this distance, with too much empty space to cross, so much more than we were used to. The pressure against my chest slacked off as the boost cut to three gravities, and I could breathe again but it wasn't a relief. Lower acceleration meant more time hanging in space, a slow, lumbering target.

I tried dipping into the command net and heard a confusing cross-chatter of orders between officers I didn't recognize to troops I didn't know, and I shut it down. If there was something I needed to know, they'd tell me. Neither Lt. Ackley nor Scotty was saying anything, which probably meant there was nothing left to say and the others were just gabbling out of nerves. Not that I could blame them.

"Sarge?" Henckel's voice buzzed in my ear. I tried not to roll my eyes.

"Don't call me 'sarge,' Henckel," I reminded him. I wasn't actually angry about it, but this was one of those times when the kid had to be reminded he was in the Marines, not a street gang.

"Sorry, Sergeant Alvarez. I just..." He trailed off and I frowned. Henckel was a lot of things, but reticent wasn't one of them. "I just wondered if, when you dropped on Brigantia, when you got the Bronze Star, were you..."

"Afraid?" I supplied.

It was the same question the PTSD counsellor had asked me, though not for the same reason. She'd been trying to get me to admit it to myself.

"Yeah, were you afraid?"

"No, not when I dropped." It probably wasn't what he wanted to hear, but it was the truth. "I wasn't afraid till later, when we attacked the base."

"Why? Why were you afraid then and not before, I mean?"

I never thought of myself as a particularly perceptive person, except when it comes to evaluating threats, but Henckel wasn't too hard to read. He was scared and he wanted me to tell him it was all right. And it was, of course. But should I tell him the truth or a comforting lie?

"I wasn't scared the first time because I thought I didn't have anything to lose," I said, deciding on the truth. "By the time we attacked the base with the civilian militia, I realized I did." And I'd lost it, lost so much of it, but he didn't need to hear that. "There's nothing wrong with having something to lose, Tom. It gives you something to fight for."

Something flashed white ahead of us, a sphere of fusion ignition. A ship had died, one of ours or one of theirs, I couldn't know.

"If we even get the chance to fight."

Yeah, there was that. The feed from the dropship cams was telling me nothing, the exchanges between the pilots coded and cryptic. I needed to access the data stream coming back from the missile cutters, but that was on the command net, locked out and available only to Captain Covington. Except for this little hack that our battalion armorer had showed me...

Thanks Mutt. I scrolled through several levels of menu until I found it, just where Chief Warrant Officer Mutterlin had said it would be. It took the universal access code I'd memorized and suddenly I was sitting on the nose of the lead flight of missile cutters, watching the approaching Tahni corvettes through their optical cameras, thermal imaging, lidar, radar and spectral analysis.

The Tahni ships were ugly and bulbous, a fusion drive, fuel tanks, shielding, and weapons pods jammed together around the smallest Transition field generator the Tahni could manufacture, with the cockpit as almost an afterthought. The Tahni religion and Commonwealth law both forbade automated weapons, and the level of ECM technology both sides had developed made remotely piloted drones impractical, and the option both sides seemed to have taken in this war was to replace disposable machines with disposable people.

We're cheaper to produce, anyway. And the last time

humans had tried to use autonomous armed drones, we'd ended up in a nuclear war, so maybe it was better this way.

The corvettes were in loose spherical formations arranged in groups of eight. Someone, maybe Top, had told me eight was like their lucky number. Their infantry squads were eight males, their squadrons eight ships, their buildings eight-sided. I don't know if it offered any advantage other than a spiritual one, but it was probably just as good as any arrangement we had, and at least it stopped the bright boys in the High Command from changing it all around every few years just for the hell of it.

Missiles launched from the corvettes, their solid-fuel rocket engines flares of white in the thermal readout, a dozen, two dozen, more than I could keep track of without the tactical computers to monitor them for me. The missile cutters responded, the first two ranks sending out swarms of torpedoes, each barely two meters long and one wide, a small fusion warhead at the business end, surrounded by a cluster of lasing tubes, Their detonations were featureless, white spheres on optical, barely visible, but the thermal and spectral analysis readings drew starburst lines of energy erupting from each of the fusion bursts, radiating away in a 180-degree arc, a hemi-sphere aimed away from the source.

Tahni missiles disappeared in fusion blasts, their warheads struck by the lasers, or cartwheeled wildly away, the rocket engines damaged, or puffed out of existence as their solid rocket fuel ignited. None were left by the time the last of the laser torpedoes had detonated, and the two forces converged, reduced to proton cannons and laser weapons at slugging distance.

Behind the front two ranks of missile cutters, other squadrons split off and boosted in toward the gas giant, leaving the dogfighting to their fellows while they did the yeoman's work of the mission. They carried the big sticks, armored anti-ship weapons they called Ship-Busters, as useful against industrial installations as they were against the big Tahni cruisers. The cutters slipped past the melee, ignoring the occasional detonation as Tahni corvettes and Commonwealth missile cutters died, spherical white fusion blasts the only grave marker their crews would receive.

Two of our human pilots to each cutter, if I remembered right. God knows how many Tahni per corvette. Probably two or three. Just flashing out of existence as if they'd never been, and their loved ones would get a pre-recorded notice and that would be it. Their lives would go on and, if they were on Earth, they'd probably never see anything of the war, barely know it was going on unless they paid attention to the news. It was that kind of war.

I switched views to one of the cutters heading in for a missile run at the gas giant, not wanting to accidentally be looking through the eyes of one of the ships when a corvette caught it with a laser blast. The shift was abrupt and jarring, from the star-filled darkness of open space to the swirling colors of the gas giant filling my view, zooming down further still until I could see the lines of the atmosphere mining facilities. Even using as much magnification as the optical cameras had along with computer extrapolation, the mine was a stick-figure drawing, tiny and insignificant against one of the churning red storms in the atmosphere.

More missiles streaked up from defense platforms in orbit around the giant planet, but the Ship-Busters were thickly armored and overpowered, each with its own fusion drive, and smart. The computers controlling the missiles could run evasion courses nearly as complex as a human pilot's, could launch countermeasures and decoys when they thought they'd be the most effective.

Space Fleet got all the cool toys.

Not all the Tahni missiles came after ours, though. Three of the cutters disappeared in expanding globes of fusion energy, and I flinched with each hit. We called the Fleet flyboys names, made fun of the perks they'd received back on Inferno, made jokes about private freezers full of vat-grown steaks they brought with them on the cruisers, but were just as ballsy as any Marine. They watched their friends die and continued the mission like it couldn't happen to them in the next second.

The cutters spun away from the gas giant, burning hot and hard to decelerate before they dropped into the orbit of Oasis, enough of them left that I breathed a sigh of relief. Between them and the assault shuttles still spread out ahead of our formation of dropships, I felt better about our chances of reaching the target area...or at least of achieving orbit.

I'd seen enough of the Attack Command experience and I toggled out of the command feed and brought myself back into my own helmet, back to the readouts from my squad. Graciano and Linebarger, the team leaders, were steady, breathing and heart rate normal according to the sensors, body temperature a half a degree below normal. The climate conditioning kept it cool in the suits.

Tom Henckel was in Linebarger's team, nominally anyway. I'd taken to having him tag along with me, since everyone, even the squad leader, had a battle buddy to watch their back. Henckel's heart rate was a bit fast, his breathing up from his usual respiration, but nothing close to a panic attack. Hopefully my words of wisdom, stolen and regurgitated as they were, had done some good.

The others seemed fine, Mullany, Reyfort, Chandra in Graciano's team all within normal limits. Pickerington and Kim, the other pair in Linebarger's group, were pushing the edge of a healthy heartbeat, but I remembered neither was very comfortable sitting and waiting in the ship. They'd be okay once we dropped. I hoped.

"Orbital insertion in five mikes," Lt. Ackley announced on the platoon net. "Run your final system checks and double-check your buddy."

I'd run mine about three times already, because what the hell else was I going to do sealed into my suit and locked into the drop gantry for the whole flight from the *Iwo* to Oasis? But I did it again, trying to be a responsible squad leader, and checked Henckel as well via the remote link. Then double-checked my team leaders, too.

"Your systems check as operational, Sergeant Alvarez," Henckel assured me.

I mumbled something in response, but I had most of my attention on the cockpit feed. I hadn't been listening to it, but I'd kept a transcription going in a corner of my HUD just in case something popped up I should know about, and the exchange between the dropship pilots and the assault shuttle was streaming up the screen so fast I didn't have time to read it. I muttered a curse and switched on the audio feed.

"...can't shake him. I need some fucking cover! Assault One, where the hell are you?"

"Transport Four, this is Assault One, I have launched inter-cept missiles, but they won't get there before the corvette is in firing range. I need you to break thirty-three degrees galactic north from the ecliptic and draw the bogie into my firing arc."

Shit. Transport Four was the designator for the dropship carrying Fourth Platoon.

I pulled in the sensor feed from Assault One, the assault shuttle squadron leader's bird and winced at the picture it drew for me. One of the Tahni corvettes had made it through the gauntlet of missile cutters somehow, a thermal flare showing a gap in the ship's reactor shielding where it had taken a hit, its drive flashing bright and then going dark for a half a second before igniting again. It didn't have much left and the Tahni crew must have been overriding the drive's safety protocols to keep it running...if the Tahni even had safety protocols. One fluctuation of the magnetic bottle at the wrong microsecond, and the ship would be glowing vapors.

I guessed the Tahni corvette didn't have any missiles left because it wasn't using them, just heading straight for Transport Four with dogged determination, as if they knew they were going to die and just wanted to take the enemy with them. Their primary laser weapon had a limited range, and the tactical computer of the assault shuttle I was accessing helpfully projected a red line in the sensor feed to show just how much farther it would have to come before it was effective.

The dropship had changed course, breaking away from the formation and trying to force the corvette to do the same. Assault One was decelerating hard, trying to maneuver into firing position to take down the corvette, but we'd already built up a shitload of momentum in the opposite direction and it was going to take too damn long for the shuttle to burn it off. Even the missiles they'd launched, boosting at thirty gravities, would take long minutes to even begin heading in the right direction.

There was no way. I wasn't a pilot, wasn't in the Fleet, didn't know that much about physics, and I could still see there was no way. They were dead.

"Third Platoon," Lt. Ackley came over the net, her voice grim, "there's a frag-o."

Fragmentary order, a last-minute change to the operations plan. The words were rote, by the book, as if this were just another training exercise, but I knew what they meant. I wondered how many others did.

"Third is no longer being held in reserve," she went on. "We're taking Fourth's place and dropping in the lead. First squad, you're on point. We're dropping into the canyon east of the base and moving up the river valley. Once we reach the base, First squad will make straight for the air defenses while Second and Third engage enemy forces and Fourth stays in reserve. Any questions?"

I had plenty of questions, but I couldn't ask them, couldn't look away from the sensor feed. The Tahni corvette crossed the red line, and less than ten seconds later, they fired their primary laser.

Did the pilots of the dropship know? Was it as obvious to them as it was to everyone watching what was going to happen? Was Lt. Costas watching the same feed I was, praying someone would save them? Or was he too scared to watch, just huddled inside his tomb, waiting for the end?

Transport Four vanished in a flare of sublimated metal as the laser split it down the middle, and hope flared in my chest for just a moment that maybe some of the troops could survive in their armor long enough for the assault shuttle to reach them. That hope went up in a sun-bright plasma when the reactor flushed violently and fatally. I had known it was coming, yet it still kicked me in the gut. I heard a low moan and wondered who was keying their mic until I realized it had come from me.

"What happened to Fourth Platoon, Sarge?" Henckel asked me. The question was subdued, as if he already knew but didn't want to believe it.

"Don't know for sure," I lied. "We'll find out after the op."

The dropship began to shake, the sort of vibration that only came from atmospheric entry. We were heading down.

"Henckel," I told him, "you think you're ready to take point?"

"Hell yeah, Sarge." Enthusiasm replaced trepidation in his voice. "I got this."

"I know you do, Tom. And don't call me Sarge."

I felt a pang of guilt, like I was throwing him head-first into the fire on his first combat op. But I also knew it was better to keep him in front of me, where I could watch his back.

The dropship shook more violently than simple turbulence could account for, and I was tempted to pull the visual feed up again, but resisted the urge. Fourth Platoon had watched death heading for them, inexorable, unavoidable.

I didn't want to see it coming.

[6]

We dropped into darkness.

This was my first combat mission as a squad leader, my first since Brigantia, and tight coils of fear wrapped around my brain and squeezed tightly. Everything outside my armor was spectacle and turmoil and confusion, rivers of fire ripping apart the night, starbursts of energy trying to blind my eyes and my sensors.

I forced order out of the chaos of my thoughts and separated the kaleidoscopic images into sense and clarity. The missile cutters were trying to hit the base with conventional air-to-ground munitions, but the warheads were being intercepted by a hail of coil gun and defense lasers, while Surface-to-Air Missiles streaked upward, seeking out any Commonwealth spacecraft they could find.

There were a lot to find. Missile cutters ranged high, their fusion drives causing auroras across the night sky, some still launching missiles, others striking from the upper atmosphere with their proton cannons. Assault shuttles swooped low, some of them below us when we dropped, air-breathing jets screaming in fury, lasers ripping ionized holes in the air on the way to targets on the ground. One of the assault birds went down just before I touched the ground, spinning wildly as something unseen smashed into it, probably a coil gun round. The walls of the canyon closed around me before the shuttle hit, but I saw a fiery glow rise above the horizon and knew its fate.

Then the darkness of the old riverbed swallowed me up and shut out the rest of the battle and I made myself concentrate on what I could control.

"Double-time, Fourth!" Scotty urged us, his voice in my ear but his IFF transponder showing him still coming down on his jump-jets. "Move it out!"

I didn't need to relay the order to my squad because we'd hit the ground running, either from instinct born of training or simply fear digging its spurs into their flanks. The floor of the canyon was dry, the river long gone, a superhighway into enemy territory, flat and easy going. Our Vigilantes ate up kilometers with long strides and the temptation was to run and keep on running, but training had taught us better than that.

"Henckel," I said, "pop up and scout ahead."

By the reckoning of the mapping software in my HUD, we only had another four kilometers before we came out into the light and we had no way of knowing what might be waiting for us. Ackley hadn't told me anything, but I didn't need her to. I could access the feed from the assault shuttles and the drop-ships the same as she could...except I couldn't. And I hadn't expected to be able to. The Tahni didn't have any of their own birds up by design, one of the few times I've seen them use a tactic that made sense. They were filling the air with anti-aircraft fire and ECM jamming, doing the best they could to make it a no-fly zone, and it was impossible to get even a clear audio signal through the electrostatic chaff and jamming signals, much less a clear tactical picture.

If we wanted to know what was happening ahead of us, we'd have to stick our heads up and look.

I was briefly running point while Henckel jetted up the twenty meters to the top of the canyon just long enough to get a read of what was around us. I could almost feel Scotty's stink-eye on me.

Not my fault, buddy.

He didn't bother to say anything. By now, he'd given up on trying to get me to stay in the center of the squad formation.

"We got company!" Henckel yelled, blasting back down into the canyon, landing directly in front of me. "Tahni High Guard in company strength, coming across the flats! Less than a kilometer out!"

He wasn't quite panicking, but he was alarmed, and I didn't blame him. We'd expected resistance. You didn't beard the lion in its den and not think they'd have more troops inside their own borders, but a whole company of armored troops for a mining facility? What the hell were they gonna have further in, closer to their homeworld?

"Fourth," Ackley ordered, "push forward out the end of the canyon, move!"

I wanted to argue with her. My first instinct was to pull everyone out of the canyon and go at them, but I did as she said almost automatically.

"Henkel, double-time, get going!"

It seemed to take forever to get going again, from walk to trot to gallop, and I was screaming at Lt. Ackley inside my head the whole time, sure that the Tahni would be jumping right on top of us at any second, ready to slaughter us like fish stuck in this stone barrel. Until I noticed the blue IFF icons on the map overlay in my HUD swarming up and out of the canyon a kilometer behind our platoon. It was First and Second Platoons. They'd dropped nearly five minutes behind us, and I hadn't even seen them enter the canyon, but Ackley was an officer and I suppose they paid her to keep track of these sorts of things.

"First and Second are hitting the enemy head-on," Ackley explained, either only now having the time to elaborate or possibly just waiting for the most dramatically satisfying time to announce the tactic. "We're going to circle around behind them and bite them in the ass."

It made perfect sense, but I didn't like it one bit. Maybe someone was hitting the enemy head-on, but it wasn't me, and when it came right down to it, I didn't trust anyone else.

"Faster, Henckel," I told the point man, feeling like I was about to run right up his back.

Everything was happening too slow and there were too few of us. The enemy had a full company, and their companies were already bigger than ours, while we were down a platoon and attacking a numerically superior force. It was all wrong, against everything they'd tried to teach me about strategy in NCO training, but there was nothing to be done about it and it wasn't impossible. But I had a gut-deep conviction we had to move faster.

Henckel did as he was told and kicked into a higher gear, his Vigilante moving at the very edge of the suit's ability. At these speeds, the limit wasn't so much the power source or the servo-motors as it was the reflexes and sense of balance of the operator...which meant Henckel and I were pulling away from the others. Technically, it was the wrong thing to do, and I expected Scotty or Ackley to tell me to slow up and stay with my squad.

"Alvarez," she said, instead, "hit them hard. Don't wait for us."

I nearly missed a step. If she was saying that, it meant she knew how fucked up this was just as well as I did.

"Aye, ma'am."

The end of the draw was in sight, the distant lights of the

base and the city beyond it barely visible, nearly drowned out by the fireworks show of the atmospheric battle still raging above us. I tried to get a quick sensor read of the flats between us and the base, just to check for more troops who might be waiting for us, but I might as well have been staring into a deactivated display. Thermal was useless, radar was useless, lidar was useless. ECM fields were killing anything electromagnetic, and burning debris from downed aerospacecraft and missiles littered the flats with heat plumes while clouds of black smoke filled the sky.

It was all hell and confusion and I ignored it. If any threats were out there, we were as invisible to them as they were to us.

So how did they know we were here to begin with?

They'd sent the High Guard after us despite their sensors being jammed as well as ours. Well, they weren't idiots. They had to know the terrain better than us, had to know that this canyon was a safe way to approach the flats without opening our forces to long-range artillery or missile fire from the base. They were getting wise to our tactics and it had only been a few months.

Henckel and I were out of the draw, curving left, and I was about to yell at him to hit the jets, but he did it before the words could form. I followed him without a conscious thought, both of us roaring up and to the left, the roaring fury of the isotope-powered turbines wrenching away our forward momentum. We paid for it, the g-forces smashing us into the padding inside our armor, but now we were up on the plateau and the enemy's naked rear was laid out before us.

The High Guard suits were functionally almost identical to ours, and form followed function, but there were stylistic differences, little things you could see even from a distance. Our Vigilantes were round-shouldered gorillas, our arms unnaturally long, legs a touch short, heads rounded and dome-like, the plasma guns we mounted for atmospheric use held like over-sized rifles. The High Guard suits reminded me more of suits of medieval armor, taller and squared off at the edges, the heads more distinct and separate from the torso, and the electron beamers that were their primary weapons built into the left arm of their suits.

Even without the IFF and the targeting computer analysis, I could have told them apart, so I didn't wait for the machines to tell me what I already knew. The first missile was loading into the launcher on my backpack when I fired my plasma gun. At less than half a kilometer away, it might as well have been point-blank range. The High Guard was arrayed in a strange diamond formation they used for their armored troops and I hit the rear-most of the suits in the diamond, the one they'd told us would be their equivalent of a squad leader. The packet of electromagnet-ically contained hyper-ionized hydrogen sublimated away centimeters of duralloy and speared through the suit's reactor shielding, which failed spectacularly.

It wasn't exactly an explosion, more a dramatic and catastrophic exothermic reaction, but the difference wouldn't have comforted the Tahni trooper in whatever afterlife they believed in. The splash of light and heat was so dramatic, I nearly missed Henckel's shot, though I noticed the Tahni battle-suit spinning away with its lower left leg burned away.

There was an old, old cartoon I'd seen once, something the director of one of my group homes had liked to watch with the kids. It was two-dimensional, hand-drawn, over two centuries old, and the main character was a fox being hunted by a pack of dogs, back when I guess that was a thing people did. The fox was smart and clever and sly, while the hounds were dopy and brainless. There'd been one part that a ten-year-old me had found amusing, when the fox had accidentally stepped on a twig and snapped it with an impossibly loud noise, and all the hounds had stopped what they were doing and swiveled toward the fox like they were orchestrated.

Something like that happened now, with most of the rear rank of the High Guard, the ones not already decisively engaged by First and Second Platoons, turning almost as one to meet us.

My first missile launched before I throttled down my jets and touched ground, a barely-controlled teeth-rattling crash because I couldn't afford to stay in the air now that they'd noticed me. Electron beams were slicing tunnels of white lightning through the air all around me, missing by less than a meter, close enough for the searing heat to bring a sheen of sweat across my whole body even through the armor. I ignored the lightning, moving left with a hop and a half-second burst of the jump-jets, sending me skating across their rank, a meter off the ground.

I wasn't thinking because thinking was too slow, wasn't reacting because reacting meant letting them act first. I'd done a lot of reading while I was in NCO school, and one of the things I'd found was a study that said once someone had enough experience and practice doing something, they did out of instinct and any conscious thought lagged behind by a fraction of a second, rationalizing the decisions their subconscious had made. I didn't let my conscious mind interfere with the process, didn't waste time figuring out why I'd done anything, I just did it and let my conscious mind watch the show.

My missiles were hitting and launching, hitting and launching until the magazine was empty and five enemy suits were down, their missile defenses useless at this range. I'd fired my plasma gun whenever a target presented itself, though I couldn't have sworn to how many times that was. I couldn't have picked out my own shots from Henckel's, or even the enemy electron beams. It was all just a blur of blinding light and raw energy. I'd taken a hit at some point, nothing vital but warning lights were flashing yellow on my HUD, telling me I'd need service on my left knee joint and left hip, and that too much pressure on either could lead to catastrophic failure.

I promised the computer I'd keep that in mind and dismissed the warning with a swipe of my left forefinger.

Time had stretched out into something elastic and meaningless, and at some point, the rest of my squad had moved into the ranks because I heard Graciano yelling at Reyfort to split wider and cut off the enemy retreat.

They're retreating? I hadn't noticed. I forced myself to pay attention to the IFF readout and saw First and Second spread out on a wide front, most of them still alive, while my squad was perpendicular to the end of their line in an L shape, catching the enemy between us. All my people were there on the display, their suits active, and some of the guilt I'd felt at leaving them behind lifted away at the knowledge.

The Tahni were trying to break through the corner of the L and the rest of Third Platoon was rushing into the gaps to keep them in the kill zone. There was barely a platoon of the enemy suits left and I felt a gut-deep shock at how many of the Tahni we'd taken out. Burning, scattered metal was strewn about the rocky highland, broken bodies buried somewhere beneath it and only God and maybe my onboard data recorders knew how many of them I'd killed personally.

My thoughts had become a haze, scattered and unfocused while I let my instincts do the fighting, but now a voice broke through the haze. It was Lt. Ackley, and I had the sense she'd been trying to get through to me for at least a few seconds.

"Alvarez," she said again, "Take First squad and get to the base, knock out those anti-aircraft turrets! Second will be backing you up. Scotty, take charge of them, I'm staying here with Third and Fourth squads to finish this up."

It was harder than I thought tearing myself away from the

fight before it was over. Every nerve in my body screamed at me to keep shooting at the enemy until they were all dead, but the assault shuttles and missile cutter crews were still dying. They'd covered our asses, now it was our chance to return the favor.

"First, on me!" I rasped hoarsely. My throat hurt and I thought maybe I'd been screaming during the battle without realizing it. "Henckel, take point!"

We didn't jet in because that would have meant putting ourselves into the firing arcs of the coil-gun turrets, and maybe they couldn't have seen us in all the burning metal and roiling smoke, but maybe they could. We ran. Again. Not quite as fast this time, and I gave in to responsibility and leadership and all that shit and kept the squad together now that it wasn't a matter of survival. It was hard for me, and I knew it was hard for Henckel because his lead over the rest of us kept growing.

"Pull it back, Tom," I cautioned him once he was a kilometer ahead of me.

"Will do, Sarge." There was reluctance in his voice, resentment, the same feelings I'd had watching the rest of my squad trying to keep up with me when I'd just been one of the grunts.

And I'd be lying if I said I didn't still feel it, but I'd gotten better at keeping it to myself.

So, I restrained myself and forced Henckel to do the same, and we kept a loose wedge formation across the plains to the base. It was a lot like running through the gates of Hell. Fire raged in every direction, smoldering beneath our feet, clinging to us spitefully as we ran through the burning wreckage of our forces and theirs, burning out with the wind of our passage and wreathing us in curls of smoke like demons charging into battle. We weren't fighting angels, though. Both sides were fresh out of those.

Bunkers were arrayed along the perimeter of the base in a half-circle, each of them spraying streams of tantalum darts from heavy KE guns, the last stand of the Tahni ground troops, the last thing they could throw at us. Anti-aircraft launch batteries crouched behind them, the squared-off, coffin-shaped missile pods scanning back and forth as if watching in impotent rage, their missile batteries empty after less than an hour of engaging our air assets. The coil-gun turrets were still a threat, the cooling jackets fat and cylindrical around the electromagnets at the heart of the weapon, filled with liquid nitrogen and still glowing red after long minutes of constant firing. Radar dishes spun beside them with desperate haste, each turn finding a new threat inbound and directing fire toward it.

"Ranger file!" Scotty ordered at about a kilometer out, and we obeyed without thinking, closing up our wedge into a straight line, a spear through the Tahni lines.

It made sense. Spreading out in the face of the emplacements just gave them more targets over a broader area. But it made Henckel our human shield, taking the brunt of the fire from the enemy gun turrets, and that bothered me in a way it never had when I had been the one on point.

"Who's got missiles left?" Scotty asked, and only three affirmatives answered him, none from my squad since we'd been in the thick of the fight against the High Guard. "Fire on my command."

I shouldn't have been able to see the incoming rounds. The tantalum darts were launched electromagnetically, no propellant to ignite, no energy pulse, just a sliver of metal smaller than my little finger zipping out of the coil-guns at three thousand meters per second. But the combination of smoke and fog and the static charge hanging in the air from the discharge of beam weapons and the ECM fields the Tahni were using must have been just right on this night. Streaks of fire scored through the haze, just the faintest ionization trail, but it was enough to follow the trajectory of the bursts as they chewed up the ground in an arc beginning twenty meters to the right of our angle of approach and heading straight for us.

"Target the closest bunker off my laser designator," Scotty said, as calm and matter-of-fact as if he were ordering us to buff the barracks floors. "Fire."

They launched, an angry swarm of fireflies arcing into the sky a hundred meters up before slamming downward. Not enough for my liking, probably not enough to bust through the ceiling of the bunker, but plenty to distract the Tahni troops manning the gun.

Did the Tahni soldiers really believe they could stop us, that there was still a chance to win this battle? Or had they known the moment our ships had Transitioned that they were going to die?

"Cam, take your squad in and trash the triple-A, we'll take care of the bunkers."

"Roger that, Scotty." I switched to my squad net. "Alpha team, break right once we're inside the line. Graciano, start blasting the anti-aircraft batteries as you go. Bravo, break left and follow Henckel and me."

The bunker was a blur of fire and smoke on my right as I broke through the enemy lines, the pounding of the Vigilante's feet taking on a different tone as the dirt and patchy grass of the open fields around the base gave way to fusion-form pavement. We were still nearly a kilometer away from the actual heart of the base, but the blue dome of the deflector shields stretched overhead, shot through with static energy as it absorbed blast after blast from the proton cannons of the missile cutters, ripped apart missiles before their warheads could come close enough to do any real damage.

The deflectors were a sword of Damocles I'd grown used to, just background noise always there, always threatening. If it came down while we were beneath it, we'd be vaporized right alongside the Tahni, yet I had faith in it as I did in my own ability, my own people, for all that it was a thing of the enemy.

What if they just turned it off, gave up and switched off the field when they saw us coming? The thought nagged at me, a tiny fragment of gravel in my shoe that I had to work to ignore. Henckel blasted a missile turret with his plasma gun, the blinding flash a mercy killing to the empty weapon and the futile searching of its crew down beneath the surface, connected via underground cables to a control room.

It still needed to be done. We couldn't take the chance they'd find a reload and take down one of our landers on its way in with a complement of Force Recon, but the real threats were the coil-guns and the next turret was only fifty meters farther along the inner perimeter. Henckel's capacitors were still recharging so I took this one, aiming my plasma gun at the cooling jacket.

The results were spectacular, the already superheated jacket failing like a grenade had gone off in its guts. Liquid nitrogen sublimated in a flash of white and bits of cooling jacket smacked against my chest armor, hard enough to gouge scratches several millimeters deep but not nearly fast enough to penetrate. The magnetic coils beneath ruptured immediately after, static electricity arcing away from the weapon, frying the motorized gimbals and the connections leading back into the control center and the emitter froze in place, smoke drifting away from the wreckage of the weapon.

Henckel was already moving to the next emplacement and didn't seem to notice the Tahni Shock-troops dashing across the pavement, moving from cover to cover, from the shadow of a storage building to the shelter of a heavy, metal construction loader, and heading for us. The powered armor was two meters tall, maybe two hundred kilos, not a self-contained battlesuit in the manner of the High Guard suits or the Vigilantes, just an exoskeleton designed to let the average infantry soldier carry heavier armor and weapons. The Commonwealth didn't bother with them because it combined the worst characteristics of regular infantry and battlesuits: it had a longer logistics train than Force Recon without the added mobility and versatility of a drop-trooper.

Still, it was easy to see the advantages of the Shock-troops for static defenses, particularly when there were two platoons of them charging at us. KE gun darts began smacking into my chest armor, each impact marked by a yellow warning flash in my HUD, but none of them enough individually to break through.

"Contact right!" I warned the others. "Enemy infantry in the open! Target with grenade launchers and fire at will!"

It was easy to forget the grenade launchers. They were strictly a secondary weapon, useless against armor or vehicles or aircraft, a throw-in to let us engage dismounts without wasting shots from our plasma guns. I'd always thought of them as a time-sink, just something else to fire at the live range and PMCS, and I hadn't used mine in combat. Until now.

The launcher was built into the Vigilante's left forearm, and the reticle floated across my HUD as I lifted and turned, leading the trooper running point by just a few meters. I touched the trigger and two rounds kicked out of the short barrel with a puff of coldgas before their integral rocket motors ignited and they homed in on the trooper I'd designated with the targeting laser. I didn't have the luxury of watching the impact; there were too many of them to stand still. I jammed down the trigger and walked the launcher backward, emptying the two-hundred-round magazine in a matter of seconds.

A line of explosions erupted along the zig-zag path the Shock-troopers had taken out toward us from the fortified entrance to the base, the rounds I'd fired joined by a barrage from the rest of the squad, nearly two thousand rounds of

Hyper-Explosive Armor Piercing plasma grenades tearing apart pavement, vehicles, buildings and enemy troops. Shock-troopers tumbled to one side and another, collapsing as their battery packs took spears of plasma and cut power to their exoskeletons, or merely freezing in place with their joints locked in death. By the time the smoke cleared, I only saw three of the Tahni soldiers still moving, and they were hobbling back to the base, barely able to move.

Overhead, the deflector shield flickered and died, leaving behind a few stray bolts of artificial lightning, and I knew Scotty and his squad had taken out the power feeds to the dish. I flinched, expecting a rain of missiles to fall on our heads, the Attack Command as heedless of our existence as the Fleet seemed to be; but, miraculously, it didn't come.

A flare of plasma from off to my left caught my attention with the crackling dome of fire that had been the overworked deflector shield down at last. It was Henckel taking out another of the Anti-Aircraft Artillery turrets, the gun throwing off a shower of sparks as its power feed burned away. I tracked around the perimeter, looking for the next one to target, but a blue icon on my IFF transponder showed Graciano and Alpha team already circling around from that direction.

"They're down, boss," he told me. "This side of the perimeter is clear."

"Triple-A is down, Scotty," I reported immediately, knowing he'd need to pass it along to the Fleet.

He didn't acknowledge, probably because he was already making that call. The roar of turbines penetrated my helmet, seeming to come from all around me, and I leaned backwards as far as I could in the armor and looked upward. Marine landers were burning in on columns of fire, their belly ramps extended before they even touched down, the Force Recon troops rushing down and leaping off the last two meters to the ground. They didn't stop to say hi, just gathered into tactical formations and headed for the base, ready to do their part in the operation. Ours was over.

And for some of us, I thought, remembering Fourth Platoon, their war was over forever.

[7]

It began snowing ten minutes before the memorial started, and by the time Captain Covington stepped out in front of the formation, the sky was solid grey and the snow was coming down hard enough that I couldn't even see the barracks. It was winter on this part of Hachiman and even though my field jacket kept my core nice and toasty, the frigid wind whipped at my face and stung my ears, and I didn't want to be out here.

"We are gathered here today," Covington said, his voice cutting through the wind like an alarm klaxon, "to pay our last respects to our brothers and sisters of Fourth Platoon."

They were brothers and sisters, fellow Marines, all that happy horseshit, but I hadn't known a one of them beyond their names, and the ones I knew I hadn't liked. Would Lt. Costas have been less of an asshole if he'd survived Oasis? Would their Third squad leader have been less inclined to cook that nasty boiled cabbage in his barracks room and stink us all out of the building?

I tried to feel guilty for not grieving, but I wondered if I would want everyone to stand in the snow and do the final roll call for me when my time came. I guess I'd just want Vicky and

Scotty to have a beer in my honor and move on. But traditions had to be served, even if the dead cared nothing for them.

"They lived the life of a Marine Drop Troop and died as they lived, died the only way a true Marine would want to die, in combat, fighting for what they thought was right."

Did the Skipper really buy into this shit? Did he really think people like me and Henckel and the other recruits from the mega-cities were fighting for what we believed in? Maybe Costas had been a true believer. He'd gone to the Academy, requested the Marines. But I know at least half his platoon had joined for the same reason I had, because the alternative was punitive hibernation. And if we took pride in our jobs now it was because we didn't want to let down our friends who counted on us to live through the next battle.

"The Commonwealth Fleet Marine Corps has a long and storied history, dating back to the days before there was a Space Fleet, before there was even a Commonwealth. We trace our history back to the United States Marine Corps, an organization that predated the country it defended and served on wooden sailing ships on the open oceans of Earth. From the halls of Montezuma, the Marine hymn begins, to the shores of Tripoli. Those battles were in the Nineteenth Century, four hundred years ago. And with each war since, the Marines have added battles, added honor, and added to the rolls of the fallen. We may mourn these men and women, but we should not regret their sacrifice, for it was given freely."

I wasn't quite sure why, but this was pissing me off. It was nothing we hadn't all heard before. Hell, after Brigantia, there'd been more Marines missing from the final roll call than had been there to show up for it. But Fourth Platoon hadn't died heroically, hadn't made any last stand with guns blazing. They'd died because some stuffed shirt back on Earth who'd never heard a shot fired in anger had decided Drop Troopers were expendable and cruisers weren't.

There was something burning in my guts and not all the snow on this shithole planet could put it out. Maybe some liquor could, if this damned ceremony would *ever* end. I'd stopped listening to Covington, letting my eyes haze over, focusing on the giant snowflakes blowing in on the blistering cold wind. But I noticed motion, saw him saluting Top, and I knew what would happen next.

"Gunnery Sergeant Holmes!" Top said in a quarterdeck bellow.

"Present!" the First Platoon sergeant responded, his reply sharp and loud.

"Staff Sergeant Lundquist!"

"Present!"

And on it went, through all the platoons until he got to Fourth.

"Gunnery Sergeant Surio!"

No response, of course.

"Gunnery Sergeant Sanjay Surio!"

Silence.

"Gunnery Sergeant Sanjay E. M. Surio!"

One last try, and still nothing, and she went down the line, three calls for each name and no reply. So many names, all met with silence. I'd felt choked up the first time I'd heard it, devastated the second, after Brigantia. This time, I only felt a dull anger. Top had been a Marine for decades. How many of these had she gone through? How much meaning did they still hold for her?

Lance Corporal Gutierrez from Third Platoon brought out the trumpet to play Taps. Poor son of a bitch had drawn the short straw and been forced to learn to play the ancient brass instrument for ceremonies, and he still sounded horrible. They could have used a synthesizer or prerecorded music, but this was traditional and the Marines were all about tradition.

I thought we'd be dismissed to quarters once the ceremony was over, but Covington returned to the front of the formation instead.

"Normally," he said, "after a mission with this many losses, we'd be taking at least a month out of the field, to shift around personnel and train up replacements. But ours wasn't the only mission and losses or no, we are part of a larger plan. And they need us back out there." Maybe it was the cold air, maybe it was the exhaustion, but Covington sounded weary to me. "We'll be picking up a replacement platoon at a staging area en route, then heading back into Tahni space. You'll be fully briefed while we're on board ship, but we leave in thirty hours. PMCS and then sleep."

Sleep. I didn't need sleep. I needed a drink. I needed a different war, because this one sucked.

———

"I thought we were supposed to be getting sleep," Vicky whispered into my ear, then followed it with her tongue.

The storage building was dark and chill, but it was insulated, a shelter from the wind and from prying eyes, and the sleeping bag I'd requisitioned from supply was enough to keep us both warm, despite the lack of heat and the lack of clothing. It even made the repurposed cargo pallet halfway comfortable.

"Is that what you want?" I asked her. "To go to sleep?" I tried to make it sound teasing, challenging, but it came out harsher than I'd intended.

Vicky pulled away and regarded me with what might have been concern, or perhaps caution in her eyes. It was too dark to tell.

"This is starting to get to you, too, isn't it?"

"You mean Fourth Platoon buying it?" I asked, as if I wasn't sure what she was talking about. "No," I lied, looking away. "I mean, a lot more people than that died on Brigantia, civilians, too."

"Brigantia meant something," she countered, grabbing me by the back of the neck like I was a misbehaving dog and forcing me to meet her eyes. "We helped people get their homes back on Brigantia. Even though that woman you told me about, Maria, died there, you seemed more okay after that than you do now."

"You're not okay with it," I said, making counteraccusations as a deflection, the way I had when I was a kid talking to psych counsellors in juvenile detention. "You told me before Oasis even that you didn't like the whole bullshit plan."

"I didn't and I don't. I don't think the Skipper likes it either, but there's nothing he can do about it. We just have to do our job."

"And hope it isn't our dropship that takes the hit." I shrugged off her hands and sat back down on the sleeping bag, the air going out of me along with the mood. "Someone's will. I was watching the approach through the feed from a missile cutter. I saw their dropship get hit. I think they had to know it was coming." I shook my head. "I'm not doing that again. I don't want to see if it's my turn."

Vicky was silent for a moment, her pale skin shining in the light leaking through the external floods. Then she grabbed her clothes and began dressing.

"I'm sorry," I said instantly, not knowing what I was apologizing for, reaching for her hand. She slipped it away from mine.

"I think you need to be alone, Cam." She stood, stepping into her boots. "And I think I do, too."

She hesitated at the doorway, looking back.

"I'll see you on the ship."

I watched her go, suddenly feeling the cold again.

"Shit."

I pulled on my clothes and fastened my field jacket, slipping on my gloves and watch cap before I headed back out the door. I opened the door a crack and cautiously stuck my head out, checking for any MPs who might be out on security patrol. The base had grown since we'd left for Oasis as other companies moved in and barracks were built for Fleet pilots, maintenance techs and all the other support troops necessary to run this sort of outpost. With the extra troops had come a ViR entertainment center, an Officer's Club, an NCO Club, alcohol, and plenty of fights. And the cops.

I didn't see any drunks or cops just now, didn't see anyone on the darkened streets. In the northern sky, a pale green aurora glowed its boreal light, snaking across the blackness. I'd freaked out the first time I'd seen it, sure it meant we were under attack until Scotty explained to me that they occurred naturally as well as being the result of nuclear weapons going off in the upper atmosphere.

I stood in the middle of the fusion-form street and stared at the lights in the sky, still amazed at the beauty out here among the death and ugliness and understanding just a bit why people left the comfort of Earth to brave the colonies.

"You can't sleep either, huh?"

I nearly jumped out of my skin before I realized it was Henckel. I wouldn't have recognized him if he hadn't spoken. He was wrapped up in what the Force Recon guys called "snivel gear," all the cold weather clothing the Marines issued and then some. I cocked an eyebrow at him and half-grinned, despite the mood Vicky had left me in.

"You just a little cold there, Henckel?"

"I'm still not used to weather," he admitted, shrugging

beneath layers of parka, field jacket and insulated underwear. "I mean, I got used to *hot* weather on Inferno," he clarified, "but I've never been in cold weather before, you know?"

"Oh, I know, Tom," I assured him. "You never got above-ground at Capital City in your whole life?"

"Not until the Marines hauled me up to the shuttle port. Just lucky they didn't slap neural restraints on me first."

"I never did ask you," I said, "but what did they get you for?"

It was a faux pas, really, a violation of an unwritten and unspoken law among the Drop Troops. So many of us had been forced into enlisting, it was worth a justified punch in the mouth to bring up another Marine's criminal history, but I didn't think Henckel would be offended, and I was right.

"The usual stuff," he said. "Drugs, pirated fabrication codes, petty theft..." He squeezed his eyes shut, as if he were trying to shut out a memory. "And attempted murder."

"Sorry, man," I said, raising a hand to keep him from continuing. "I didn't mean to bring up bad memories."

"No, it's okay." He leaned against the wall of the storage shed, stuffing his hands in his pockets. Top would have ripped him a new one for that, but I didn't give a shit. Wasn't like there'd be any officers around to salute at this time of night. "It was just..." His chin went down to his chest. "It was just there was this girl who lived a few doors down, and I liked her. But she got involved running product for one of the gangs and I tried to talk her into stopping. So, she went to Remy, the guy in charge of the block, and she asked him if she could quit."

"Fuck," I said under my breath. Stories like that never ended well. No one quit the gang any way except feet first. I couldn't see Henckel's eyes anymore, and it was probably better that way.

"Remy must have liked her, because he didn't kill her. He didn't even beat her up. Just told her she had to do one more job, to pick up a package in the Kuratong Baleleng territory and bring it out. And then he sent a message to Kuratong Baleleng and let them know she was coming."

He fell silent and I thought he might stop there, *hoped* he would stop.

"They never found her. The word is that they burn the remains and then dump them into the composting pits. But they let the family know. They always do." I couldn't see his eyes, but I could see the smile. It was feral, a baring of teeth. "I waited for Remy, staked out his girlfriend's place and got him on the way out, played him like a fucking bass drum, man. The only reason I stopped was I thought he was dead." Henckel slammed an elbow against the sheet metal wall of the storage building, the impact a hollow thump. "I wish he had been. But they found him and saved him. And here I am, and I guess it's as good a place as any, huh?"

"Is that what's keeping you up?" I asked him. "Were you thinking about her?"

"No." He looked up and I thought I saw a glistening of something in the corner of his eye. *Shit. Why did I ask? They have these unwritten rules for a reason.* "I mean, I think about her all the time, but that's not why I'm out here." He shook his head. "I'm afraid, Sarge."

"Yeah, I can understand that. I mean, this is a quick turn-around, and the last mission was tough." And I'd been told in NCO school that the stress wasn't just cumulative, it was exponential, but I wasn't sure if Henckel knew enough math for that to matter to him. "I can't promise you we'll all get out of this, but if…"

"No," he said quickly, cutting me off. "I ain't afraid of dying. You been where I was, you know dying doesn't seem so bad. Thing is, I know you're counting on me. I don't want to sound like I think I'm hot shit, but I've heard people talking. They put you and me up front because they *need* us up front." He hissed out a clouded breath, the vapor trailing away from the sides of his mouth. "I'm afraid I'm going to let you down. This is the only thing I've ever been good at. I don't want to fuck it up."

The words punched me in the gut and I felt unworthy to hear them, somehow. I wanted to reply with something meaningful, but I was barely twenty-one and fresh out of profound sayings of my own, so I settled for one I'd heard Top say.

"Tom, there's only one good thing I can say about war. It lets you really know who the guy fighting beside you is." I put a hand on his shoulder, squeezing hard. "If there's anything I can be dead certain sure of, it's that I am not worried about you letting me down."

[8]

I'd told Vicky I wasn't going to tie into the external cameras anymore, but I couldn't help myself. I had to see.

"This is going to be the largest operation of the war to date," Captain Covington had said, and I'd been skeptical at the time, watching the briefing on board the *Iwo Jima* just after we'd Transitioned away from Hachiman.

Not anymore. The *Iwo Jima* wasn't alone this time. The *Tripoli* floated off her port side, an identical twin, carrying three full companies of Drop Troopers and a full battalion of Force Recon, and that wasn't even the most impressive part. Ten squadrons of missile cutters shielded our approach, a glittering starfield of fusion drives in the darkness, and I knew their carrier waited somewhere behind us at the farthest Transition point in the system. I hadn't seen it, but an image of it had been part of the briefing. It was a skeletal thing, all framework with reactors and Transition drives and long, narrow struts to allow the cutters to dock, and a pair of habitation modules at opposite ends of the ship and nothing else. No weapons, no fusion drives, nothing. It existed only to allow the cutters a longer reach and its response to any attack would be to Transition out of the system immediately.

Which sounded like a damned good plan and I wished to hell I'd been forced to join the Space Fleet instead.

Between us and the cutters were the slightly dimmer glows of a full wing of assault shuttles, and I should have been impressed by all the power the military had brought to bear on this one target, but I wasn't. I knew better. If the High Command had committed all these ships to one target, it was because they'd thought we'd need it.

In the distance, dark against the glare of the system primary, was our target. I knew what it looked like. I'd seen it in the briefing a week before.

———

"The target's military designation is Confluence," Covington told us, motioning toward the holographic image of the blue and green planet. "It's right in the heart of the system's habitable zone, with a temperate climate and a large civilian population. Three quarters of the planet's surface is underwater, with one fairly large continent and the rest of the land mass split up between half a dozen island chains. While there are a few industrial farms out on the coasts, and some minor settlements in the islands, the main area of habitation is a medium-sized city along the shores of the continent's largest river. It's one of the Tahni's oldest colonies, established just after they developed the Transition drive. Intelligence estimates show a permanent civilian population of nearly a million, and a transient number of approximately half that."

"Half a million tourists at a time?" Scotty blurted from where he stood near the front of the ship's situation room. "Do they have like a theme park or something?"

"It's a religious site," Covington explained. "It has something to do with their god granting them the power to expand the Imperium beyond their system, with this being the first of the habitable worlds they discovered. There's nothing intrinsically valuable about the planet other than its biomass, so it's not as heavily defended as many of their other colonies, but there's a temple here, one of their largest."

I raised my hand and Covington nodded at me.

"If there's nothing that valuable here," I asked, "then why are we bothering to launch an assault on it?"

"The whole purpose of the strategy we've adopted," he reminded me, sounding very much the teacher, "is to get them to draw their forces away from our occupied colonies. This is a morale war as much as anything, and this is a morale target. They will consider our very presence on the world akin to sacrilege, and if our intelligence analysts are reading this right, it should enrage them and shake their faith in their god."

I said nothing, but felt skeptical that our intelligence analysts could tell their asses from a meteor crater.

"This is our target." The view changed to an image of some sort of complex. Its design seemed to make no sort of logical sense, like a maze had fucked a Moebius strip and had a mutant child. "It's their temple built to celebrate their expansion to the stars."

"A civilian target?" Ackley asked, and I thought from the look on her face that she was genuinely shocked, as if she thought we were better than that, somehow.

"Their religion is deeply intertwined with their government and their military," Covington told her, "in ways it's hard for us to understand given our culture. No one lives in the temple, and we're fairly certain they'll evacuate civilians from the area once we Transition into the system, so collateral damage should be minimal." He shrugged, the corner of his mouth quirking downward. "There is some sort of housing area not too far from the base, centrally located between it and the temple, and we're going to try to be precise in our air strikes, but taking this target is our priority and we will accomplish the mission."

"We're going to destroy it, sir?" That was Lt. Victor, Costas' replacement. His platoon had come aboard from the *Tripoli* when we'd rendezvoused with her and the rest of the strike force. He was younger than Costas, just out of the Academy, and had less of the late platoon leader's bluff and arrogance, and perhaps less of his confidence, too. "Is that...I mean, isn't it against the laws of war?"

There were a few harsh chuckles at that until Top stomped on them.

"At ease!" she barked, and even the officers stopped grinning.

Covington didn't laugh, or smile, or look impatient. He answered the question with the same sense of sincerity with which it had been asked, which I thought was a mark of a patient officer.

"The laws of war are standards we apply to ourselves. There are no third parties in this war, no independent monitors, no one to enforce any standards except the winners. We avoid civilian casualties when possible for the very pragmatic and selfish reason that we don't want to provoke the Tahni into slaughtering our own populations. But they lack those restraints and they've already demonstrated it. They murdered half a million people on the squatter colonies at the start of the war." He snorted humorlessly. "This particular iteration of the war. Their concepts of morality and ethics are different from ours, the product of a different history and different biology."

"But they're so close to us in appearance, sir," Victor objected. "In my Academy xenobiology course, the professor said we're almost sure they're related to us."

"Genetically, yes," Covington agreed and my eyes widened. I hadn't heard this at all. "But that's a whole line of academic debate, and even if the idea of Panspermia is true, we're talking about related back when RNA was the most complicated building block of life. Hell, let's get real crazy and say the wild theories about ancient aliens creating life and terraforming planets are true. We'd still have less in common with the Tahni than we do with chimpanzees."

The Skipper raised a hand as if to forestall any further questions.

"The point is, the Tahni don't have our society's delineation between civilian and military targets, and this temple is one of those areas where the lines blur. Priests in the Tahni society are part of the Imperial government and pilgrimages to the holy places are required for promotion to high office or senior military rank. That's the final word, and if you don't feel, in good conscience, that you can participate in this attack, you need to come see me in private after the briefing."

That shut everyone up, including Lt. Victor. I didn't give a shit about bombing some Tahni church. Or maybe I might have, if I'd been willing to waste any time thinking about it, but I was more interested in hearing something that would convince me I was going to be alive at the end of this op. I snuck a few glances at the others, wondering how they felt about it. Ackley still seemed troubled and even Scotty was frowning. Vicky was stone-faced. I hadn't had the chance to talk to her since we'd boarded the *Iwo Jima*.

No, that was a lie. I hadn't *tried* to talk to her. I was pissed at her and I didn't know if I had any right to be, and thinking I might be in the wrong was just making me even more pissed. I still wasn't sure why she'd left, if it was me talking about the likelihood we'd die or maybe me saying Fourth Platoon getting killed didn't bother me. The whole thing made my head hurt and I couldn't decide if Scotty had been right about her and she just wanted something light and impersonal and I'd made it too personal.

"The target is guarded by a Tahni destroyer as well as at least three squadrons of corvettes and an unknown force of dual-environment fighters based on the planet near their primary spaceport. We have no data on how many ground troops are stationed there, but if the ratio of ground troops to space assets remains similar to our past experience, we should expect at least a battalion of High Guard and another of Shock-troops, plus various service and support soldiers who will fight at need."

"Sir." Ackley had raised her hand.

"Lieutenant?"

"Aren't we violating doctrine and the principle of concentration of force? Shouldn't we have a three-to-one ratio against the defenders?"

"Bottom line, we don't have the ships or personnel available to assemble that large a force," Covington told her, not holding back. "And if we wait until we've built up those forces to strike at the Tahni, we're ceding them time to consolidate their gains. That's time we're not going to get back. It's to our advantage to keep the situation fluid, stay inside their OODA loop."

"We're expendable," I murmured. I hadn't realized I'd said it aloud until Henckel threw me a sharp glance. He seemed alarmed at the thought and I felt guilty for a moment, but shrugged it off. He wasn't stupid. He had to see it.

"Here are what details of the target we've been able to glean from long-range reconnaissance and Scout Service probes."

The image in the holographic display at the center of the compartment changed from the welcoming blues and greens of Confluence to a tighter view, just a few hundred meters above the surface of the city. Did their cities have names? They never told us the city names in the briefings. Maybe naming cities was a human thing, or maybe we just didn't have detailed enough intelligence to know. Confluence would have made a better name for the city than the planet. It was built around the confluence of the broad, cross-continental river coming out of the western mountains and heading down to the ocean and a small tributary. The buildings were different than I'd seen before, less boxy and utilitarian than their military bases, some thin and spindly in clusters of spikes dug partway underground, some blinding white spheres built on octagonal bases. They seemed more like works of art than buildings and I wondered how practical they were.

Art or no, the Tahni obviously valued the temple more than the city, since the deflector dishes were spread out between the military base and the temple and barely covered the edge of the city. They did protect that cluster of boxy structures near the temple and I wondered if those were some sort of public shelters.

The base itself was like every one I'd seen so far, but bigger. The Tahni might have some cool architectural ideas, but they were strictly pragmatists when it came to their military installations. Squared off buildings were built low and heavily shielded, and mostly underground except for the hangars where they kept their fighters. Sometimes shipboard, when I didn't have anything better to do, I'd just run through subjects on the central database at random. A few weeks ago, I'd seen photos of excavations on Earth in the Middle East, ancient fortresses with crenelated battlements and these could have been built by the Assyrians or Babylonians brought forward in time.

"Delta, Bravo and Charlie Armored Infantry companies and 4th Battalion of the 37th Force Recon will be dropping under cover of the missile cutters and assault shuttles." His eyes searched out the crowd, the company packed shoulder to shoulder into the briefing room, the ones farthest back hanging out the open hatchways. "I know some of you are concerned about the presence of the destroyer, but in the short term, it could work to our advantage. As much as it exists to guard the planet, the corvettes exist to protect it. The Fleet Attack Command analysts believe the corvettes will concentrate their fire on the cutters to prevent them from getting clean hits on the destroyer. Our main worry will be the fighters once we hit orbit. We'll have to count on the assault shuttles to clear the path for us there."

Covington traced a line on the screen of his 'link and red circles appeared in the hologram around the temple, the military base and the deflector shields.

"Unlike previous operations, Force Recon will not be waiting for us to clear out armored resistance before they land. It's believed the skies will be too dangerous for them to keep circling. Instead, they're going to touch down on the far side of the city and march in from the east to hit the main military base, taking out air defenses near the city along the way. Although the primary target is the temple, the base is a secondary target and we still plan on destroying all enemy forces on the planet before we withdraw."

He pointed to the temple and the deflector shield.

"Charlie and Bravo are going straight for the temple to take out the air defenses. Which leaves the deflector dishes for us. We have high confidence that the enemy will deploy most of their own battlesuits and any artillery to the temple area, to defend the deflector dishes." His face was grim. "This is going to be a bloody bastard of a fight, ladies and gentlemen. I want you to look to your left and right and mark the faces there well, because some of them won't be coming back from this."

Henckel was staring at me and I gave him an elbow.

"Don't get your hopes up," I told him in a soft hiss and he chuckled.

"The detailed op order will be disseminated by your platoon leaders and squad leaders, and you'll have the opportunity to run simulations in the pods before we Transition. Don't waste the time we have. An extra hour's practice could be the difference between a successful operation and a disaster."

———

Staring at the Tahni destroyer, a silver wedge across the face of Confluence, I was betting on disaster.

"...four, three, two, one...launching!"

I hadn't even heard the five-minute warning, and barely had time to suck in a breath before the boost from the dropship's drive shoved me into the padding inside the Vigilante suit. It was another hard boost, pushing the edge of nine gees from the tunnel vision and audio exclusion that hit me immediately, and I wondered how long we could keep this up. Dropships weren't assault shuttles, all fuel and weapons. These birds had a shitload of cargo to carry and usually didn't have the fuel stores for violent maneuvering in space. Maybe they intended to refuel them on the ground. I found I didn't care about the fate of the bird, didn't much mind the crushing acceleration. I just wanted to be on the ground as soon as possible.

I wasn't watching the external cameras anymore. I didn't know how the hell the cutters were going to take out the massive hulk of the destroyer and I didn't care to see them die trying. I kept trying to convince myself it wouldn't be a bad way to go, just taking a missile right up the center of the dropship, a clean, painless fusion explosion and everything would be over. Blackness, or Heaven, or Purgatory, or Hell, or Valhalla or whatever. I don't know that I believed in any sort of afterlife, despite the strict Catholicism my mother had drilled into us when I was a child. If there was a just and beneficent God running this universe, I certainly hadn't met Him yet.

"Jesus," Henckel's rasping groan sounded over a private channel between us, "is this fucking boost ever gonna let up?" He sounded like an elephant was sitting on his chest and I think the actual weight pretty much lined up with that.

And as if on cue, it did. I couldn't have said how long it lasted because I'd been doing my best to avoid looking at the clock, but once it ended, the air rushed back into my chest. We were still at two gravities, but that seemed like nothing compared to the initial boost, though my chest still hurt bad enough I thought I'd cracked a rib.

"Shit, we're close now," Henckel said and I cursed because he was making it harder for me to keep my promise to myself not to look at the camera feed. Sure, others in my squad might be gabbing about it, but they were doing it on their own private channels and not bothering me with it. "Oh, my God! Do you *see* that?"

"Damn it all, anyway." I opened the feed to the dropship's external view and nearly swore again.

Yeah, we were close all right. Close to the planet and oh so *fucking* close to the Tahni destroyer. She hung off the circle of Confluence, her plasma drive sputtering irregular flashes of fusion flame as the magnetic containment fields began to fail. Atmosphere vented from half a dozen rents in her hull and caught fire as it evacuated, and a jagged, charred chunk had been bitten out of her stern. I didn't know much about space combat or the physics involved, but I could guess that one of the Ship-Buster missiles had detonated close enough to overload the destroyer's deflectors in one spot.

Another of the huge missiles slammed into the ship as I watched, and she had nothing left to stop it, not a flicker of deflector screens nor a single round of anti-missile fire. A smaller ship, what I assumed was one of the Tahni corvettes, made a run for the missile, but the laser it fired might as well have been a water gun for all the damage it did to the missile's thick armor. The fusion explosion whited out the camera view to nothing for several seconds before the feed returned.

Where the destroyer had been was an expanding globe of white fire and not so much as a splinter of the huge ship remained. The corvette that had been trying to save her was gone as well, nowhere to be seen against the blue of the planet. I gritted my teeth, not wanting to know and yet *needing* to know.

I gave in and tried to tie into the tactical transmissions from the missile cutters. There'd been ten squadrons of the things and I thought sure one must be close enough to communicate with the *Iwo Jima* and they'd be sharing the feed with the drop-ship pilots to show them the situation in the battlespace. I found nothing.

I tried dipping into the comm channels for the dropship and heard nothing.

Okay, jamming had to be pretty fierce this close to a major colony. I checked the sensor feed, hoping to pick up some IFF transponders if nothing else...and got nothing, not a single transponder, which was also understandable if the jamming was that bad. But I also saw nothing on the sensor screen's visible arc that the tactical computer could positively identify as a missile cutter.

They couldn't *all* be gone, could they?

An explosion flared somewhere in high orbit around Confluence, roughly where the briefings had told us the orbital defense platforms would be, and a sensor blip snuck up behind the blast. There. That was a cutter. And another just to the port of it, the wingman.

"I think that's the last of the platforms," someone in the

cockpit transmitted. A pause and she spoke again. "*Two*, are you reading me?" She didn't bother to take her thumb off the transmit button before she made the next comment to her copilot. "Still not getting through. I wonder if she's even back there, still. If she's not, it's going to be a long walk home."

"Don't worry about it," the copilot said, voice taut with dark humor. "The Fleet carrier can give us a ride. She'll have plenty of room, now."

The voices cut off with the click of the transmission ending.

"Transport squadron," an incoming signal lit up the commo board again, "this is Assault One." The Wing commander of the assault shuttles. A full Fleet captain if I remembered right. "We are detecting a full fighter wing making for orbit from the city."

That would be sixty birds for a Fleet assault shuttle wing, probably about the same for the Tahni except it would be divisible by eight. Sixty-four maybe, against sixty of our assault shuttles, assuming we hadn't lost any already.

"Roger that, Assault One," the dropship pilot replied, his tone laconic and calm. "We'll keep our eyes open and our guns hot, but we'd appreciate it if you could keep those bastards off our six."

"We'll do our best, but we're going to have to divert a couple of squadrons to suppress the air defenses. Good luck, Transport One."

"Can you see what's going on, Sarge?" Henckel asked me. I didn't even bother to remind him not to call me 'Sarge.'

Oh yeah, I could see it, all right. Darts of dull-grey metal were rising from the day side of Confluence to meet us, bristling with missiles. Individually, they weren't particularly formidable, not heavily armored nor massively armed nor all that fast or maneuverable outside the atmosphere that was their true home. But there were just so damned many of them...

I was about to try to explain to Henckel what was going on,

when an announcement over the dropship's PA system took care of it for me.

"Attention all Marines," the dropship's crew chief announced with the voice of a weathered veteran who knew what to expect and wasn't too happy about it, "prepare for evasive maneuvers. And for what we are about to receive may the Lord make us truly thankful..."

.

[9]

"Oh, Jesus," I moaned involuntarily, and it wasn't a curse.

Boost at six gravities, no boost and microgravity, a sustained banging on the hull like a giant wanting to get in as maneuvering thrusters kicked us to the port, another six gees of acceleration, microgravity again, more maneuvering thrusters and nine gravities and close to blacking out, except I *thought* we were decelerating now...

Over and over again for what could have been hours but was probably only minutes. I tried to keep the feed dark so I wouldn't have to see it, but the constant maneuvering combined with the view of the front face of my helmet was giving me motion sickness despite the best the anti-nausea meds could do and I *had* to bring the external view back up.

Just in time to see us entering the atmosphere. If the zero-g maneuvering had threatened motion sickness, then the aerobatics demonstration the dropship pilot put on once the pull of Confluence began fighting against the push of the drives for dominance over my stomach basically put a gun to my head and told me to throw up or else.

I bit down and tried to trap the bile before it escaped. Vomit burned in my throat, greater agony than the nine-gravity burns, but I clamped my teeth shut and swallowed it back down because I couldn't think of anything short of death that would be worse than spewing my lunch all over the inside of my helmet.

The clouds outside were spinning, trading places with the navy blue of the atmosphere's edge every half-second, and when the spinning stopped, the horizon only remained straight until the dropship plunged straight down, a high-g dive that peeled my lips back from my teeth. The only reason I didn't piss my pants was because I didn't have any piss left.

Keeping my eyes open took a supreme effort, focusing on anything even more so, but I finally saw the enemy. Just a few contrails streaming into a bank of cirrus clouds, then a black shape zipping by so fast it might have been my imagination. Loud thumps shook the fuselage and panic surged along with the thought we'd been hit, but out to the sides of the bird I caught the edges of bright flashes and glittering white puffs of chaff and I realized the pilots had launched countermeasures. Electrostatically charged chaff and thermite charges were churning the air behind us, trying to draw away the Tahni missiles from below and above.

How many SAMs did they have down there? A hundred? A thousand? The assault shuttles were trying to take them out but it only took one to get through. A clean, quick death wouldn't be terrible, but the fall.... I thought about the fall from the dropship on Brigantia and the lake I'd found and what would have happened if it hadn't been there. It would be cleaner if I didn't try to use the jets to slow myself, a single, smashing impact and then nothing. But I wouldn't be able to do it. I knew myself well enough to know I'd hit the jets and try to abate the fall and I'd hit hard enough to break every bone in my body and *not* die. That was the nightmare, the worst-case scenario, and the best was instant death and I didn't care for the whole spectrum of possibilities.

We pulled out of the dive close to another dropship, its bulbous, ungainly lifting body shape a twin of our own and I wondered how the damned things even stayed in the air, much less handled this sort of maneuvering. I tried to identify the bird but we were both moving too sharply and violently for me to read the tail numbers. And then it was gone.

Our bird shook like it had been physically struck when the shockwave hit us, the mass of superheated air from the death of the other dropship, and we spun away. I jammed my eyes shut, sure we were in our death spiral, that we wouldn't be pulling out of this one. I didn't know our pilot's name, but if we made it out of this, I was going to find her and buy her the most expensive drink they served in the officer's club, because somehow, she brought the dropship back to stability. The huge aircraft bobbed up and down like a cork in the ocean but we weren't in the uncontrolled spin and I couldn't see anything else in the air with us.

"Is that it?" Henckel asked me, his voice a rasp. He gagged halfway through the question, but I caught the gist of it. "Are we through?"

"There ain't no through until we're on the ground."

We fell into formation with four other dropships and their chin-mounted turrets flashed white, spitting laser pulses at a flight of Tahni fighters climbing up from the surface. It didn't seem so far down now that we were through the thickest of the cloud layers, and the indistinct blurs of green and brown were clarifying into rolling hills, and open plains cut with the striations of river valleys.

Flashes of white and red ignited above the river valley like a fireworks show, a fascinating spectacle until I realized it was the residue of our assault shuttles duking it out with the air defense emplacements. Was each of those detonations one of our assault shuttles dying? Or one of the Tahni fighters, or an intercepted SAM? There was no way to know, and when I tried to listen in on the chatter from the flight crew, I got nothing but an earful of incomprehensible jargon until one, unmistakable word.

"Incoming!"

Reality curved around me in a descending spiral and everything outside turned into a multicolored blur punctuated with flashes of fire and at least three solid, rending cracks that sounded so wrong and so bad they couldn't be anything but damage to the fuselage. We stopped spinning and twisting and rolling for a half a second, just long enough for me to see something I would never be able to un-see, something I'd go to my grave wishing I'd never witnessed.

One of the dropships had been torn apart by a missile, ripped in half in a cloud of billowing smoke, and Marines were tumbling out of it like the discarded toys of a bored child. I heard someone screaming at the Drop-Troops to hit the jets and realized after a half a second that it was me. None of them did. In retrospect, I suppose their suits had been damaged badly enough in the explosion that none of them could have, and at this altitude, it probably wouldn't have saved them.

But I watched them drop, hoping to the very last second when the ship rotated away and they disappeared off the camera view that one of them would try to fly.

I was praying. I couldn't remember the last time I'd prayed in earnest, and I hated myself for my weakness. God had shown very clearly that He didn't give a shit about me or my family, or all those helpless kids in the group homes. He'd shown me through inaction and indifference that the only justice in this world is what we can take with our own hands. And yet I prayed to this apathetic, uncaring God with all my heart, not asking to live through this day, just asking Him to get me to the fucking ground. Once I was there, once things were back in my hands, I could take care of the rest, but I wanted down.

God said yes.

"Drop! Drop! Drop!" God sounded a lot like Lt. Ackley.

I fell into the stillness of a Confluence morning.

And it was still; no wind, no rain, not a cloud in the sky over the city except the black pillars of smoke from what had once been anti-aerospacecraft batteries. It was eerily quiet until I triggered the jump-jets and the suit pushed back up against me with a whine of raging, desperate turbines. My descent slowed and I began paying attention to my sensors, my IFF display... and my eyes.

We were low, but I could still see all the way across the city from up here. It was deserted, a ghost town haunted by the specters of something so close to human, but not. The spires and pyramids and spheres seemed to emphasize the differences, even as their positions on either side of the broad, green-brown river showed our similarities. I wasn't sure if the Tahni civilians were inside their homes or if they'd been moved to shelters once their military had detected our Transition, but they were smart enough not to be on the streets, which put them one up on me.

Past the city stood the Tahni military base, a kilometer farther up the river and even further from the artistic designs of the civilian buildings. It wasn't deserted, though there was no casual traffic. Firefights were already raging in the neatly-arranged streets between the base's larger structures, small clusters of Force Recon Marines engaging Tahni Shock-troops.

I frowned, remembering the Force Recon companies had been intended to touch down on the far side of the city and march in on foot. There was no way they could have already made it that far...

Then I noticed the dropship crashed just outside the base perimeter, half its starboard wing sheared off and its vertical stabilizer on that side shredded by the same explosion. Without any way to steer, the huge aerospacecraft was left with just its belly jets and those could only take them up or down. They'd chosen down and now the plan had gone the way of all battle plans when they first contact the enemy.

More Drop Troopers were coming down behind us, by squad, by platoon, some falling faster than the book dictated, desperate to get to the ground. Two of them weren't fast enough. Something invisible to the naked eye, probably a burst of coil-gun rounds, smacked them out of the sky one right after the other, only a few dozen meters apart, pieces of armor and Marine raining down out of the sky, the fiery debris of the explosion leaving the burning gas behind, hanging in the sky like a tombstone.

None of the IFF transponders for my platoon winked out after the destruction of the two Vigilantes, and there wasn't enough space on my HUD to list even our whole company's identifiers, much less Bravo and Charlie. I didn't know who had died and might not have recognized their names if I had. I felt better about that, then felt guilty that I'd felt better.

Our targets, the two huge deflector dishes, loomed higher than our current altitude, a hundred meters tall and powered by their own dedicated fusion reactor built underground beneath them. I was used to seeing Tahni deflector dishes lit up blue and gold like Christmas tree ornaments, crackling with the energy of incoming attacks, but these were quiescent, a mild hum in the air and a heat-mirage shimmering just above the dishes the only indication they were active.

That was bad on so many levels. First and most obviously, the lack of incoming Fleet attacks on the shields was bad because it meant we didn't have the missile cutters left to throw significant firepower at it. I knew we had some left and they must have at least enough missiles to take out the temple once we disabled the defenses, or we would have aborted already.

But it was also horrible for us because we usually counted on the feedback from the deflector shields to disrupt the Tahni sensors and camouflage our approach. Without it, not only would they know we were coming, they'd know exactly where we were and we could expect...

"Contact right!" Henckel snapped a half-second before I could get the words out. "Enemy armor and dismounts at 1200 meters!"

Oh yeah, there was contact all right. Back in Tijuana, I'd once watched a farmer and his family knock down an old storage shed that had originally been set down by a tractor on concrete blocks. They wanted to clean it out and pour a new cement foundation for a newer and bigger building, but the minute light shone on the ground beneath the old shed, rats had swarmed out from beneath it, where they'd built a nest years before, eating grain that had been stored inside. The Tahni High Guard battlesuits swarming out of underground bunkers at the center of the military installation didn't quite have the numbers of that rat's nest, but it was a near thing. Behind and around and among them, Shock-troops in smaller, powered exoskeletons scuttled beside their older brothers, nearly useless against a Vigilante but determined to get in on the fighting.

"Private Henckel," Ackley said with calm, dry humor, "you have a gift for understatement." Her voice went hard and serious, a splash of cold water in the face of our insipient panic. "Platoon wedge formation, First squad on point. We're the tip of the spear as usual, Third. The rest of the company is forming on us. Hit the ground running, boys and girls."

She wasn't really that calm. She'd just gotten really good at burying her fear under a calm exterior. I knew because I was doing the same thing, and it was damned hard. Things had been so much easier when I didn't care if I lived or died, and the temptation to fall back into that shell was nearly overwhelming at times like this.

"Henckel," I said, my voice just as calm as Ackley's, despite the turmoil in my gut, "you're on point. Graciano, your team behind me and Linebarger at the base."

"Come on, Cam," Julio Graciano whined in my ear, "let me up front for once. You always hog all the fun."

I smiled thinly. Graciano was a hard-charger, young and gung-ho and ready for battle. That I was less than a year older than him was irrelevant, he was young on an emotional level that I had never been. He was a good Marine, and he'd become better since he'd been training under me and Ackley and Scotty, but Henckel was better and I was better than either of them.

"Next time, Julio."

The ground rushed up and the jets cut off. There was no more time for talking.

There was a qualitative difference to the landscape once we were connected to it by gravity, a feeling of really being there, as if we could have changed our minds and jetted back to the drop-ships right up until the dirt crunched under our feet. It seemed that the Tahni felt the same way, since they didn't launch missiles until we touched the ground. Once First squad landed, smoke trails streaked up from the rumbling mass of enemy armored troops, arcing toward us from a kilometer and a half away and ours crossed them in mid-air.

The suits reacted automatically, the grenade launchers in our left arms firing without having to be told, each launching a spread of chaff warheads, miniature versions of the countermeasures the dropships carried. I didn't have time to watch the results, just sending my fervent hopes and good wishes after the rounds and trusting them to do their job. I was too busy targeting and launching my own missiles, one after another, each target designated with the suit's laser rangefinder and the data programmed into the missile's warhead just before it launched. Inert coldgas kicked each missile free of the launch tube, straight into the air above me, the weight of the warhead pulling the rear end down just slightly before the solid-fuel rocket ignited and sent the weapons downrange. There were four of the meter-long missiles stored in the armored bay on the side of the Vigilante's backpack and I didn't hold them back, figuring I wouldn't have a better use for them.

They were gone in seconds and I was running at full speed. Their warheads would hit or they wouldn't, and the same with ours, but now there was only one way to keep from being targeted by missiles or beamers or coil-guns from some unseen enemy: be so close to the Tahni lines that no one else could shoot at me without hitting their own troops. Yes, it had its drawbacks, but no tactic is perfect.

Electron beams and plasma blasts crossed each other's ionized wakes and turned the air into a crackling cloud of static discharge and heat mirage for hundreds of meters around us, as if conspiring to distract me from the target in my crosshairs. The targeting reticle flashed uncertainly, unable to get a solid lock on the enemy battlesuit through the interference, and I overrode it with a grunt of impatience and fired manually.

It wasn't quite a center-mass shot, off by over half a meter, but if I was going to miss, I'd missed in the right direction. The plasma blast caught him at the elbow joint on his weapon arm and the power junction shorted out spectacularly and blew the lower half of the limb off the suit. I didn't know if it had taken the Tahni's arm with it, but it couldn't have done him any good and he stumbled away off balance and out of my field of view.

I left it to someone behind me to finish him off. He wasn't a threat and there were so damned many others who were, too many to count, too many to keep track of.

There's a reason that so many combat soldiers are obsessed with luck. Sure, there's the tried-and-true six P's: Proper Preparation Prevents Piss-Poor Performance. But wading through a battalion of High Guard battlesuits in a kinetic strike planned by brasshats light-years away, with missiles from both sides raining down around us, electron beams passing so close that I got a contact burn on my right arm through the armor, the difference between the dead and the living came down to blind chance.

I lashed out with a metal fist and grunted in pain as it connected, sending a vibration ringing through my suit, but I was already firing with the other hand. That was two threats down but there was a whole fire team of Tahni suits aiming their electron beamers at me from only a hundred meters away... I was a half-second from leaping up on a blast from my jump-jets, knowing it would only buy me the barest of respites and might make me a bigger target, but living through this fight from one second to the next and leaving the next worry for the next second. And then the Tahni battlesuits disappeared in a ball of fire and I stumbled backwards from the concussion of the blast, staring dumbly at the assault shuttle as it pulled out of its firing run. I'd never seen the missile that had saved me, but I didn't sneer at the luck. You never turned down good luck.

"First squad," Ackley ordered, terse and breathless, "cut left, cut left."

I didn't ask why, didn't have time to try to peer at the IFF display and figure out how the company was doing. I echoed the command to Henckel, catching a brief glimpse of him in action. Watching him make that Vigilante dance like a ballet virtuoso was almost enough to make me forget to fight my own battles. The kid was a natural, moving with a flow you just couldn't teach, a smoothness that would take years to learn unless you'd been born with it. The trainers had said I had it, and I wondered if that was what I looked like in a fight.

Henckel curved to the left, incorporating the move into his attack on a team of High Guard troopers, and I moved off a few degrees farther to the left of him. I'd fallen into a rhythm: fire the plasma gun, slam a fist into a metal face, side-step, half-second blast of the jets to take me out of the firing arc of anyone who'd zeroed in on me while I struck. If the field had been less crowded, an enemy trooper might have read the pattern, anticipated my movement and put an electron beam right through my chest, but there wasn't that sort of time available to plan, not for me or for them.

I was barely able to keep an eye on my squad by not concentrating on any one thing, letting my eyes go a bit out of focus, absorbing the information from the sensors and transponders as a sort of wave of information washing over me, leaving behind a big picture awareness I couldn't completely understand and wouldn't have been able to explain. I just *knew* where they were like I knew the position of my own body. Graciano was on my far right, his team completing an arrowhead with Henckel at the tip, while Linebarger and his team stretched out even further to the left, a bit out of line and messy.

"Tighten up Bravo team!" I snapped, as if the words punctuated the hammer-fist thundering into the left knee of a High Guard suit.

The suit fell, tumbling sideways to the ground and I stomped into its beamer emitter. Capacitors blew in arcs of electricity and curls of black smoke and I kept moving. Movement was life.

Another big-picture realization hit me and I realized we were nearly under the easternmost deflector dish. The hum of the electromagnetic fields was audible through my suit, a static charge making my hair stand on end. I hoped to hell *someone* in the company had saved enough ordnance to take these things out, because I knew no one in Third Platoon had as much as a fucking grenade left.

"First squad!" Ackley said, as if reading my mind. "Headquarters Platoon is moving up! Cover their advance!"

Headquarters Platoon? The Skipper's coming up here to the point?

HQ Platoon was Captain Covington, the XO Lt. Bradley, Top, and Lance Corporal Chen in the special commo suit that can connect to ships in orbit...and also Lance Corporals Madoff and Czarnowski in the Fire Support Suits, the Vigilante XBs, what everyone called the Boomers. I had forgotten about them because I'd not once seen them used, not in training and certainly not in a real fight. Headquarters Platoon and the Boomers were kept at the rear of company formations and usually far away from Third, who was always in the front.

If the Vigilante was a metal gorilla, the Boomer was a gorilla playing a pipe organ. The regular suit had a single missile launcher, built flush into the side of the suit's backpack, but the Boomers had twin launchers, one at each side, protruding nearly a meter above the head of the suit. Flanking the launchers were another set of paired weapons, fat and cylindrical, extending back a meter behind the Boomers' shoulders and forward another meter. They were coil-guns, slow-firing and too cumbersome for general use and they made for a big-ass target, but devastating and handy for the special weapons team.

If anything could take out the deflector dishes, it would be one of the Boomers.

They lumbered across the field, weighed down by the bulk of their extra weapons, escorted by our top officers and NCOs, and for the first time, I actually got to watch Top and the Skipper in action. If Henckel was a prodigy, those two were virtuosos, masters of the art approaching it from different philosophies. Covington was a dancer, a martial artist putting on an exhibition for the crowd, sidestepping electron beams as if he was moving faster than the relativistic blasts of charged particles because he could anticipate the shots. His plasma gunfire was a punctuation on every sequence of moves, as if he'd planned and practiced the dance for years and the Tahni were simply playing according to his choreography. None of them even came close to touching him.

Top, well, she was no dancer. She was a hammer and the Tahni were nails sticking out, waiting to be pounded. She used her jump-jets to turn her suit into a cannonball, striking the enemy with foot or shoulder, hitting them at just the right place to knock them off-balance and finishing them off with her plasma gun or even a quick flurry of punches.

I don't know why the two of them didn't take point for every battle. But orders were orders.

"Alpha and Bravo team, take the flanks!" I said, throwing my Vigilante forward on a one-second burst from the jets. "Henckel, plow the road!"

People were dying. I knew it, even as I tried not to think about it. IFF transponders were winking off in other platoons, two, then three, and I refused to look at the names listed beside them. Our platoon had taken some damage, but we hadn't lost anyone yet, and I thought, counterintuitive as it was, it was because we were up front. We were the point of the spear, scattering the enemy, and by the time they'd reorganized and managed to collect themselves for a counterattack, we were past and the base of the wedge formation was in their sights.

That advantage was about to disappear. The tip of the spear was running into the ground here at our destination, our target, the deflector dishes. The surviving enemy troopers had given ground to our charge until their backs were up against the wall and they were clustered together in a knot of massed fires, electron beams stabbing outward in a scattershot of charged particles. Plasma blast counterpunches flared in at the Tahni and the raw energy ripped apart the air itself. The ambient temperature outside my armor shot up past seventy degrees Celsius and sweat began pouring down my back and collecting in my boots faster than the cooling system could evaporate it.

At this range, no one could miss, and they didn't. I didn't see the one who nailed me, just felt the blistering heat and an unbelievable, searing pain in my right arm and all up and down my right side. I stumbled, my vision disappearing into starbursts of agony, unable to think or fight or even stand, knowing only one thing for sure.

I was about to die.

[10]

I was down on a knee and I didn't remember falling. It was hard to fall in a Vigilante. The thing was designed to keep us upright, because a tumble forward or backward would take long and potentially fatal seconds to recover from. I should have hit the jets, should have kept moving, but the pain was consuming thought, consuming time I didn't have.

But I didn't die, and gradually, I began to realize a suit was standing over me, pouring plasma fire out at the High Guard troops around us. I didn't realize who it was until his voice finally penetrated through the haze of fire blanketing my brain.

"Get up, Sarge!" Henckel was yelling. "We've got to move now!"

"I'm up," I gasped. The pain was receding, the drugs from the suit's onboard medical systems automatically injected and finally began to take effect. And with coherence came a grasp on grim reality.

It was bad, I could tell from the damage display. The suit's right arm had taken a direct hit and the plasma gun was trashed, but, more importantly to me for the moment, the beamer had penetrated my armor and my right forearm and hand were so much burned toast. I couldn't feel it anymore, thank God, but I was going to be spending a few days floating in a tank of biotic fluid if I lived through this.

"We got you, Cam!" Graciano said, and I could see the squad surrounding me, guns firing outward.

"No, guard the Headquarters Platoon," I croaked, trying to yell but lacking the breath and strength for it. Even as I said it, I was dimly aware that the enemy fire was dying down and their numbers had dwindled at least in our area.

"I think we'll be fine now, Sergeant Alvarez." Captain Covington must have been listening in on our squad frequency, which made sense, but his pronouncement shocked me almost enough to bring me back to full coherence. "Get your people moving. These dishes are about to come down."

"Aye, Skipper," I said as clearly as I was able. "Henckel, move it out."

The flats around the deflector dishes were a sea of smoke rising off dozens of burning High Guard battlesuits, and dozens more Shock-troops I hadn't even noticed dying, and we were a band of travelers in the land of the dead. I limped sideways, waiting for my squad to form up, and saw the Boomers open fire on the deflector dishes. The sight alone was almost worth the pain.

The discharge of the coil-guns was a flat, humming snap followed by the hollow thump of the heavy, tungsten rounds breaking the sound barrier before they slammed into the power feeds at the base of the deflectors. Sparks exploded out of the massive emplacements and the fields shut down with a crackle of static charge bleeding away into the air.

I don't know how I hadn't noticed the throng of civilians before. It might have been the selective attention I'd learned to apply in battle, letting unimportant data slide off me and only grabbing hold of the vital information. They weren't hot on thermal, they didn't have armor and they weren't vital to my mission, so I had totally missed the throng of them pouring out from the compound built between the deflector shields and the temple until they were nearly among us.

It took a moment longer for me to understand they were all females.

From what I'd been told of the Tahni society, the males and females lived separately out of biological necessity. The males would go into heat at the scent of any female of reproductive age who wasn't already pregnant, becoming violent and unreasoning in their presence. Mating was a negotiated thing, arranged through third parties and at specific times. The children, male and female, lived with their father, raised by his father and brothers in multigenerational homes in the cities, until the girls reached puberty. At that time, they would join the other females who lived in a collective outside the city. Only the matriarchs, the females past the reproductive age, mixed with the males, negotiating mating visits and attending to the needs of the females.

The structures outside the city, I deduced at the sight of the throng of young adult females, was one of those collectives. And apparently, they were every bit as fanatical about protecting the temple as the men.

"What the hell are we supposed to do?" Graciano demanded, his suit grinding to a halt as the females swarmed around him.

"Keep moving," I ordered him. "Don't hurt them if you can avoid it, but don't let them hold you up, either. That goes for everyone. They can't hurt us, but don't let them tie us down to make us easy targets for their reinforcements."

They grabbed at my legs and I walked anyway, sweeping a half a dozen of them off their feet, sending them sprawling. Someone screamed, an eerily inhuman sound, and I thought I might have accidentally stepped on an arm or a foot, but I wasn't going to stop and check.

Behind me, a flight of missile cutters rumbled across the sky at a thousand meters up and something small and dark separated from each of them, growing larger and taking shape as it grew lower and closer. They were air-to-ground missiles, each packed with nearly fifty kilos of HyPex, chemical hyperexplosives.

The temple was nearly a klick away, but when the missiles hit, the ground shook and the temple was engulfed in billows of black smoke rising high into the sky. Through the black clouds of smoke and dust, I caught glimpses of the walls of the temple complex crumbling around it and I knew the strike had done its job.

The females were all screaming now, louder than the one I'd injured, some of them pounding impotently at our armor, some ripping at their own clothes, or scratching bloody gouges in their own faces. Twenty of them rushed in at me and I brushed half of them away with a sweep of my left arm, sending a few sprawling and tumbling. A couple didn't get up.

Only twenty meters away, Henckel was also being swarmed, and I'd taken a single step toward him to help him clear the civilian females away when I saw one of them pushing something against the torso of his suit, just below his left arm, something amorphous and putty-like with a metal cube set in the center, something that looked very much like a block of HyPex...

"Henckel!" I yelled, just before he died.

It was a shaped charge, but the concussion wave from the explosion was enough to rock me even inside my suit. The females gathered within twenty meters of us were mown down like wheat beneath a scythe, the closest ones vaporized while the unlucky had their organs burst and their eyes pop right out of their skulls.

The fireball had been orange-white, but it disappeared as quickly as it had ignited and left me wading through yet more black smoke, blinded, confused, and desperate. There was, I thought, still a possibility he had survived. The armor was tough, meant to take a lot of damage. It only took a glimpse through a wind-blown gape in the clouds to know neither of us had been so lucky.

The female had placed the charge just right, under the arm in a weak spot for the armor, and it had ripped right through. Henckel's left arm was gone at the shoulder and a nasty, ragged, charred hole had been burned through his chestplate, angling upward. I didn't have to guess whether he was dead. I could see through the hole in his armor, see the dark, blood-stained absence where his head and upper torso had been.

A roaring filled my ears and nothing seemed able to make it past the sound, past the haze of rage, the mist of pain. I wasn't sure whether the pain was in my arm or inside my chest, but it could only have one outlet. I charged into the half-stunned crowd of females and swung my left arm in a broad, arcing stroke. Bones broke, skulls cracked and bodies flew meters away and still I waded through their ranks, dozens of them, stomping and smashing, coating my battlesuit with their blood.

I would have thought they'd run, but they didn't. They threw themselves at us and no one would take the chance there were more with the HyPex charges, ready to kill us in the way they had Henckel. Plasma blasts ripped them apart, burned them to charred husks in great swathes, but I kept smashing any who would come close enough, then chasing down the ones who wouldn't. It didn't seem real. *They* didn't seem real, separated from reality by the thickness of my armor, and Henckel's corpse was an artifact in a ViR simulations.

But their screams, those ululating, inhuman wails, seemed irritatingly real, setting my teeth on edge, and I had to keep pounding, stomping and crushing until the screaming went away. The dirt and gravel were invisible now, buried under a carpet of bodies and an ocean of blood.

Finally, there were few enough left that they hesitated, perhaps realizing they were all dying for nothing, or perhaps thinking they'd need breeding-age females to repopulate the colony. I don't know. I couldn't figure out their motivation any more than I could my own. I took a long, lumbering step toward them, fully intent on killing every single one, but a Vigilante suit blocked my way.

I wondered who it was with the dull curiosity of a brain in a painkiller haze, and would have checked the IFF signal if she hadn't spoken. The voice was soft in my ear, soothing yet firm.

"Cam," Vicky said. "That's enough. They're not a threat anymore."

I stared at her through the display, seeing the featureless grey of her helmet and not the person within. She saw the same view of me, I knew, but the difference was, I think she was seeing the real thing.

"Oh Christ, look at that shit!" I thought it was Graciano, but it might have been someone from another platoon. Those not saying it were thinking it.

The rest of the females, the ones who'd withdrawn away from us, the ones Vicky had tried to stop me from going after, were killing themselves. I hadn't seen the knives, hadn't noticed any weapons while they'd been trying to cling to us, hold us down. But they all had them, short and wickedly curved and looking sharp as hell, and they were all using them to slice their forearms open up the wrist. Their anatomy must have been similar enough to ours to make the arteries there a convenient target for suicide.

"That's some fucked-up shit right there," Scotty said, shaken enough to rubber-neck with the rest of us for a moment.

"Third platoon," Lt. Ackley's voice cut through the shock and horror. "We still have work to do. Move out. We've been assigned to pull security for Force Recon at the military installation." A pause. "Except First Squad. Alvarez, get your people to the LZ and dust off with the first available dropship."

I tried to single her out among the grey gargoyles milling around in an ocean of blood and death, but they all looked alike.

"I can stick it out, ma'am," I insisted. The words sounded a bit slurred in my own ears and it seemed to take an effort to say them. On some level, I knew that meant the suit was upping my dosage of painkillers, which was probably a sign I'd made things worse on my rampage through the Tahni females. "I'll be okay."

"I can see your health readings from here, Alvarez," she reminded me. "And this isn't a debate. In fact, Corporal Graciano, take charge of the squad and get Alvarez upstairs for medical treatment."

"Aye, ma'am," Graciano acknowledged. "Come on, Cam, let's get you looked after."

Graciano slid up beside me, guiding my suit with a metal hand on my metal shoulder. But I dug in my heels. There was something else, something I couldn't forget.

"Ma'am," I said to Ackley. "What about Henckel's body?"

She said nothing for a long second, and I thought she might be ignoring me, but then she answered, her words dragged down with sadness.

"The same as for all of us, Cam. We already triggered the self-destruct on his suit."

I knew what that meant, should have known to expect it. The thermite charges were built into every Vigilante, ready to burn the suit clean if the trooper had to abandon it...or to dispose of the body if he died in place during a battle. Henckel was gone, burned to ash.

And I was halfway there myself.

"Why the hell didn't we just nuke this place?" Graciano hissed, and I wasn't sure if he'd meant to transmit it.

I looked over at the Tahni females, down on their knees now, bleeding out rather than survive the destruction of their holy place, and I laughed until it turned into a cough, then had to clear my throat before I keyed my radio and answered his question.

"Because," I told him, "we didn't want to be the bad guys."

[11]

"You're good as new, Sergeant Alvarez," Dr. Fournette assured me, probing gently at the pink, baby-smooth skin of my right forearm.

It didn't look new, it looked damned disturbing, the pink butting up in unnatural joinder with the pale brown a couple centimeters north of my elbow. But it felt the same as my other hand, which was, I suppose, the best I could hope for.

"You may experience pins-and-needles sensations periodically for the first few days," Fournette warned me, motioning towards my uniform shirt laying across the examination table. I slipped it on, grimacing at the way the fabric set against the tender, hairless skin. "That should fade on its own in a week, but if it doesn't, come see me. The other burns were fairly minor and you won't even notice the repairs there."

The auto-doc squatted on the other side of the examination table, somehow exuding an air of self-satisfaction in the job it had done on me in the two days I'd floated in its transparent cylinder, engulfed in oxygenated biotic fluid, letting medical nanites repair me. I shuddered just slightly at the thought of breathing the stuff, and I was glad they'd knocked me out for it.

We'd been back in Transition Space before they woke me up and I was glad of that, too. The disorientation coming out of it had been bad enough without adding free-fall to the mix. I wondered why the artificial gravity only worked in T-Space and I resolved to look it up. I did that every time I thought of it, and I always forgot.

"Take it easy getting up," Fournette warned me when I began pushing off the table. "You may feel normal, but your body has been floating in a tank for two days and it's going to take your inner ear a little time to readjust."

"Don't worry about it, Doc, I got him."

I hadn't heard Scotty enter the *Iwo's* sickbay, but it was a busy place two days after Confluence. There'd been, or so Fournette had assured me, fifteen wounded Drop-Troopers and half again as many Force Recon WIA, mostly burns, and most of them not severe enough to warrant the limited auto-doc cylinders. Instead, they rested on treatment beds, arms or legs or in one case, half a man's face wrapped in smart bandages healing the flesh more gradually than the biotic fluid would, though just as surely.

He hadn't mentioned how many KIA there'd been.

"How're you feeling, Cam?" Scotty asked, grabbing me beneath my repaired arm and hauling me to my feet. "I stopped by a couple times before but you were still a floater so I had to wait until you were ready to flush."

He'd been expecting me to rise to the dig, either with an insult of my own or at least a chuckle. I said nothing, just let him guide me out of the sickbay. Fournette had been right about my sense of balance, and I definitely needed assistance. Scotty took me to the lift banks and we rode the car alone. I leaned against the wall of the elevator and closed my eyes, not because I was tired but because thinking I was might make Scotty less inclined to make small talk.

"You hungry?" he asked when the silence had apparently grown too thick for him to stand.

I was about to issue an instinctive denial, but the fact was, I was starving. He'd known I would be. The nanites had to get the raw material to fix me from somewhere. They started with blood sugar then worked their way to body fat and God help you if they needed more.

"Yeah, I could eat something." Like half the mess hall, for instance.

Scotty programmed a new destination into the lift controls and we exited on the deck with the ship's mess. The whole deck was usually a constant buzz of activity during a Transition because the ship's crew stood watch in shifts and one was always getting on or off and heading for chow. To make sure no particular shift got crowded out by Marines heading for breakfast or dinner, the troops on board were divided into different shifts by platoon and sent to eat between the crew shifts. There was still almost always a crowd in the mess.

There wasn't now. A handful of Force Recon troops were clustered into about a quarter of the tables against the far bulkhead, huddled close and eating between brief attempts at muted and hesitant conversation. We were the only Drop Troopers here and there was no line at the processors. By the time I had my tray and plates, I was able to stand on my own and I programmed one of the processors for chicken and rice, for values of chicken and rice that included soy disguised as chicken patties and spirulina powder shaped into rice. It wasn't so bad if you could forget you'd ever eaten real food.

Scotty led me to a table on the other side of the compartment from the Force Recon platoon and I began digging into my meal as if it actually tasted good while he picked at his. He'd probably already eaten and had just grabbed something to be polite.

"Tell me something, Scotty," I said, taking a drink of fruit juice to wash down a mouthful. His face seemed to brighten at my attempt at conversation, and I felt bad for causing it to crash back down again. "How many?"

At least he didn't pretend not to know what I meant. He hissed out a sigh, rubbing both hands over his face, covering his eyes like he could shut out reality.

"We lost four dropships on the way in." The words were a punch in the gut. "One Force Recon company and...." He winced in anticipation of what he had to say. "...pretty much all of Charlie Company."

"Fuck." The food lay heavy in my stomach, a solid, unappetizing mass, yet I kept eating because I knew I'd just come back later if I didn't. "And on the ground?"

"Thirty dead for Force Recon, mostly from booby-traps."

"I thought the Tahni didn't believe in uncrewed weapons," I said, dully argumentative. "Doesn't their religion say a living hand has to pull every trigger, or something like that?"

"It does," he acknowledged. His usually expressive face was carefully neutral, his tone almost robotic. "From what we were told, the explosives were triggered by volunteers who held out and suckered the Straight-Legs into the trap, then blew themselves up."

I wanted to swear again, but I didn't want to repeat myself. It shouldn't have surprised me after what I'd seen from the females. I waited, looking at him, knowing he'd only told me half the story but not wanting to press him for the rest.

"We lost seven KIA from our company. All but one from Second Platoon, all of them on the assault on the deflectors. Bravo took twelve KIAs, most of those on the drop."

Holy God. No wonder the place looked empty. We'd lost half the Marines we'd brought on the fucking op.

"The flyboys got hit harder than us, percentage-wise,"

Scotty allowed, his tone a bit grudging, as if he didn't want to admit the Fleet pilots were as hard-core as Marines. "Two whole squadrons of assault shuttles are gone, and the cutters..." He shook his head. "God, they were slaughtered, Cam. Two thirds of them were taken out, mostly trying to nail the destroyer."

I let my fork drop to the tray with a clatter, less from lack of hunger than the fact I'd lost the emotional fortitude to hold it. It was worse than I'd imagined, and what I'd imagined had been pretty bad.

The raw numbers should have made me feel less focused on the loss of Henckel, but they didn't. All they did was shine a laser designator on him. He'd died for the same reason all those other poor sons of bitches had died, because someone up the chain had decided they could afford to lose us.

"I'm not hungry anymore," I told Scotty, unable to meet his eyes. "I think I need some rest."

It was half a lie. I didn't need rest, I needed unconsciousness. I needed not to talk, not to think. Scotty knew it, I could see it in his eyes, but he nodded anyway.

"Sure. Get a good night's sleep. Lt. Ackley wants to talk to you, but that can wait until morning." He sniffed a laugh. "Not that morning means anything here."

Not that anything did.

———

I lay alone in the dark and tried to remember what Thomas Henckel looked like.

Henckel had one of those faces, unremarkable, almost nondescript. If I'd seen a personnel photo of him among a hundred other male Marines, it would have taken me a few seconds to pick him out. Henckel was distinctive by his expression, by the twisted grin, the cynical glint in his eye. But when I tried to think of him, tried to remember him, the image was flat and impersonal, not Thomas Henckel, just an anonymous face on some cheesy, holographic memorial.

I stopped trying to imagine his picture and thought instead about the conversation we'd had on Hachiman the night before we left on the *Iwo Jima*. His face had been alive with expression, tortured by self-doubt, by the worry he'd let me down, that he'd fuck up and I wouldn't respect him anymore. Like anyone should have been worried about losing my respect.

I opened my eyes and the memory faded with the intrusive light of the door security panel. Scotty wasn't here. He'd left me in the compartment alone to get some rest, but sleep had eluded me. I felt utter physical exhaustion, but my brain wouldn't shut down, wouldn't stop throwing accusations at me in the dark. Every time I'd almost succeeded in lulling it into quiescence, my newly-repaired arm would catch fire with the pins-and-needles sensation the doctor had warned me about.

The Doc would have some drugs that could knock me out, and the way things had gone on this op, I was fairly certain he'd give me as much as I asked for. I swung my leg off the bunk and slipped into my boots. I hadn't bothered to get undressed. It hadn't seemed worth the effort, and for once, my gut hadn't steered me wrong. I don't know why the hell I kept listening to it. I couldn't think of a single decision I'd made in my whole life that hadn't ended up a complete disaster.

I squinted my eyes against the light outside in the passageway and still had to stand in the hatch for a good thirty seconds for my vision to adjust. No one passed by in the ghost ship the *Iwo* had become.

Second time in a year. Second time we're coming back with half what we left with.

Was the *Tripoli* this empty? They'd lost more Drop Troopers, but fewer Force Recon, so probably. How many NCOs were wandering through her corridors, searching for a way to stop thinking about the battle? Had it been a battle? Would the history classes of the future say anything about the Battle for Confluence or would it just be the "raid on Confluence?" Or maybe just a footnote reference in a larger section on the "series of kinetic strikes into Tahni territory?"

Shit. I was being optimistic assuming we'd even be around to write the histories. A vision of the Tahni females slicing through their veins flashed across my memory. How were we supposed to fight *that*? All we'd done so far was try to make them mad, and God alone knew what they'd do if we succeeded.

I halted in mid-step, suddenly aware I was nowhere near the sickbay. I'd wandered aimlessly, letting my subconscious take me where it wanted, and it had led me to the docking bay. It was dark down here, the same as it usually was in T-space, but I thought I saw a glow in the open airlock of one of the dropships. I walked toward it, not sure why...or not willing to admit why.

Tony, Andre and Terry. The three Straight-Legs I drank with on the way to Oasis, weeks ago now. I hadn't seen them since, but they were on the ship. Or they would be if they'd made it through. Would they be there, along with their friends, having a drink to celebrate surviving the battle?

The boarding ladder was extended down from the side of the utility airlock and I climbed it as silently as I could. I still couldn't feel much with my hand. They hadn't told me how bad it had been, and I was sedated before they pulled me out of the armor, but I was fairly sure I'd lost most of the hand and the nanites had regrown it, because even the fingernails were a bright pink. I had to watch the fingers wrap around each rung of the ladder before I could be confident that they would hold me.

The light was brighter from the inside of the open airlock, but I didn't see the people until I stepped out into the utility bay. They were sitting cross-legged on the floor just in front of the passenger seats, a portable lantern between them, and they all looked up when I took the first step onto the stairs down from the utility bay. Three faces, but none of them were Tony, Andre or Terry.

They had a bottle, though, and it was frozen in mid-motion as one of them, a stocky, raven-haired woman was about to pass it to a shaven-headed man. They wore Marine fatigues but none of the three had interface jacks, which made them Force Recon.

"Sorry," I said, stopping between one stair and another. "I thought you might be somebody else."

The three of them looked at each other, as if trying to get approval, and finally the woman held the bottle up.

"I think there's a lot of that going around," she said. "Come on down and have a drink."

I hesitated for just a second, but it felt right. Maybe this had been what I was looking for. I took the bottle and fell into a squat between them before I took a slug from it. The liquor was the same quality as last time, a torch in my esophagus trying to burn its way out.

"What's your name, man?" the bald guy asked me.

"Cam," I told him, my voice a rasp after the shot. I didn't bother to check his rank. It didn't matter.

"And what were their names?" That was the third guy, gangly and skinny, all arms and legs. Probably not old enough to be drinking this shit.

"I never did find out their last names," I admitted. "And you know, right now...I don't even want to know. So many people are gone, I want to be able to think someday, on another op, I might find them down here sharing a bottle."

I took another shot and handed it back to the woman.

"Then here's to finding your friends getting drunk." She toasted me.

"You know," the young, skinny kid said, "before the war started, I thought I was going to wind up working some boring job on Aphrodite for the next fifty years, until they forced me out and I found some other boring job." He took the bottle from the woman and sipped it, gasping a little for breath as the liquor worked its way down. "My great-granddad always goes on and on about how the anti-aging treatments everyone in the core colonies gets is such an incredible thing, how when he was a kid, no one lived past a hundred or so. But all I could think about was what a nightmare it was going to be." He handed the bottle off to the bald guy. "Right now, though, I wouldn't mind living a boring life for a couple hundred more years."

"I never figured I'd even live *this* long," I said. It didn't feel like me talking, more like I was watching someone else saying the words. "I've been running away from death since I was a little kid, and every time I think it's finally got me, it takes someone else instead. Someone who didn't deserve it."

"You think you deserve it more?" the woman asked, pushing the bottle back at me. I assumed she was talking about death, but she could have meant the bottle. I wasn't sure of my answer to either question, but I took the bottle.

"I've done some bad things," I admitted.

The alcohol was untying knots inside me, numbing some of the pain to the point where it nearly felt tolerable. I thought about the jobs I'd pulled, the cons, the rip-offs, the gang hitter dying on the subway track coming after me. If there was a God, would He hold those against me? Would He condemn me to Hell for my doubts, for my lack of faith? And what Hell could be worse than this?

"But not as bad as others," I went on, trying to be honest with myself. "It's not that I think I deserve to die, it's just that sometimes I think it hurts more to go on living."

"You know any history, Cam?" the bald man asked me. I

regarded him carefully, trying not to let the thickening haze over my senses blind me to what I was seeing. He was older. Even with the anti-aging treatments, you could tell someone who was past their thirties. It was something in the way they carried themselves.

"Not much," I told him. "I try to audit the courses they have on the ship's net when I get a chance, but the only history I've read is military history. Mostly about the Marines, when I went to the NCO school."

"I know a lot of history. My pop is a professor of Earth history on Hermes and my grandfather was one of the curators at the New Smithsonian for twenty-three years. History was all I heard about before I joined up to get away from it, because I thought it was boring as shit."

I nodded to encourage him to go on, though I just had the barest idea of what the New Smithsonian was. A museum, I thought, somewhere on the Atlantic coast.

"What we got now," Baldy went on, "people think it's always been like this, and it's always gonna be like this, but the fact is, humans were around for hundreds of thousand years before anyone figured living in a city and writing shit down was a good idea, maybe seven or eight thousand years ago. And we were still riding horses and swinging swords at each other until about four hundred years ago. People born before the first airplane flew lived long enough to see a man walk on Earth's moon, and people born before those men walked on the moon, well...." He shrugged. "Their children lived long enough to see the first humans walk on Mars, and some of them are still alive, because the anti-aging treatments came along. But for most of the history humanity, this...." He motioned around them. "...was the rule, not the exception. Oh, not the starships and the Gauss rifles and the aliens, but war. Dying violently. Suffering and watching your friends suffer. In fact, it used to be a lot worse.

Wars meant famine and plague and more civilians died than soldiers."

I thought about Maria and snorted a bitter, humorless laugh.

"A lot of civilians still wind up dying."

"They do. But not percentage-wise. There's something like nine billion people living on Earth and another ten billion off it, between the Solar System and the star colonies. How many have died in this war, do you think? A hundred million, maybe? That's a horrible number," he admitted, "a number we can't even fathom, but what is it against nineteen *billion*? A half a percentage point?" I didn't know. Doing math in my head wasn't a required skill for a Drop-Trooper.

"You're saying I should just stop whining and be glad I wasn't born four hundred years ago?" I asked, starting to get annoyed with the man.

"Naw, bro," he assured me, raising his hands in a quelling motion. "Everybody's got their own pain and I respect that. What I'm saying is, people back then, when things were so much worse, they had every right to wonder if life was worth living, worth the pain. It was seventy or eighty years if you were lucky, and near the end, your whole body was breaking down and every day hurt worse than the last, and living to an old age just meant you watched your friends and loved ones die around you. But they kept going. They played the hand they were dealt."

"Man, I was born with people like that," I said, grabbing the bottle again. "Where I'm from, there wasn't any government medical care or free food. Everyone either scratched out a living from the ground or stole what they could from the cities and made themselves the boss by being the only ones around who had fabricators, computers, entertainment, or drugs."

"Why did your people keep going, then?" Baldy wanted to know. "Why didn't they give up?"

"Momma used to say our reward was in Heaven." I couldn't taste the alcohol anymore, so I guess it was doing its job. "She had her chance to find out. So did my father and brother. I've always thought I was the lucky one, but maybe they were."

I handed the bottle back to the woman.

"I should get going." I pushed myself up to my feet. "Thanks for the drink."

I climbed down with exaggerated care, my whole body numb and not just my hand. Maybe I could sleep now.

"Cam," Baldy said, head sticking out of the airlock. "If you ever want to hang out with us and talk some more back on Hachiman, look for us in Foxtrot Company. I'm Marshall... Xavier Marshall. People call me X."

I nodded, waving to him as I stumbled away, but I wished he hadn't told me. We were both better off with me not knowing.

[12]

Hachiman was cold as hell when we got back. Snow covered everything, the roads, the buildings, the equipment, wherever the deicers hadn't sprayed, the powder was packed fifteen or twenty centimeters tall, and the drifts against the side of the barracks and hangars was up past two meters.

I marched my Vigilante into the storage hangar, the rest of First squad lined up behind me, grateful for the heating elements built into the suit. We were the first off the dropship, led by Lt. Ackley, with Scotty at the rear, and what might have been a victory parade felt more like a chain of pall-bearers. I stepped backwards into the maintenance cradle and powered down the Vigilante, popping open the chest plastron and giving my arms room to move before I yanked out the interface cables, letting them spool back into the helmet.

When I'd first gotten the sockets implanted, they'd seemed huge and obtrusive, giant metal-rimmed holes in my temples, something that would define my identity for the rest of my life, but now I barely noticed them. The hardware would be there forever. My nerves had grown around it, wrapping it in brain and bone and blood vessels, and trying to remove it would require dangerous fucking around with my brain tissue. The docs back on Inferno had assured me I could have the sockets covered up if I wanted, after I got out of the military, but at this point, that seemed a million years away.

The flat, stinging hand of the raw cold slapped me in the face and wished I could have worn a field jacket inside the suit. Now I'd have to make a run for the barracks in sub-zero temperatures to get warm.

"All right, Third Platoon," Ackley said, clambering out of her suit, standing before us all with her hands on her hips and not shivering. I wondered how much determination it took to keep yourself from shivering, wondered if she thought we'd consider her weaker for doing it. Officers were weird. "I know everyone wants to get settled into their barracks and get warmed up, but I wanted to give you all a quick heads-up on the schedule. PMCS at 1330 local, which is in three hours, so make sure you grab some lunch first. No training today or tomorrow, but we are going to be plugging into the pods for at least an hour a day after that, until everyone's suits are back in top condition."

I couldn't help the flicker of my eyes towards the right hand of my Vigilante. The techs had slapped a temporary field repair on it en route, but the patches and welds looked sloppy compared to the rest of the suit. The maintenance crew here would do a better job.

"After that...." Ackley hesitated, a bit of the starch and self-assurance leaving her in that second. "After that, the word is, it's going to be a few weeks, minimum, before we head out again. Obviously, some replacement troops are going to have to come in from Inferno, and the new Fourth Platoon we picked up is going to have to go through training and quals before they deploy with us again."

The last was said with a tinge of bitterness seeping through the professionalism. I understood why. The story had filtered down through the rest of the company during the trip back, but I hadn't heard it until I'd been popped out of the biotic fluid. Our replacement Fourth Platoon had totally screwed the pooch during the assault and not only dropped in the wrong sector but wound up attacking an industrial facility instead of the military base.

"I know we've all lost people these last couple missions," she went on, and I thought she was looking directly at me when she said it, "and if anyone needs to speak to the psych counsellors, there's plenty of time to do it now. Don't feel like you have to be all Spartan and tough. We're all human, and we all need help dealing with loss." Now I *knew* she was looking right at me. "Don't make me make it an order."

You're going to have to. I thought the words hard enough at her that I might as well have been screaming them. I'd had enough counsellors in my life, and not a damned one of them had done a bit of good. Though that might have been because I got so good at lying to them.

"Use this time," Ackley urged us. "If you found something that needs fixing, either in your suit, your technique or yourself, now's the time to get it fixed." She nodded. "You're dismissed."

Graciano and Linebarger were staring at me, but I didn't have anything for them. They'd heard the same thing I had, and if they couldn't figure out when chow started, they'd better get their shit together or have some ration bars in their locker. I headed across the street to the barracks, wrapping my arms around myself and clenching my teeth against the cold.

No one, as it turned out, had thought to run the heaters in the barracks while we'd been gone, and there was a thin film of ice over every metal surface in the room. I cursed in three languages as I stabbed at the temperature control on the wall and only heard the fans kick in after I'd ripped into the sealed containers of personal gear that I'd never had time to unpack and pulled out a field jacket. It wasn't adequate to the task, but it warmed me up enough to stop shivering and actually take a look around the room.

I hadn't had the chance to do anything but dump my gear there and it was still bare and unfinished and impersonal. That was okay, though. What was I going to do to personalize it? Put up videos of my family? They were lost to time. I could barely remember what they looked like, and every memory I did have was from recurring nightmares.

I dug through the personal gear and began separating it into categories to better fit it into the lockers they'd provided us with. Fix stuff now, Ackley had said, while we had the chance. And yeah, she'd also said we'd have weeks before we went out again, but that shit could change in a second. That we very badly *needed* a break was beside the point. The brasshats didn't give a damn what we needed; they just knew what they needed *from* us.

I'd almost gotten everything stowed away when the knock came. I barely had time to look around before Vicky walked inside. I stood there with a pair of underwear in my hand and stared at her. She looked angry, hands against her hips, cerulean gaze as harsh and unwelcoming as the weather.

"What's up?" I wondered. "We got a formation or something?"

She slammed the door shut behind her and closed the distance between us, hands clenching like she wanted to grab me by the collar and throw me against the bulkhead.

"Why have you been avoiding me?" she demanded. "I tried to talk to you over and over on the *Iwo Jima* and you blew me off."

I realized my mouth was hanging open and I closed it. Was she for real?

"The last time I talked to you," I reminded her, "you told me you needed to be alone, and so did I."

"I meant right then, not forever!" she said, hands going in the air as if the words were exploding out of her. "We were about to go on an op and you were psyching me out! I was trying to blow off some steam and get my head clear, I didn't need you being a damn buzzkill."

I nodded, remembering what Scotty had said about Vicky and I wanting different things from each other. I hated when Scotty was right.

"Sorry I was harshing your buzz," I told her, not even trying to keep the sarcasm out of my voice. "God knows I'd hate to be an inconvenience to you."

Jesus, why couldn't she just get out of here and leave me alone? I'd been hoping what I said would piss her off enough to leave, but she set her jaw and widened her stance, as if she was preparing for a fistfight.

"You're a real prick sometimes, Cam," she told me. "I get it, you're hurting because you lost a friend. You think the rest of us haven't? You think it didn't hurt when I lost just about everyone else in my squad on Brigantia?" She bared her teeth in a snarl. "What? Do you think those people weren't important because *you* didn't know them? Because they weren't *your* friends?"

That was a kick in the balls, and I deserved it. All my righteous indignation fizzled out as my perspective shifted. It didn't make me hurt any less for what had happened on Confluence, but I realized I'd been thinking more about myself than Henckel.

"You're right," I told her, my shoulders sagging. "I'm sorry. I know everyone else is hurting, too. I just..." I collapsed onto my bunk, letting the gravity and the exhaustion drag me down until I was lying flat on my back. "I'm not used to this, Vicky. It was a lot easier when it was just me."

I had my eyes closed, but I felt the bunk sag under her weight as she sat down next to me, felt her lips touch mine.

"It's okay," she whispered in my ear. "It's easy for me to forget where you came from. I guess it's not fair for me to expect you to react the same way I would. I'm sorry, too."

Then she was pulling at my clothes and I opened my eyes, frowning.

"Now? We have to be at chow in less than hour!"

She paused, cocking an eyebrow at me in a look full of skepticism.

"You really think you're going to last an hour?"

———

I'd been so eager to get inside into the warmth, I hadn't noticed the base had grown while we were gone. When we'd left for Oasis, the whole installation had ended at the chow hall, but now there were more barracks carved out of the rock and into a cleared area of the forest, and more administration buildings between them with the Fleet logo emblazoned over the front. The landing field had also been expanded, the brush and trees burned off and a few small hills flattened out by heavy equipment. Missile cutters and Fleet landers were packed into the new sections, practically wing to wing. They might need time to replace the Marines who'd died, but it looked to me like they'd already brought in fresh meat for the Attack Command.

"The Engineering Corps have been busy little beavers, haven't they?" Vicky asked, following my gaze as we headed for the chow hall.

It took every bit of effort I could muster not to hold her hand, to make sure I stayed the right distance from her rather than touching shoulders. I watched other clusters of Marines and Fleet personnel wandering toward the mess hall and idly wondered how many of them were doing the same thing, maintaining the fiction that we were all good little regulation-obeying boys and girls who didn't drink, or do drugs, or have sex with anyone in our unit.

"Makes me think we're here for the long term," I agreed, and the thought sank low into my gut. Being here long term meant doing just what we'd been doing, over and over. How long until we wound up with a hundred percent replacement rate for the whole company? The battalion? Except for the Skipper and Top, of course. They'd never die.

My squad was already at their table, or what we'd claimed as our table anyway. We hadn't eaten here yet, so it was all up for grabs. Vicky and I grabbed trays and joined them.

"What about your squad?" I asked her.

"They're my squad, they'll come to me."

"Hey Cam," Graciano said, waving as we sat down, his rounded, baby face breaking into a smile. "You know, I heard the mess techs are trying to requisition some actual frozen meat in the next shipment. Wouldn't that be great? It'd have to come all the way from Loki, but I am so damned tired of soy..."

I shrugged, taking a bite of what advertised itself as a hamburger. It wasn't bad.

"I tell you what, you can do a whole lot worse than soy and spirulina. Try eating rat a couple times, and you'll be glad to steal someone's ration card to eat a damn soy burger."

"You ate rat?" Chandra said, her eyes going wide. "Like, an actual rat?"

"I killed it with a stick," I confirmed, sneaking a grin at Vicky. "Then I cooked it over the exposed heating element of a moisture evaporator."

"Ew, gross." Mullany made a face. "I mean, rat..."

"No, I think the kinetic strike strategy is working. Yeah, there've been losses, but nothing we didn't expect."

The conversation was happening at the table behind us and I supposed it had been going on for a while now, but someone had become a little too loud at just the wrong time, and the two sentences cut through the cross chatter. I turned in my chair and wasn't surprised to see a sea of blue Space Fleet uniforms at the other table. None of them wore the Attack Command patch on their chest, so I assumed they were the tenants of the new admin buildings I'd seen on the way in. I couldn't tell which of them had spoken until a tall, lantern-jawed type with hair at the edge of regulation length, styled as much as he could get away with out here, opened his mouth again.

"It's what they planned for, right? Admiral Sato basically invented the Attack Command so we could take losses without it crippling our ability to defend our core systems. I hear they're cranking out a hundred cutters a day in the shipyards." He laughed, the sort of rough snicker of someone who knows they're being a douchebag but thinks it makes them sound edgy. "And as long as the justice system is working back home, we won't run out of Marines."

That was one of those jokes a Drop-Trooper could have gotten away with making and maybe even gotten a few laughs. A Force Recon Marine could have slammed the Drop-Troopers with it in a bar and started a healthy exchange of insults if he sounded like he was kidding, or punches if we decided he wasn't. But a Fleet admin puke?

I stood up, the legs of my chair scraping against the raw, concrete floor.

"Tell me something, desk pilot," I said, louder than I had to, as loud as he'd been speaking, "how many combat missions have you been on?"

"Cam...," Vicky said, hand brushing against my arm in a restraining motion.

"I said," I went on, taking a step closer to the other table, ignoring both her and the number of Fleet admin pukes at the table, "how many combat missions have you been on?"

If the guy hadn't been a total shitbag, this would have been a perfect opportunity to back down. All he would have had to say was nothing. Instead, he pushed his chair backwards and stood up...and kept standing up until he was nearly a head taller than me. He was a gym rat like a lot of the rear-echelon staff pukes were, since they didn't have anything better to do while we were off dying.

"Maybe they don't send people like me out on combat missions," he sneered, "because they know I actually have a functioning brain and an IQ over room temperature. Otherwise, they would have put jacks in my head and stuck me in a fucking suit, right?"

I've known guys who when they get angry, they just red out. That is, everything goes red inside their brain and their conscious thought shuts down and they lose it. They charge in headlong and don't give a damn what happens next. I've also known guys who never get angry. They're always in control and they're usually able to avoid a fight, but if not, they take as few risks as possible and try to get away from it.

Me, though, when I get really angry, everything goes cold and I start calculating the quickest and easiest way to disable whoever's standing in my way. It was probably a good thing I very rarely got angry.

I was pretty fucking angry now.

"You need to sit down and shut up, keyboard commando," Vicky said from a hundred klicks behind me. "This isn't the fucking time."

"What are *you* gonna do about it, you jackhead bitch?" he asked, eyes on her instead of me. That was a mistake.

He was tall and hard-muscled and hitting him anywhere the muscles gave him protection would have been pointless. And I was low anyway. I punched him in the balls. The angle was wrong, and I couldn't put as much force into the strike as I would have wanted, but just the shock of it was enough to bend him over, exposing his throat to my uppercut. He crashed back into the table, hands at his throat, gagging and choking.

And then, of course, it was on. Even the Marines who hadn't heard what douchebag had said originally had heard what he'd said to me, and that was enough for them. And the Fleet boys and girls had seen me chop down their golden boy like tomorrow's firewood and they weren't about to let that go.

Someone slammed into me from the side and I grabbed them by the belt and squatted low, trying not to get taken down, using their momentum against them. We weren't Force Recon, but they still showed us some unarmed combat in Basic, at least more than they'd taught the Fleet assholes. Whoever had tackled me went tumbling across a line of abandoned chairs, sending them crashing to the floor and I never did get a look at their face, couldn't even tell if it was a man or a woman.

Other bodies were flying and most of the fights were devolving into individual wrestling matches on the ground, because that was where most fights went if they made it past the first flurry of punches. I'd found that out when I was ten, and none of the rules had changed since. I'd also found out the hard way that the ground was the *last* place you wanted to be when you were outnumbered, and I endeavored to avoid it because I was almost always outnumbered.

I wasn't actually sure about the numbers in the chow hall. I hadn't tried to get a head-count when I'd walked in, just noticed the patches of blue among the clusters of brown and green, but there was one of me and I couldn't count on help from anyone else because they might have their own battle to fight.

Another dumbass in blue Fleet utilities swung at me with an awkward roundhouse and I didn't even bother to hit him, just gave him a hard push in the shoulder and sent him sprawling. He'd very obviously never been in any sort of fight and had the soft, scared look of a button-pushing clerk and he scuttled away at the first opportunity. I'd watched him retreat just a half second too long, and I nearly tumbled over myself when someone rammed into my side. I cocked back my arm for a punch as I spun around, but found out it was Vicky. She was a bit disheveled and had what looked like a nascent bruise over her right eye, but I thought she might have been enjoying this.

"Back to back," she told me and I nodded, putting my shoulder against hers and facing outward.

"Break it up!" a foghorn bellow cut through the din and the yelling. "Break this shit up now or I will bash your fucking heads in! If you assholes want to fight, you can take it out on the fucking Tahni!"

A Force Recon Marine stumbled backwards at the swipe of an arm at gut level and a Fleet technician rolled forward from a rough push, clearing the way for a short, wiry woman in a spotless, neatly-creased set of Marine Drop-Troop utility fatigues. Her face was carved from ancient teak by the claws of some extinct cave bear and sanded and polished by the sands of a million years, and anyone who thinks I'm exaggerating has never met Top. Master Gunnery Sergeant Ellen Campbell had been a Marine longer than the Commonwealth had been in existence and I had a feeling she'd still be a Marine when all the matter and spacetime in the universe had contracted to a point and was ready to explode again.

"Who the fuck started this shit?" she demanded. Her eyes scanned the crowd and when they lit on me, it was like an enemy laser designator had settled on my chest and the missile was about to be fired.

"I did, Master Gunnery Sergeant," I said, straightening to parade rest. No use dragging all this out. She could have checked the security cameras if she really wanted, but that would have just made the shit deeper.

"Top," Vicky objected, jumping to her feet beside me, "those fucking Fleet admin assholes were calling us..."

"Shut the hell up, Sergeant Sandoval," Top snapped at her, eyes still locked on mine. "I want you and the rest of our company pitching in and cleaning up this shit right now!" She glanced at the Fleet admin crowd with utter contempt evident in the sneer passing across her face. "As for you desk patrol types, you might want to help clean up and keep your fucking mouths glued shut or I will personally have Chief Grundig, your senior NCO, review the video from this little dust-up and take whatever actions against you he feels are appropriate. You got me?"

"Yes, Master Gunnery Sergeant!" The response was ragged and antiphonal, but what it lacked in coordination it made up for in respect.

Top fixed me with a sidelong glance, her eyebrow going up, the eye looking at me somehow wider than the other.

"Now, Alvarez."

I followed her wordlessly, gulping.

Oh well, if I was going to die, at least I'd gotten laid first.

My ears were ringing.

Even in Basic, I'd never had a Drill Sergeant yell at me loud enough to leave my ears ringing, but Top had managed it. I think her office must have been soundproofed, or else the duty NCO was just used to her screaming so loud the walls shook, because otherwise someone would have been running into the office with a gun drawn, certain that the Tahni were attacking.

Finally, the onslaught petered out and Top's shoulders were actually heaving with the effort of the verbal barrage. I honestly couldn't have repeated back a single word she'd said to me because once a word is yelled loud enough, it loses coherence.

"Goddammit, Alvarez," she said, somehow making the curse a mild, almost affectionate word. "What in the hell am I going to do with you?"

I stood at parade rest, eyes straight ahead and didn't give her any suggestions.

"Oh, at ease for fuck's sake," she said, almost in surrender, waving a hand at me and sitting back against the edge of her desk, nearly knocking over a cube with a hologram of a little girl playing in a park. I wondered if it was her daughter. Or grand-daughter, or great granddaughter.

I relaxed slightly, but not by much. I was still in deep shit.

"I'm sorry, Top," I said, meaning it. "I should've kept my shit together. It was just a bad time for me to hear an admin fuck tell me how Marines were expendable criminals."

Her eyes pinched slightly at the words, maybe in anger, or maybe in pain. I couldn't tell.

"Alvarez," she said, sounding calmer and more philosoph-ical than I'd ever heard from her, "the toughest thing about lead-ership is watching young men and women die doing something you told them to do. I've been in long enough to see it over and over and it should have left an impenetrable callous over my soul, boy, but instead, each death rips the scab away."

I was speechless for a moment. It wasn't something I'd thought I'd ever hear Top admit. She was being honest, so I decided to do the best I could to be just as honest.

"I've had so many people die around me," I said, the words rushing out like my confessions to our local priest when I was a little boy. "My whole family, friends, kids I ran with on the streets...the people I knew and cared about on Brigantia. And somehow, Top, none of them hurt like this."

"That's because you've never been responsible for their lives before." She felt around behind her and picked up the cube, tossing it in her hand without looking at it, as if she had the images memorized. "It's like having kids. You train them as best you can, you love them in your own way, then you have to send them into a heartless world and the whims of fate, and it's even worse in war. In life, you worry they'll get hurt emotionally. In a war, you know some of them are going to die."

I blew out a sigh, the whole idea of being responsible for other people's lives a weight pressing down on my chest.

"That's not very comforting, Top."

"It's not my fucking job to comfort you, Alvarez!" she barked, coming to her feet, and sending me instinctively back to parade rest. But her voice softened as she continued. "And it's not your job to keep every newbie alive. You can't. I know it and you know it, and if they don't know it, they'll find out soon enough. It's their job to complete the mission. That's why we're here."

I couldn't keep the words in, even though I knew I would have been wiser not to speak them. They burst out like bile.

"The admirals and generals and the President are throwing the lives of their pilots and Marines away because they're afraid to lose their damn cruisers."

"And they're fucking right!"

I blinked at her declaration, disbelieving, but she didn't back down from it, getting in my face, her nose about level with my chin.

"That's their job, to figure out how not to lose the war, to use the assets they have in the best way possible." She backed up a step and waved around us demonstratively. "That's what we are, assets to be used." She shook her head and paced back around the other side of her desk, fists on her hips. "I know you well enough to know you've accepted that about yourself, but you have to accept it about the Marines you lead, boy. Or else I'll have you busted back to a line shooter, which would be a waste."

She collapsed back into her office chair, the air going out of her, tension melting away from the set of her shoulders.

"Now get out. And don't make me haul you in here again."

Vicky was waiting for me outside the company offices, the look on her face full of trepidation.

"Is everything okay?" she asked, fingers clenching like she wanted to grab me but was forcing herself not to.

"I'm not going to the brig," I said, shrugging. "And she didn't mention an article 15 or Non-Judicial Punishment, so I guess I'm in the clear for the fight. Though I'd bet I'm going to be assigned every shit job available while we're here in garrison."

I looked up and down the street. Things were getting back to normal.

"We have to get to the hangars for PMCS," she reminded me. "We'd better hurry before we wind up in the shit with Lt. Ackley, too."

"I can't leave it at this," I admitted, falling into step beside her.

"Leave what?"

"We are *not* fucking expendable, Vicky. There has to be a better way."

She laughed sharply, then seemed to regret it.

"Come on, Cam...maybe there is a better way, but do you really think any of us can find it?"

"Probably not," I admitted. "But that doesn't mean I'm not going to try."

———

I'm sorry, that information is classified.

I hissed out a sigh and barely restrained myself from throwing the tablet across the barracks room. It would have felt satisfying, and the tablets were cheap, but then I'd have to go back to the rec center to grab another and it was too damned cold outside for that. I chewed on my lip and tried again.

"What is the closest a Fleet Attack Command missile cutter can emerge from Transition Space to a planetary body?"

The tablet's cursor swirled in a tiny whirlpool as if it were considering the question, though it was probably just trying to access the base's datanet.

I'm sorry, that information is classified.

"Damn it." I leaned my head back, staring at the ceiling, the bunk creaking at the movement. "Okay, what is the closest to a planetary body that a Commonwealth starship has emerged from Transition Space?"

I'm sorry, that information is classified. However, the minimum distance for Transition as per Commonwealth Transportation Safety Council regulations is nine planetary diameters of the body in question, unless the gravitational pull is compounded by the presence of a larger mass within the nine planetary diameters.

It went on with a long list of mathematical formulae and diagrams and my eyes began to glaze over, but I tried to pay attention anyway.

Why was so much of this shit classified? Who did they think I was gonna tell? Did they think the Tahni were going to send one of their people disguised in a trenchcoat and broad-brimmed hat and slip one of us a few Tradenotes to look up technical information they could figure out from their own Transition Drive ships? Morons.

Nine planetary diameters. Okay, I knew the Earth was like 12,700 kilometers in diameter. I'd looked it up earlier. Nine times that was...

Shit. I used the tablet's calculator and came up with a bit over 114,000 kilometers. But that was just what the regs for commercial vehicles said. Those would probably have a lot of fudge factor in them. I didn't know how much, but I knew when it came to the suits, the safety limits were usually underestimated by about twenty percent. So, call it maybe 24,000 kilometers of safety factor and say we could come out of T-space 90,000 kilometers from our target, minimum. That was a long way to travel in open space, a lot of time for the enemy to take potshots at us on the way in for an assault.

I tried to picture the battlespace in my head, the cutters

jumping into a system ahead of the troop carrier, the carrier launching assault shuttles and dropships and falling back. I wondered if they'd tried arming the troop carriers, but something told me they weren't any more willing to lose those than they were the cruisers. They were big, expensive and time-consuming to build.

There was exactly zero chance anyone was going to get the Fleet to build anything different, either. At least no one I knew. Anything I came up with would have to be a different way to use what we had.

No one is going to listen to you, dumbass.

I squeezed my eyes shut, believing for a moment I'd read the words on the tablet screen, but they'd just been inside my head. I shook them away and tried to come up with another tack to follow. Everything related to modern space warfare and tactics was classified except in the broadest terms, the sort of bullshit they'd broadcast on the scansheets to make concerned citizens think they had any idea of what was going on with the war.

But they'd taught me some military history in NCO school. Not a lot, but enough for them to drive home the point that war never really changes once the boots hit the ground. If that was true, then what about previous wars? Space was space, but before we'd left Earth, they'd fought wars on the oceans. It wasn't a perfect analogy, because the battlefield was bound by gravity, and there were separate battlespaces on the water, under the water and above the water. But before they invented submarines and airplanes, people made war on the oceans for centuries. How did they get close without getting spotted?

"Show me anything you have about naval tactics from the Twentieth Century and earlier," I said to the tab. "If it's not fucking classified."

This information is not classified.

Computers have no sense of humor. It's why the Commonwealth doesn't allow research into sentient AI's. Who wants an all-powerful computer with no sense of humor running the universe?

There are several distinct eras of naval combat, the tablet told me, *ranging from the nuclear aircraft carrier back to diesel navies, coal-powered steamships and three separate ages of sail. Where would you like to start?*

Good question. The tablet had provided a timescale for each of the possibilities it had listed, along with different conflicts that had occurred in those time periods. I had no idea which to pick from, so I chose at random.

"Tell me about World War One." Whatever the hell that was.

———

I'd never seen one of the missile cutters up close before. There was an ugly utility to the design, something cookie-cutter generic, but they had a certain charm. They reminded me of a mutt my mother used to throw scraps to after dinner, so ugly he was cute. Not that anyone would call one of the missile boats cute.

They were lined up wingtip to wingtip in the valley below the base, massive, bulky delta shapes built around a fusion drive bell in the rear and a proton cannon at the nose and two hollow missile bays to either side. The Transition Drive was jammed in beside the fusion reactor, a hump-backed shape between the vertical stabilizers, and the whole thing had an ad hoc, jury-rigged feel to it.

The flight crews and maintenance techs were swarming around the craft, arming sleds hauling missiles and lasing cartridges for the Gatling laser turrets and crew chiefs yelling with motherly protectiveness when someone came close to dinging the hull of one of their babies, and they all ignored the lone Marine walking amidst them. The ships were about a hundred and twenty meters long, half that wide at the broadest, and ten meters tall not counting the landing gear. They were tiny compared to a cruiser or a troop carrier, barely longer than an assault shuttle, not as bulky or bulbous as a dropship, but to me walking beside them along the fusion-form pavement, they seemed huge and intimidating.

And mysterious. Which was why I was there.

I watched the workers and the armorers and the techs and tried to decide who I needed to talk to. If the Fleet Attack Command was anything like the Marines, then the ones who really knew the deep, dark secrets would be the NCOs. Not one *too* high up the chain, though, or they'd think their shit didn't stink and they wouldn't be bothered to give the time of day to a Marine buck sergeant.

I cruised up and down the lines, popping the collar of my field jacket against the chill wind coming out of the north. The morning sun hadn't made its way over the mountains yet and my ears were already going numb. The enlisted techs were trying to keep warm by moving fast, probably afraid to sham and stick their hands in their pockets under the watchful eyes of their NCO supervisors, who hid their own misery under a stoic exterior. Not them. They'd know their specialty, weapons or fuel or reactor maintenance.

I could tell the officers, the Attack Command pilots, because they were staying nice and warm inside their boats, popping their heads out the utility airlock or scuffling halfway down the boarding ramp whenever someone had a question and otherwise staying out of the wind and drinking coffee. Not them, either. They'd know how to fly the ship, maybe a bit about how it worked, but they wouldn't be as interested in pushing the physics limits. They needed to keep formation and watch their wingman and work the op order like all officers.

No, the ones I needed to talk to were the ones hanging in the background, watching the crews do the work, eagle-eyed to make sure no one bunged up *their* boat. Petty officers and Chief Petty Officers, the missile cutter's NCO, called the crew chief for admin purposes though the crew consisted of just them and the pilot. I squinted at ranks, looking for one sort in particular, a lower-ranked petty officer who was nonetheless toward the older range for the rank, someone who knew their shit but wasn't a go-getter looking for advancement, someone who was a little too laid back for their own good.

And there he was. He was tall and gangly with a long, horsey face and what seemed like it must be a perpetual grin if he was able to wear it in this weather. His hands were stuffed in his jacket pockets and he offered nods and cheerful hellos to the maintenance crews instead of barking at them to be careful. His rank tab was three stripes, one rocker, CPO but only the lowest of the CPO ranks and he had the air to him of a man in his forties at the youngest.

"Chief," I said, stepping up onto the bottom of the ramp of his boat and offering a hand. "I'm Sergeant Cam Alvarez. Could I bother you for a second?"

He shook my hand, a bit of bemusement in his eyes. He wore gloves but his grip was strong and firm.

"We don't get too many Marines out here on the flight line, Sergeant," he said. "I'm Steve Machate. What can I do for you?"

I squinted against the wind blowing a flurry of snow into my face.

"This is gonna seem a little strange, Chief Machate, but I just got back from our second op under this new kinetic strike strategy the Fleet's been using, and I've been trying to figure out some things about how it all works. I was wondering if you might be able to answer a couple technical questions I've been kicking around when I can't sleep."

Machate shrugged, smiling a bit wanly.

"I suppose I know these boats as well as anyone, since I've been around from the time they designed the damned things. And it'll be nice to have someone ask me something *not* involving maintenance checklists for once. I'd invite you inside," he said, his tone apologetic, "but I gotta be out here to supervise or the Commander gets upset."

"That's okay," I assured him, though I would have paid money to get out of the damned wind. "What I was hoping to find out, Chief, is how close to a planet can one of these things Transition? I know what the commercial regs say, but I also know we've come in closer than that in battle."

Machate laughed softly, leaning against the support strut for the ship's belly ramp.

"That's one of those questions that can't be answered simply or without a lot of math, Sergeant. Y'see, the exit wormhole can't form if the gravimetic field generator is too close to a gravity well of a certain strength. It's complicated, but for the sake of discussion let's call it anything larger than a small asteroid. I mean, if you had a space station out in the same orbit around the primary star as a planet but on the opposite side of the ecliptic, you could jump in right next to it. But a moon or a big rock like Ceres back in the Solar System? That's a no-go. Now the military regs say we're supposed to be nine planetary diameters out, just like the commercial limit, but I've been there when we jumped out from as close as seven, so I'm thinking we could jump in at seven, too, but no one wants to try it."

"Well, that doesn't sound too complicated...," I started to say, but he raised a finger for me to wait.

"Thing is, though, there's almost never just *one* gravity well to deal with. Look at Earth, for example. It's not just Earth, it's the Earth-*moon* system, right?"

I nodded understanding, fascinated. The man was really getting into it, like a lecturer in a college. I thought he would probably make a good military instructor if he ever got the chance.

"Well," he went on, "you might think that the moon's gravity would like, add itself to the Earth's and that would mean you'd have to jump in even farther away, but you'd be wrong. If you could find the exact spot where the moon's gravity cancelled out the pull from Earth, what they call the Lagrangian point, you could safely form a Transition wormhole right there and jump in a *lot* closer." He sniffed, his nose going up in the air. "Lot of us want to start trying that on these attacks, and I think the brass might let *us* do it, but they'd never risk one of your big troop carriers on something like that. Too easy to wind up jumping right into the missile range of an orbital weapons platform and then, boom! You're dead as last month's fashion trend." He grinned broadly. "Deader, because fashion trends can still be going on in the colonies after they're buried and rotting on Earth."

Damn. There went that idea.

"Okay, then tell me something else. I read that the Transition kills all pre-jump momentum. Is that right? Is there any way to carry any of your speed with you? Or any way to accelerate once you jump in without using your drives?"

"Oh, jeez, let me think," Machate said, rubbing a gloved hand over his face. "All I can think of that *might* work is if you come out in the same orbit as a planet or moon or large asteroid, as close as possible and just sort of use maneuvering thrusters to nudge yourself into its gravitational pull, then use it as a gravity slingshot." He shrugged. "It might work, might not, I'd have to put in some computer time, and I'd have to be more specific about the gravitational values."

"Chief Machate, who the hell is this and why is he on my flight line?"

I knew from the tone of her voice she was an officer. No NCO could ever sound quite as self-important. I turned and went to attention, then saluted the Commander's rank she wore on her collar, ignoring the petulant sneer on her pinched face. She returned the salute out of habit, with a grimace of irritation like I was wasting her time with the military courtesy.

"I'm Sergeant Alvarez, ma'am," I said with crisp precision. "I'm sorry to intrude, I just..."

"This flight line is restricted, Sergeant!" she snapped. "Who's your commanding officer? Do they know you're out here? Do you have any sort of authorization to be here?"

"Ma'am, I wasn't trying to cause any trouble. I can get out of here right now and you'll never see me again."

"He was just asking some technical questions, ma'am," Machate added, just trying to be helpful, I supposed, though I wish I could have told him to shut the hell up. "It was no big deal."

"What sort of technical questions?" she asked, her tone sharp. "What did you tell him, Chief Machate?"

"It's nothing top secret or anything, ma'am, just shit like how close to a planet we can Transition. Standard stuff."

"I shouldn't have to remind you, Chief Petty Officer, that information is classified. It may be common knowledge for you and me, but a Marine sergeant is not cleared for it." She pulled her 'link from her belt and tapped a control. "This is Commander Johansen. I have a security risk on the flight line at slip 46 Alpha. I need an MP patrol here immediately."

"Ma'am," I protested, raising my hands palms out, "that isn't necessary, really! I'm not a security risk, I was just curious! I didn't realize I was asking anything I wasn't supposed to know. If you let me, I'll get back to the barracks..."

"You're going to wait right here, Sergeant. Whether or not you're a threat to security will be up to the MPs to decide."

I thought about running. She wasn't armed, and I was fairly sure I could outrun a Fleet pilot. It was what I wanted to do on a gut level, what instincts ingrained since my childhood told me to do. But they knew my name, knew where to find me, and all running would accomplish would be to make me look more guilty...of something.

I ran a hand over my face, moaning. Top was going to *kill* me.

[14]

"Tell me again what, exactly, you were doing on the flight line, Sergeant Alvarez," the MP officer repeated for what had to be the third time in the last hour, leaning across his desk toward me, arms resting on top of the inset touchscreen display.

"I've already told you everything, sir," I said, leaning back in the chair.

It wasn't a comfortable chair, probably on purpose. The whole room was designed to be uncomfortable, to make anyone brought in here ill at ease, from the pasty white of the wall color to the up-and-down straight metal of the furniture to the slightly-too-warm temperature that would make someone just a little bit nervous sweat down the small of their back. Not that I'd know that first-hand or anything. I wondered what effect it had on the people who had to work here every day.

"Tell me again, anyway," the 2nd Lieutenant insisted. He'd never told me his name, but the tape across his uniform chest read Lucas.

Lucas was following some book, I could tell by the bored expression on his face. He knew this was a waste of time, but the MP interrogation book said to keep asking the same questions over and over until the suspect contradicted themselves and then pounce on the inconsistency. It was the same book the cops back in Trans Angeles followed, and I'd been in this uncomfortable chair many, many times.

"I was just curious," I said, a sigh creeping out beneath the words. "I've been on two missions using the new tactics and I wanted to know more so I could do my job better."

Lucas grunted, making a mark with his finger on the touch screen. I thought maybe we were done, that he'd given up, but the exterior door to the Military Police station opened with a blast of cold air, and with the chill came a younger man dressed in black. He was a prick. I knew it before he opened his mouth. When you've met as many pricks as I had through the years, you get a sense for them. It was in the set of his dark eyes, the hint of a smirk on his narrow mouth.

"I'm Lt. Darian," he announced, as if that explained everything. "Fleet Intelligence," he added, just in case it didn't. "I was notified there was a security breach."

"There was unauthorized personnel on the flight line," Lucas explained, then frowned. "I mean...no. Personnel is plural, isn't it? What's the singular?"

Oh, Jeez, this guy is a winner.

The prick thought so, too. Darian rolled his eyes and motioned toward me.

"Is this the security breach?"

"Oh, yeah," Lucas said, nodding. "This is Sergeant Cameron Isaac Alvarez, Delta Company, Fourth Platoon of the Marine Drop Troopers here on base."

Darian punched something into his tablet, frowned at it for a second, then looked around the mostly-empty office, catching the eye of a Corporal who was sitting at a nearby desk. He looked from the Corporal to the extra chair and back again and the woman sighed and pushed away from her desk, grabbing the chair and hauling it over to him.

Prick.

Darian took the chair, spun it around backwards and straddled it, like every douchebag authority figure who ever wanted to look tough.

"So, tell me," he said, "exactly what were you doing on the flight line, Sgt. Alvarez?"

I let my head roll back, eyes raised to the featureless ceiling like God was up there and I'd finally broken down and was asking for His help.

"I was curious." I enunciated every word very carefully. "I've led my squad on two missions using the new tactics and they kept asking me questions I couldn't answer. Like how close to a planet could we jump? Is there any way to jump in and get closer without the enemy seeing us?" Which wasn't exactly true, but it sounded likely and was easy to remember. "I just wanted to have a handle on the bigger picture, that's all."

"The bigger picture?" Darian repeated, snickering at the words. He waved his tablet in front of me, showing me an open personnel file—mine, I assumed. "Sergeant Alvarez, you are a hood rat from Trans Angeles, and before that a deadender in some broken-down ruin of a city no one has ever heard of. The only reason you're here at all is the Marines are desperate for warm bodies. What the hell makes you think you could even understand the bigger fucking picture?"

That blue filter seemed to fall over my vision again and I began to think of the quickest ways to hurt Lt. Darian. This wasn't going to end well, because I was going to be in the brig for the foreseeable future and this asshole was going to be floating in a vat of biotic fluid, regrowing his trachea and I just didn't give a shit.

The only thing that saved him from days of pain and me

from the end of my military career was the door opening again. Only this time, the icy blast didn't blow in another douchebag, it blew in Lt. Ackley...and Captain *fucking* Covington.

Shit. I am so dead.

I sprang to my feet, as did Lt. Lucas and the MP corporal, all of us stiffening to attention. Darian rose slowly, with a notable lack of deference to the Skipper.

"You have one of my people in custody," Covington said quietly, nodding toward me. "If you're planning to file charges, I'd like to know the substance of them. If not, I'm going to take him back to our company area."

"Nobody's taking this man anywhere," Darian said, every bit as self-important as any Intelligence prick ever, "until I am done questioning him."

Out of the periphery of my vision, I saw Lucas' eyes go wide and I thought that, for all the MP officer's failings, he still understood what a bad mistake Darian had just made.

The Skipper crossed the distance to Lt. Darian in a single step, towering over the shorter man, looking down his narrow, aquiline nose at him, fixing him with blue eyes as frosty as the crust on the snow banks outside.

"Who the hell are you." It wasn't a question, it was a statement, but Darian wasn't smart enough to realize it.

"I'm Lt. John Darian, the Fleet Intelligence liaison assigned to this base," he announced with all the officiousness he could squeeze out of the words. "I'm responsible for evaluating security risks to..."

"*Lieutenant,*" Covington interrupted, spitting the rank out as if it were a curse word, "if you honestly think a Marine sergeant with a Bronze Star with a V for Valor for his service in the liberation of the Brigantia colony is going to somehow smuggle the secrets he got from an Attack Command junior crew chief out to the Tahni, then you are somehow more of a fucking moron than I imagine you to be." The man's lip was curled in a snarl and I realized this was probably the first time I'd actually seen him angry. "And frankly, that would be a Goddamned miracle."

"I don't care who you are," Darian said, puffing up, shock in his expression, "you can't talk to an Intelligence officer that way! I'll report you to Intelligence Command on Inferno!"

"You do that, you little pissant," the Skipper snapped. "And while you're at it, tell your boss Colonel Murdock that Phillip Covington says hello. And if he asks you which Phil Covington, you can tell him it's the same one who taught him platoon tactics at the Academy when he was a cadet."

Darian swallowed hard, as if the mention of his CO's name was some sort of word of power invoking forbidden magic.

"There's a car outside, Alvarez," Covington said, eyes still locked on Darian's. "You and Lt. Ackley wait there for me."

"Aye, sir," I said.

Ackley was already moving and I followed her out, not waiting to see what new dumbassery Darian was going to pull out of a hat next. Ackley barely waited until we were out of the building before she unloaded on me, the white-hot flare of her anger almost cancelling out the winter blast funneled down through the streets of the base.

"Alvarez, do you know how many times I've gone to bat for you?" she said, yanking open the rear passenger's side door of the car and waving me into it. "Do you know how many times I've had other platoon leaders and platoon sergeants itching to file complaints against you for going out of your way to embarrass them in training exercises, how many training officers wanted you written up for a failure to respect the range limits?"

The upholstery of the car seat was cold against my legs even through my fatigue trousers, and I shivered involuntarily until she slammed the car door shut and walked around to the other side. She sat down beside me and had to unclench her teeth before she could speak again.

"And I didn't mind, because you're a hell of a Marine, and you're becoming a good squad leader. But pulling stupid shit like this and embarrassing me in front of the fucking *Skipper* is pushing things too far! What in the hell did you think you were doing stirring up trouble with the Attack Command zoomies?"

"I didn't mean to embarrass you, Lieutenant," I said, sullen resentment at being chewed out again for something so innocuous warring with guilt at getting Ackley in trouble.

She'd been a good platoon leader, or as good as I was likely to find, anyway. She was about due to be promoted to First Lieutenant and bumped up to XO somewhere and then I'd have to deal with some worthless shavetail right out of the Academy or, more likely, Officers' Candidate School. There weren't enough Academy grads to go around in the Marines with the war.

"Well, you *did*," she said. "It would have been bad enough if the dumbass bitch pilot had called *me*, but she called the Skipper. I had to find out there was a problem by having Captain Covington come to my office and inform me we'd have to drive down to the MP station to pick up *my* squad leader!"

She ran fingers through her hair, gripping hard as if she wanted to tear it out.

"I've been cutting you as much slack as I can because I understand you're probably still experiencing post-traumatic stress after Brigantia, but you've pushed things too far. If Captain Covington doesn't do it himself, I'm going to have to replace you as squad leader."

Her door was yanked open and Captain Covington blocked out the wind, towering above us.

"Drive, Lt. Ackley," he ordered.

Ackley gave me one last, disappointed look as she slid out of the car and went to the front. The military didn't do self-driving cars, perhaps because they were worried about worms and hacks, or perhaps because they had too many personnel and not enough jobs for them. I wondered if Ackley had driven them on the way here or if Covington had taken the wheel himself. This leg of the trip he'd spend in the back seat, next to me.

Ackley pulled the car away from the curb, the tires scraping against the packed snow and ice before they caught on the pavement. I kept my eyes straight ahead, but I could feel the Skipper's glare on me and even as I dreaded what he'd have to say, I wished he'd get on with it and say it.

"Why were you there, Alvarez?" he asked, his voice calm and lacking the anger I'd expected. "What were you hoping to find out?"

I tamped down the surge of irritation at hearing the same question again, knowing the Skipper wasn't like the morons in the MP station. He deserved my respect and my honesty.

"Top told me something the other day, sir," I told him. "She was talking to me about Henckel, trying to help me not feel guilty about him getting killed."

"He was killed by an IED, by the females." It wasn't a question. Covington knew every detail about every man and woman who'd died under his command, probably since he'd joined the military. I nodded anyway. "There was nothing you could have done. If you'd opened fire on them unprovoked, I would have begun the court-martial proceedings myself."

"That's what's been eating at me, sir. The fact there was nothing I could have done. Top was trying to tell me it's not my job to keep my people alive, that it's not possible. And I realized she was right. I can't keep them alive and neither can you, and neither can the Fleet Attack Command pilots. I kept wanting to blame someone, someone besides myself, and the only way I could be sure there was no one to blame was to try to understand the bigger picture."

"And do you understand it now?" The question was almost gentle.

"I understand why we're doing what we're doing, but I don't think anyone has put enough thought into whether there's some way we can use the same strategy and still mitigate our casualties. We're risking everything every time, just throwing ships and troops into the fire and hoping enough make it through to get the job done." Anger and frustration were rising up like bile in my throat and it was getting harder to keep from spewing them out. "It's like no one is even trying to find a better way."

Covington eyed me sidelong.

"You say that as if you've already thought of one."

"I've been researching military history. Our problem is we have too much open space to cross, too much time for the Tahni to target us on the way in, and I figured they must have had the same problem back when Earth navies fought on the oceans. Have you ever heard of a Q ship, sir?"

"I have," Covington said, a shadow of a smile passing across his face, as if he was pleased that I even knew the term. Ackley turned slightly in her seat, frowning in confusion, and Covington explained. "It was a term applied to warships disguised as merchant vessels, Lieutenant, used to bait enemy vessels into attacking, then it would sink them." His attention returned to me. "The concept doesn't exactly translate to our situation, Sergeant. We aren't having any problems getting the enemy to show themselves and attack us, so there wouldn't be any advantage to disguising a military vessel as a merchant ship."

"Yes, sir," I agreed, "but it gave me an idea. These are Tahni systems, not occupied human colonies. There have to be regular supply ships coming in from their core worlds. I mean, if they're anything like our colonies, there's no way they can be totally self-sufficient, not this far from their core worlds. They have cargo ships coming in and maybe they wouldn't be all that suspicious about one of them Transitioning into their system or making orbit around one of their worlds."

"We don't have a Tahni freighter handy," he said, but I could make out the interest underlying the words. "And we don't have their security codes, even if we could build one that looked the part."

"But they do," I pointed out. "And I think hijacking a Tahni freighter has got to be easier than running the gauntlet of their defenses every fucking time we attack." I shrugged. "I mean, Force Recon's got to be good for something besides fitting into tight spaces, right? Sir."

Covington pinned me with a sharp glance and for a moment, I thought I'd blown it, that he was going to do just what Ackley had suggested and bust me back to private, take away my squad. When he finally spoke, though, his words were quiet and thoughtful.

"Here's what's going to happen, Sergeant Alvarez," he said. "We're going back to the company area and you're going back to work. Your squad's replacement trooper will be arriving in the next shuttle down and I expect her to be up to speed by the time we deploy again. And I want your word that you won't talk to anyone about this, not a soul, until I get back to you."

My breath caught in my chest. Was he saying what I thought he was saying?

"You have it, sir. And thank you. But does that mean...." I trailed off, unwilling to say the words lest I get my hopes up.

"I'm not making you any promises, Sergeant. It's a wild idea, a risky one. Not a risk of lives and equipment, which the brass is always more than willing to take, but one of reputation, which is a much harder gamble for anyone above the rank of major to make. The likelihood is that I'll get laughed out of the battalion commander's office." He inclined his head toward me. "But I'll try. I owe Private Henckel that much." His eyes lost focus, and I wondered what battle he was thinking of, light-years away and decades ago. "All the Private Henckels."

"Cut left, Dixon!" I almost yelled the words, though it would have accomplished nothing. The helmet radio would have reduced the volume of the transmission for the sake of clarity, and Dixon wasn't going to cut left in time even if I'd been standing a centimeter from her ear, screaming.

She was cresting the hill, skylining herself just the way I'd told her *not* to in the pre-mission brief, just running right over the top of the rise instead of skirting the crest and staying just below the hilltop. And if the enemy was where I thought they'd be...

The targeting laser from the First Platoon suit struck Private First Class Marina Dixon's Vigilante dead-center and her IFF display flashed red for a moment before fading to black.

"Dammit!" PFC Dixon cursed plaintively from inside the frozen battlesuit. "I'm sorry, Sergeant Alvarez."

She was notionally dead, so I ignored her apology and blasted ahead of Lance Corporal Graciano on a burst of my jump-jets. I'd had Dixon running point for him and, with her down, his fire team would be a trooper short.

"Contact front!" I announced. "Enemy armor in platoon strength!"

First Platoon wasn't going to wait. Their ambush was blown and they were coming to us, sprays of snow kicking up from where they were kicking free of their concealed positions and spreading to intercept our advance through the mountain pass.

"Assault through, First squad!" I ordered, knowing what Ackley would do without having to hear her commands.

Breaking contact would have meant taking even more casualties, and taking the chance the enemy hadn't sprinkled our back trail with more surprises, and the mission depended on completing this mission and reaching the Tahni spaceport on the other side of the pass. Or so the tactical exercise's op order had told us. There wasn't time for anything fancy, not with enemy troops coming over the hill, so assaulting through was the only tactic that made sense.

And it was all a colossal waste of time because Dixon had gone and gotten herself killed *again,* and the main purpose of this outing was to judge her capabilities and get her synched up with the rest of the squad.

I went through the motions anyway, blasting away at First Platoon with the full virtual wrath of my neutered weapons, softening up their front lines for the rest of my squad. At least Graciano and Linebarger were improving, probably from their experience in actual combat. They followed my example and unloaded on the opposing force, taking what targets they could hit and then barreling through their lines, giving First Platoon the choice of letting us get behind them or ignoring the bulk of Third Platoon charging up the hill toward them, guns blazing.

It ended quickly to the call of "index," and we all recovered from our simulated damage and straggled back down to the collection point for the After-Action Review.

At least it was pretty out here. With the expansion of the base had come the mapping and establishment of training grounds a few kilometers from its borders, up in the hills. The mountains in the distance were cloaked in snow, narrow veins of rock still standing out from it here and there, while the foothills were magical crystal fairylands of frozen streams and waterfalls, spoiled only by the footprints of our suits and a few animal tracks.

That this place even had animal life was almost a miracle. It hadn't evolved here, the scientists were fairly sure of that. The life here had been based on the same genetically-engineered terraforming cyanobacteria we'd found on hundreds of worlds, left there in the distant past by a civilization we knew next to nothing about. People called them the Predecessors, or the Ancients and extrapolated the content of dozens of documentaries and movies about them from the scantiest of evidence. Hell, cults had formed around them, people worshipping statues of idealized humanoids without the slightest of evidence of what they'd looked like.

Their work here had been brief, but effective. The algae had spread enough to make the atmosphere breathable, and the Tahni had taken over from there. From what we understood, or what the intelligence reports claimed we understood, the Tahni didn't go in for genetic engineering on themselves, but they held no such compunction about plants and animals. Tahn-Skyyiah, their homeworld, was warm, like a wetter version of Inferno, but they'd genetically modified plants and animals from that warm, wet place until they were suited to live on this snowball world.

I wasn't sure what I found more disquieting, the fact that the animal life here was so alien to me or the fact that most of it had been introduced less than a century ago. We were playing in someone else's genetic laboratory.

Dixon's suit was parked next to the shelter the Engineering Corps had constructed at the end of the road leading up to the draw. She was already inside, her Vigilante's chest plastron hanging open like she'd blamed the armor for her failure and abandoned it in the road out of spite. I stepped up beside it and swung my own plastron forward, pushing the helmet up and back and clambering out of the suit. The blistering cold wind of the winter morning slapped me in the face and I forgave Dixon her haste; I wanted to get out of this shit, too. But I had an example to set, so I shut the chest plastron after me and then closed hers as well before I headed into the shelter.

The interior of the dome was raw, grey buildfoam, poured by automated construction bots, and so were the benches that seemed part of the floor, squared off lumps of the cheap, malleable building material chopped and sanded and better than standing the whole time, I supposed. Chemical heating coils were built into the foundation, which made the place practically balmy compared to the outside, though it was probably only a few degrees above freezing and I could still see my breath.

Dixon was huddled under her field jacket away from the rest of our platoon and as far as possible from the First Platoon op-for. She stared at the floor, her mouth set in a sullen frown, and I could just see in the set of her dark eyes the conviction that the exercise hadn't been fair and that she'd been set up to fail. The look on her face practically screamed "it's not my fault!"

"Marina," I said, sitting down beside her, flinching just a little at the deep-settled chill in the material of the bench. I wanted to start in with the ass-chewing immediately, but I had a sense it would be the wrong move and just make her more defensive. "You doing okay?"

"Do you think that exercise was realistic, Sergeant

Alvarez?" she asked, confirming exactly what I'd guessed about her train of thought. "I mean, would we really just blunder into an ambush like that?"

"Oh, no, it was unrealistic as shit," I admitted readily. "Things have never, not once been as easy as it was today." She blinked, mouth half open as if she'd been expecting another answer. "In real combat," I went on, "we don't get to sneak around, not since we don't have orbital bombardment from Fleet cruisers to use for cover. Instead, we get to jump straight into the fire and just pray to whatever gods we believe in that *our* drop-ship will be one of the few that makes it through."

She looked as if she wanted to interrupt, but I didn't give her the chance.

"And then, for the ones lucky enough to actually reach the ground alive, we get to be totally outnumbered almost every time, and I honestly think the only reason we've won so far, or at least accomplished the stated mission, is that the Tahni just aren't as good at fighting as humans." I laughed at the absurdity of it. "I mean, they're ruthless, ready to kill civilians, ready to die for their god-emperor, but when it actually comes to tactics and strategy, they're amateurs. They haven't had to fight any internal wars for centuries. Humans were fighting each other right up to the point we formed the Commonwealth and went to the stars, and we'd probably still be fighting each other if we didn't have the Tahni around to keep our attention."

I was trying my best to sound authoritative, even though everything I was telling her was coming directly from the intelligence briefs. Covington had begun sending me declassified intelligence reports on the Tahni Imperium every single day since my little misadventure with the Fleet Attack Command, the MPs and Fleet Intelligence, and I'd studied them more dutifully than I ever had a school lesson as a kid.

"If they're so bad at fighting, why haven't we beaten them?"

she demanded, sounding skeptical about the whole thing. "Why are they still sitting on Demeter and Canaan and the other colonies? How did they manage to take out our shipyards at Mars?"

"Because of that whole part where they've had a unified government for centuries," I reminded her. "It means they might not have much experience in war, but it does mean their Emperor could put all their economic power into building ships and training troops. And quantity has a quality all its own, as Joseph Stalin once said."

"Who's Joseph Stalin?" she wondered.

"The point is, Marina, you're going to be outnumbered and even though we're getting better and more experienced in fighting them, you can't count on it. You have to use your head. So, tell me, why did you run straight up the hill instead of heading to the left and staying beneath the crest, like we discussed in the briefing?"

Finally, there it was, the air going out of her along with the stubborn pride as she realized she'd fucked up.

"I got excited when I heard about the ambush," she admitted. "All I could think was that I had to get in there and break it up before they got the rest of the platoon."

"And that's the right thing to do and the right feeling to have," I said, trying to be encouraging. It was hard. Encouraging wasn't my default setting. "But you won't do the squad or the platoon any good by getting yourself killed in the first two minutes of a battle. Our living through the fight might be secondary to accomplishing the mission, but we aren't going to accomplish the mission by losing half the squad before we even get started. No matter how bad things are, there's always time to think."

"Yes, Sergeant," she said, not quite smiling but seeming a bit relieved.

My gut twisted. I was doing my job, but was I really doing her any good? Henckel had been ten times the drop-troop she was, he'd listened to every lesson I'd taught him and learned it faster than her, but it hadn't kept him from getting killed about as senselessly and pointlessly as possible. Was I helping Dixon to survive or just keeping her alive long enough to be useful?

"So, got ourselves killed, did we?" Scotty asked, shaking snow off his field jacket, grinning broadly despite the temperature. "Don't sweat it too much, Dixon. Not everyone is an idiot-savant like Alvarez here, some of us actually have to practice and get better."

"That's just 'savant,' Gunny," I told him with a scowl that was only skin deep.

"That's not what I heard," he insisted. "Private Dixon, allow me to tell you a story about your squad leader when he first arrived in our poor, benighted platoon and I had to save his ass from getting beat up in the shower..."

Lt. Ackley slipped through the door and I stood, waving absently to Scotty and Dixon.

"I'll be right back," I told them. "But go right ahead with your bullshit story, Gunny. I'm sure it sounds better this time than the first ten times you told it."

He shot me a bird and sat down beside Dixon, but I'd already focused on Ackley. She had her tablet out and was already tapping something into it, probably preparing her section of the AAR.

"Ma'am?" I said, catching her before she got too deep into it. "Could I talk to you for a second?"

The corners of her mouth turned down at the sight of me, the same sort of reaction I'd received every time I'd been around her for the last three weeks. Covington might not have been angry with me for my transgression, but Ackley clearly hadn't forgiven me, and it was beginning to bother me.

"What do you need, Alvarez?" she asked, the words flat and clipped.

I checked around us to make sure no one was close enough to overhear before I answered.

"Ma'am, I haven't had a chance to say it since everything happened, but I just wanted you to know how sorry I was about making you look bad. I didn't mean to embarrass anyone or cause trouble for you."

She looked as if she wanted to cut me off, to cut the conversation short and dismiss me, but I pressed on before she had the chance.

"I guess I've never been great with authority figures," I admitted. "They were always either a joke or a threat, something I had to get around. But I respect Top and the Skipper, and I respect you, too. And making you think I didn't was the last thing I wanted to do."

Those words might have hurt to say, once upon a time. They weren't exactly easy even now, and I think Ackley understood that, from her slow nod.

"It's easy for me to forget how young you are, Alvarez," she said. She sniffed a quiet laugh. "Not that I'm ancient, but I did have the benefit of the Academy, and the one thing they pound into your head there is that every action you take has unintended consequences. It's like a pebble thrown into a pond. You've spent most of your life not having anyone to count on except yourself, right?"

"Yes, ma'am," I admitted. "Until recently."

"And since that's changed, I'll bet you've mostly thought about how that affects *you*, but it also means you affect everyone else. You're part of a larger whole now, and I don't just mean this platoon, or even the Marines. Do you know what I'm saying?"

"I think so," I said, though I wasn't sure if I was lying. "I was part of the platoon and the company and, I guess, the Marines. But beyond that..."

"When I was in my senior year at the Academy," she said staring down at the tablet as if she were reading the words off of it, "I fully intended to go Space Fleet, to be the captain of my own ship one day. It was all I had ever wanted, from day one. My father was Fleet..."

"I heard he was an admiral," I blurted out, repeating the rumor Scotty had told me when I'd first arrived at the company.

"No," she said, her smile fond and full of memories. "He might have been. He was the captain of a troop transport, the *Belleau Wood*. It was in the shipyards in Martian orbit for service when the Tahni attacked."

She blinked hard, maybe squeezing back a tear or maybe not.

"The next day, once I heard...." She trailed off. "Once they called me out of class and told me, after I'd called my mom and taken a few hours to scream and cry and pound my fists into the wall, the first thing I did was to go into the commandant's office and change my branch request to the Marines. Because it didn't matter what *I* wanted to do as a career, what mattered was where the Commonwealth *needed* me."

"I guess maybe I don't understand, ma'am," I confessed.

"Right now, you're doing this for your brothers and sisters in this platoon, this company," Ackley told me. "And that's fine for a squad leader. Even a platoon sergeant. But at some point, Cam, you're going to have to understand that we're doing this for the Commonwealth, for *people*. People like those colonists on Brigantia. They aren't just unfortunate victims of the war who you had the chance to help, they're the *reason* we're here. We do what we do not so we can go live among them once this is over, but because we're giving up that chance to make sure they can live their lives." She gestured outward. "All those nameless, faceless billions on Earth, the ones who wouldn't have pissed on you if you were on fire, every one of them is a son, a daughter, a mother, a father...just as much as those people on Brigantia. And you might despise them, might think they're blind fools who don't understand the war and don't care about us, but we're out here so they never *have* to."

"Yes, ma'am," I said. I wasn't sure if I totally agreed with her, but I understood her, which was, perhaps, more important.

"How's Dixon working out?" Ackley asked, changing the subject abruptly enough that I understood she'd done as much talking about herself and her motivations as she felt comfortable with. "I mean, aside from throwing herself into the enemy guns like a dumbass?"

"She's your typical noob. Came here thinking graduating armor school meant she was ready to face the enemy and got pissed off when she wasn't even ready for a pretty basic tactical exercise." I blew out a frustrated breath. "She'll be okay. She's ready to listen and learn, anyway. If I'm being totally straight with you, my biggest problem with her is that she's not Henckel. And the squad's not as effective without him."

"You got too dependent on Henckel," she said. It wasn't so much an accusation as an analysis, her tone clinical and didactic. "You and him would hit the opposition and the rest of the squad would just be support. Without him, you're going to have to use the strengths of your whole squad...which means you have to *know* their strengths. Private Dixon isn't the only one who's going to have to listen and learn. Get Gunny Hayes to help you with it. I've found him very perceptive in identifying natural talent."

I laughed, part self-deprecation, part honest amazement at how clearly she saw the problem I'd been chewing on for weeks.

"I'm glad I wound up in your platoon, ma'am," I said. "It could have been a lot worse."

She motioned with her tablet as she headed for the front of the room.

"Remember that," she cautioned me, only half joking, "when I'm reaming your ass in the AAR."

[16]

I didn't like leading from the rear, not even when the rear was in the middle. I'd spent most of the last two years either running point or just a few steps behind someone I trusted just enough to let them get shot at first. Watching Alpha team trace a broad wedge ahead of me across the river valley, while Bravo maintained an identical formation behind me, and let someone else be responsible for spotting the enemy seemed not just unnatural but positively dishonorable.

I was, I could say without any danger of my judgement being clouded by ego, the best in the platoon at operating a Vigilante. Except for the Skipper and maybe Top, I was probably the best in the company. I should be up front, keeping anyone else from playing Russian mine detector, the phrase my trainer at Armor school had used for a Marine who was only good at tripping ambushes.

"Dixon," I ordered the underqualified Russian mine detector out at the point of the spear, "push forward another twenty meters ahead of the squad. You need to hit the draw before the troops on the wings have to close in."

"Aye, Sergeant," she said. She never argued with me in the

field, but I could hear just the slightest tone of resentment poorly hidden in her words. I wanted to be angry with her, but she was saying and doing the right things when corrected and I wasn't going to fix her attitude by yelling at her.

She was far enough ahead of me that the wind-blown sheets of snow concealed her from even my helmet's thermal imaging, and the only way I could track her, or any of them, was the IFF transponder signal glowing blue on the map overlay in my HUD. The weather had gone from unpleasant to nearly uninhabitable over the course of the last month and I was beginning to wonder if the winter here would ever end. The forecast called for another four to six weeks of the really nasty storms until something resembling spring would finally set in.

It wasn't so bad if you could spend your days huddled indoors, pulling PMCS or running simulations in the pods, but Lt. Ackley preferred training in the suits and so did I. The simulators couldn't replicate the physical experience of running and jumping and flying in the suit, much less the emotional impact of being in the real world. The simulators added a filter to things, removed a level of consequence and reality and made everyone just a bit more blasé and reckless than they would have been otherwise.

Dixon needed training and so did I, so out into the deadly cold and driving snow we went, almost every day for the last month. And every day, I wondered if this would be the day I'd hear something from Captain Covington, even if it was just the final denial from the Battalion Commander, or the Brigade Commander, or the Fleet admiral in charge of this sector, or maybe straight from Intelligence. By this time, I was sure they'd all seen the Skipper's proposal, crafted from my wild idea. They were probably laughing it from one office to another, passing it around attached to official memos like the joke you wanted everyone to hear from you first.

No, I wasn't bitter or anything. Why do you ask?

I wrenched my mind away from the same worn rut I'd paced mentally for weeks now and concentrated instead on the map. The broad river valley ran into a draw as it narrowed on its way uphill from the inland sea where it terminated, through the surrounding hills as they closed in around it back up into the mountain glacier where it originated. This time of year, it was hard to tell the river from the land when both were frozen and covered in ice, but the mapping overlay assured me I was pounding my way across solid ground, the legs of my Vigilante post-holing in the deep snow with every step.

In another kilometer, the draw would be narrow enough for the Marines on the flanks to have to move into a staggered column, which would be the perfect place for the op-for to hit us. If we'd been running a platoon-level operation, with one of the other platoons as op-for, I would definitely have expected the attack to come there, because the other platoon leaders were nothing if not predictable.

But this was a squad scouting mission and the opposing force was Fourth Squad, and their squad leader was Vicky Sandoval. The fact we were occasional lovers was secondary at the moment due to the fact she knew how I thought tactically and could generally think rings around me. She'd know I expected an ambush at the narrows, but would she change her plan based on that knowledge? Was there any better place for an attack?

I scanned the map past the draw and tried to look at it the way she would. If the weather were better, it might make sense to try to have her squad up beyond the crests of the hills on either side of the draw, have them swoop down on top of us as the last of Bravo team entered the narrows. But with the snow buildup in the draw and the brutal cold removing all background heat, they'd stand out like signal flares on thermal the second they approached the crests of the hills. And if I knew that, so did she.

The only place that made sense was where the draw dead-ended at a waterfall. We'd be forced to jet up to the top and skirt the course of the river to reach our objective, an imaginary Tahni observation and listening post on an imaginary occupied colony. Vicky would, I thought, have her squad at the top of the waterfall, ready to fire on us the second we hit the jets. And if the only objective had been to survive the ambush and carry on the notional mission, the easiest thing to do would have been to change routes and bypass the waterfall. But the real aim of the training exercise was to teach the squad how to fight together without me and Henckel to do the heavy lifting, so I'd let them walk right into the ambush, as much as it galled me.

"Dixon," I said, not wanting to cheat by warning her but needing to do something besides watch her lead the lambs to the slaughter, "what do we do when we reach a choke point?"

"Slow up and let the rest of the squad catch up," she said, the words sounding rote enough that I thought she must have the manual memorized. "Prepare to synchronize fires to open up a gap in enemy forces in case of an attack."

"Got it in one," I said, trying to sound impressed. I'd really be impressed if she could remember to do it when the time came. Or recognized a choke point without me having to tell her. "Graciano, keep your eye on Dixon and if she slows down, push up and stack your fires."

"Will do, Cam." He was cheerful and upbeat, as usual. The man gave Lance Corporals a bad name, always happy and optimistic, even pulling one training mission after another in shitty weather. He needed to complain more.

Despite my concern for Graciano's attitude, I wasn't worried about him fucking up tactics. He'd been in enough combat for him to have a sense of which direction to shoot when the bullets started flying. Reacting fast enough to avoid being cut off and wiped out, that was something beyond knowledge and skill, something training could improve but only ability could ensure.

"You're not their conscience, Cam," Scotty said, his tone dryly humorous. "Stop sitting on their shoulders nagging them to do the right thing."

"That's a funny thing for you to say," I shot back at him, looking off to the right, unable to see him or even detect his IFF transponder, but knowing he was there. "Since that's exactly what you're doing."

"The difference is, I *am* your conscience on this exercise," he reminded me. "That's the whole reason I'm here."

I couldn't argue with that. He was in armor because he needed the Vigilante to survive the cold and keep up with us, but Scotty wasn't officially involved in the exercise, neither as a participant nor a trainer. He was only there to try to advise me on my leadership style, and even that not openly or officially. Not that I was loathe to admit I needed help, but Scotty and Lt. Ackley had decided it wouldn't do my squad's confidence in me any good to make them think I needed someone looking over my shoulder, so Scotty stalked unseen in the driving snow, my personal Ghost of Christmas Present.

The map showed the valley closing into the draw before I could even make out the surrounding hills through the storm, and Dixon's blue icon blithely proceeded into the narrows without so much as a backward glance much less any announcement. I wanted to scream at her, but Scotty would have slapped me down, figuratively anyway.

Come on, noob. Can't you see the walls closing in on radar? Slow the hell down.

But I wasn't being fair. I *knew* what was coming, knew the terrain and wasn't staring into the blinding snow, seeing

181

phantom battlesuits behind every flake. It would take her a moment, but she wasn't stupid. Just a few seconds. Maybe a few more.

Maybe a minute...

"We're coming into some narrows here, Sergeant Alvarez," she said, finally, nearly three hundred meters into the draw.

Gosh, you think?

"Corporal Graciano," she went on, "you're going to have to shift to a staggered column to make it through here. Maybe you should move up the team."

"I'm coming, Dixon," he assured her. The blue icons of Alpha team closed in and picked up their pace as Dixon slowed hers down, letting them catch up. I could barely make out the nearest of them passing in front of me, just a ghost on thermal and perhaps a shadow in the sea of white.

Now I could react, since I actually had something to react from.

"Bravo team," I called to Linebarger, "I'm moving up on Alpha. Keep your interval and be prepared for fire support."

"Roger that," he replied. He sounded taut, nervous, despite this being just another training run. Maybe he expected what was coming, just like I did. Maybe, I thought with a flash of insight that was very unlike me, he was afraid of letting me down, the way Henckel had been.

It felt wrong. I didn't deserve that sort of loyalty. I'd done nothing to earn it.

Do something now. Be the leader they think you are.

It took me a moment to figure out it had been my conscience advising me inside my head and not Scotty whispering in my ear. The two sounded remarkably similar.

"I'm not picking anything up on thermal as far as the sensors can track," Dixon reported. "I'm checking upslope, too."

"Roger," I said to her, hoping the curt reply would give her the hint that she didn't have to tell me every single time she *didn't* see the enemy. "Let me know if you spot anything."

It was hard to imagine the u-shaped draw as the course of a river. The spiny, stunted mutations the Tahni had foisted on this place instead of trees were completely buried under meters of snow and even the rocks and ruts were a smooth powder. I'd seen videos of rich people skiing on slopes like this for sport, one of the many things rich people did for fun that I found incredibly stupid. I'd never seen one of them trudging up it in a metal suit, so maybe they had that on me as far as intelligence went.

Here and there, life would punch through where the snow covering had collapsed, a section of frozen stream barely visible beneath the powder or the questing branches of the genetically-engineered flora sticking out with just a spray of green among the white. I kept a close eye on the squad's line of travel, worried about one of them straying onto the river and cracking through the ice. The suit would still protect them, but if they got trapped down there at an angle where they couldn't use their jets, it would be tricky as hell pulling them out.

At least the storm had slacked off, the snowfall down to flurries and most of the wind shut out by the surrounding hills.

"Getting steeper up here," Dixon said, always helpful.

"I know you want to tell her to shut up," Scotty said just as I'd opened my mouth to utter the words, "but don't. Better she tells you too much than not enough. Talking is helping her stay observant."

I clenched my teeth and stayed silent. Dixon was about three hundred meters from the waterfall on the mapping software, and I was finally close enough to see her and the rest of Alpha team. Their Vigilantes climbed steadily up the pass, frost giants from some Norse myth assaulting the goddess of winter's stronghold. They were clustered together, probably too close, but I let it slide. If we got hit, it would help to mass fires.

The smooth, unbroken blanket of snow began to fold and kink and crinkle as the slope increased and the jutting ledges of rocks on either side of the waterfall shed the white buildup to reveal their grey granite. The falls themselves were forty or fifty meters tall, most of the flow frozen in a shimmering, crystal curtain, just a narrow gap in the ice at the center showing the actual water buried beneath. Below the ice, the faster moving water crashed and the deeper sections of river still flowed and someone had told me there was still life down there at the river bottom, even at this time of year.

I was more worried about the life at the top.

"Dixon, hold up," I said.

Maybe I was wrong, maybe I should have let her stumble into what I suspected was coming, but would I have done it in a real movement to contact? I might not have been the best squad leader in the Corps, but I wasn't an idiot.

"Graciano, I want you to send up your whole fire team at once, spread out around the perimeter of the falls. Linebarger, hit the jets the same time they do and describe a higher arc, get a firing angle from above to give them cover."

"Got it, boss."

There were, I knew, some units in the Corps who insisted on what they called "radio discipline," using only approved call signs for communications. "Alpha One, this is Charlie One Actual for Alpha One Bravo, over?" That sort of shit. They'd taught us the system in Basic and I'd yet to hear anyone using it ever since Armor School. I'd asked a trainer about it in NCO school and she had explained with great deal of scornful amusement that the concept was ancient, from a day when humans were only fighting each other and signal intercept was a real possibility. Using names had been considered a breach of operational security because the enemy could use them to match people to units, perhaps track down their loved ones for leverage.

Signal intercept was a fantasy with modern communications, particularly when everything up to company level mostly used laser line-of-sight, but there were some by-the-book sticklers who still insisted on the old way. To me, it just added a layer of mental filtering, needlessly slowing down the communications process.

"Spread out at the base of the falls," I instructed. "Jump together on my signal."

The IFF signals were laid out like chess pieces and I regretted for a moment never taking up the game. I recalled watching older men playing it outside the bars and tobacco shops of downtown Tijuana when I was a kid, but it wasn't a popular pastime in the Trans-Angeles Underground.

"Go."

I didn't jump in the center of them, knowing that was exactly where Vicky would expect me to be. Yeah, maybe that was cheating, but as my old Armor School instructor had said, if you ain't cheatin,' you ain't tryin.' Instead, I pushed off to the left, just a dozen meters back from Mullany out on that side of the wedge. The scream of the jump-jets seemed muted inside my helmet, drowned out by the alarm klaxons sounding in my head. The sheets of ice crawled by in slow-motion, leaving us hanging in mid-air for way too long.

"Contact front!" Dixon yelled the word in my ear, as if the sheer volume would make the threat diminish, but I'd seen them before she'd managed the shout.

It was Fourth squad, aligned along the rock ledges on either side of the waterfall's banks, far enough back to prevent us spotting them from below, just the way I would have set them up. My first instinct was to fire, and I did, blasting notional missiles out at the Vigilante farthest out to the right, just outside minimum arming distance. But I had to think of the squad's fight, not just my own.

"Mullany, Dixon, with me on the left! Graciano, you and Chandra hit the right! Linebarger, head up and over the middle and give us fire support!"

I was only repeating what we'd gone over a hundred times in simulators and dry-runs and even dismounted walk-throughs back in the squad bay, and maybe no one was listening. Maybe they were simply reacting, going from instinct and I was talking to hear myself talk. But if they were only reacting, then at least they were reacting the way they'd trained and did what I said even if they didn't hear me saying it.

This was the hard part; the part I wasn't sure I'd ever get right. I'd become used to letting the data in the HUD flow over me, catching and holding only the useful bits, like those videos I'd seen of bears catching fish from a waterfall. It left my mind free to concentrate on the fight, on my next move and the move after and the one after that. Here, I didn't have that luxury. I had to pay attention not just to my own movements and the motion of the enemy around me but also the arrangement of my whole squad, and their next move. It stretched me thin and boxed me in all at the same time and left me a step slow.

And got me killed.

I didn't see the shot that tagged me, couldn't tell which direction it had come from. One moment I was blasting at one of Vicky's troopers with the targeting laser and the next, my armor was frozen and motionless and I was face-down in the snow. I was so surprised I forgot to curse. My HUD was dead, my comms were dead and the only thing I could see straight ahead was packed, white snow.

I blew out a breath, disgust rising in my gut like bile. It had been a long time since I'd gotten tagged in a training run, and I wondered how long it would take me to live this down.

"Okay, index," Lt. Ackley said, her voice the first sound in my headphones for nearly five minutes.

My armor's systems flickered to life and I pushed up from the snowbank as a Vigilante sauntered up to me. The IFF system was reading the op-for now that index had been called and I saw it was Vicky.

"Oh, be still my beating heart," she said, laughing throatily. "I actually got a kill on Cam Alvarez. Mom will be so proud."

"You're a riot, Vicky," I told her, then switched to Graciano. "What was the butcher's bill?" I asked him.

"Just you, boss," he told me and I blinked in momentary disbelief.

"Just me?" I repeated.

"We kicked their asses!" Dixon enthused and I looked around for her Vigilante, wondering if she was jumping up and down like a kid who had scored the winning goal at a school soccer game. "Got all but two of them!"

"Great job, everyone," I said over the squad net. "I just wish I'd been alive to see it."

The Vigilantes were milling around like shoppers at the Zocalo, waiting for someone to tell them it was time to go to the rear for an AAR, and so was I. That was usually Lt. Ackley's job for a squad-level exercise, and she'd just been on the horn to index us. So where was she? I didn't have her IFF transponder in my display for this exercise since she was a trainer on it, not a participant, and she wasn't one of the armored troopers I saw shuffling in the snow at the top of the waterfall, either.

"Scotty," I called. "Is the LT around?"

"Yeah, wait one," he told me. "She's on the horn."

Which meant her comms were tied up by a call from base, since there was no one else out here today but us.

No one dumb *enough to be out here but us.*

I was getting antsy and considering asking Graciano to send

me his battle cam footage so I could review the fight in my helmet display when Ackley finally piped up.

"Alvarez," she said, "Scotty is taking your squad back to base. You need to come with me. We have to catch a transport to the spaceport."

"Why, ma'am?" I asked. "What's wrong?"

"There's a planning session in four hours on the Fleet carrier *Bonaventure*, and Captain Covington wants you there for it."

"A planning session, ma'am?" I said, not comprehending. "Planning for what?"

"Your idea," she said, and I felt the hackles rising on the back of my neck. "Apparently, it's been approved. And you just got volunteered for it."

[17]

I don't know if I'd ever seen so much brass in one compartment, and it scared the hell out of me. I squirmed in my seat, grateful at least for the seat and the centripetal force that held me there. I was in the one ship in the whole system that rotated for gravity and my gut was already roiling enough without dealing with microgravity.

"Welcome to the *Bonaventure*, ladies and gentlemen," the tall, wispy woman said, nodding to the small group of officers and one stupid junior NCO gathered in the situation room of the Attack Command carrier. "For those who haven't had the pleasure yet, I am Captain Hightower, commander of this ship and the Attack Command wings on board. We also have with us today Colonel Arora of Force Recon." The straight-leg battalion commander was almost the prototypical Force Recon grunt: square-jaw, buzz cut, broad shoulders and clear blue eyes, straight off a recruiting poster. "As well as Colonel Voss of the Armored Command."

I'd never met Covington's boss and just looking at the woman made me think I hadn't missed anything. I might have been judging a book by its cover, but I'd read enough books to know my covers by now. She had the perpetual frown and pinched face of someone who lived by the book and would rather die by it than deviate. I'd seen it so many times before that the look was burned into my brain.

"Just for the record," Voss said, confirming everything I'd decided about her, "I want to state once more that I opposed this half-assed, half-baked excuse for a plan."

"Yes, Caroline," Arora sighed. "We know. We heard it the first dozen times. But the decision has been made and now we move on. Captain Covington is here, of course, as this is his operation, along with the field commanders who are being sent on the infiltration mission, Lt. Brian Davies of First Force Recon and Lt. Joyce Ackley, Third Platoon, Delta Company, Fourth Battalion of the 187th Marine Expeditionary Force."

Ackley looked, if possible, even more uncomfortable than I was. Maybe she had a right to. I was set decoration amidst all this brass, part of the background noise. She was just high enough in rank for one wrong word to shitcan her career. This Davies guy might have been calm, or it might just have been that I didn't know him well enough to tell when he was nervous.

"And lastly," Hightower finished, "our Fleet Intelligence liaison, Captain Cerrano."

I was so relieved by the confirmation that Hightower wasn't going to try to introduce me that I almost forgot to spare a look for Cerrano. She was nondescript, medium everything, with one of those faces that could blend into a crowd. Only her Intel black uniform stood out among the blues and greens.

I wasn't the only one who'd escaped notice, of course. There were two Fleet Lieutenants busying themselves in the background, working the data terminals for the compartment's central holographic display projector and Voss and Arora had both brought along their Executive Officers, majors both of them and neither, apparently, worth noting.

The whole lot of us were squeezed into the compartment with a massive holotank in the center, surrounded by an interactive table, while the bulkheads were inset with flat displays of star maps, troop projections, Transition Points and orbital maps of a dozen different worlds. And one with the face of a Tahni male, the face I so rarely got to see even having killed so many of them. Dark eyes set deep beneath bony brow ridges, jaws like steam shovels, ears and nose set flat into the skull and heads shaven except for a Mohawk ridge growing down into an impossibly long queue wrapped around the throat. It was a good reminder of the fact that there were aliens inside that enemy armor, that they might not necessarily react the way humans did in training.

"For the Marines among us," Hightower went on, "I'm terribly sorry to drag you out this far, but this ship can't go beyond the closest Transition point and I'm damned reluctant to bring her even that far into the system given how easy it would be for the Tahni to turn her to scrap with a couple of their corvettes. I don't want to waste your time, so let me get right to the heart of the matter."

Her fingers danced across the interactive tabletop and a star system coalesced in the projection, dual stars orbiting around a common center of gravity, with ten planets scattered from an orbit that seemed closer than Mercury's all the way out almost to their cometary halo.

"I'll let Captain Cerrano give you a rundown of what we know about the target system."

The black-clad Intelligence officer nodded, moving up to the table and gesturing toward the image in the projection.

"This is EHS-5679, a system closer in to the Tahni Imperium core worlds than any other we've attempted to strike so far. Our target for this mission is the one habitable." The fourth planet out from the twin suns expanded outward in the

191

image, showing a vast field of ocean-blue with the browns and greens of land scattered and spotty. "Our name for it is Ambergris. It's basically a strategic resupply world for their expansion, an agricultural colony, though not for the benefit of their civilian population. The sea farms on Ambergris provide food supply for most of their military, and there's an orbital transport facility to handle loading the cargo onto regular supply runs to their military outposts and those of our colonies they've occupied."

Cerrano sought out the eyes of each of the officers gathered around the hologram, and mine too. I wondered if she knew who I was and what I was doing there.

"I don't know how deep your knowledge of Tahni society runs, but you have to understand their diet is highly restricted by rules so deeply ingrained they might be religious. They get all of their protein from a plant native to their homeworld of Tahn-Skyyiah, and the consumption of it involves some sort of ritual they follow even out on the occupied colonies, involving communal dining led by their senior officers, who sort of act as priests."

She waved a hand at the table and the image of a plant appeared, a bulbous root of some kind, fuzzy and purple and decidedly unappetizing.

"The point is, denying them resupply of the plant is more than just a logistical strike, it also adversely affects their morale. And since the Tahni are not idiots, they know this as well as we do and this planet is heavily defended. Most of the defenses are static and land-based, though there are three large orbital weapons platforms, as well as at least one destroyer in-system, possibly two."

"Jesus," Arora muttered. "That's a tough nut to crack."

"Which is where your Marines come in," Hightower interjected, motioning for Cerrano to continue.

"Though the planet is rich in biosphere," the Intelligence

officer went on, "it's rough on equipment. The sea-water is abnormally corrosive and it plays hell on their gear and makes fuel separation for fusion reactors problematic. Their solution is to run regular cargo shipments from the asteroid belt and the gas giant just beyond it. Their schedules are as regular as clockwork, and perfect for Captain Covington's plan."

"I am old school when it comes to battle plans," Hightower admitted, a deep frown creasing her long, horsey features. "I prefer simple and direct. Anything else adds unnecessary complication and nearly always gets more people killed." She closed her eyes for just a moment, as if considering a painful memory. "However, direct and simple has been having its own problems lately, and I am prepared to risk a few lives for the possibility of saving many more. This is Captain Covington's plan, so I'll allow him to lay it out for you."

Despite their superior rank, it seemed to me that every one of the Fleet captains and Marine colonels and majors paid complete attention to the Skipper, as if his age and record outweighed his rank. Covington stood, as commanding and in charge as he was at one of our company-level AARs.

"Thank you, Captain Hightower," he said, nodding to the woman. "I prefer simple and direct myself, for the record, and I understand Colonel Voss' doubts, but this is a target we'll break our teeth on if we try to take it in a straight-up fight. And while this plan involves subterfuge, it is still fairly simple. Here...." He splayed his fingers against the table's touch screen and a cluster of asteroids grew into the dimly-lit collection of loose rock they were. "...is a cluster of small asteroids that is all that's left of a collision a few tens of thousands of years ago. They're not in the main belt, they're at what are called the Trojan points, close to Ambergris' largest moon. They're in a loose orbit around a larger piece of rock that is unstable in the long run and will ultimately lead to the smaller pieces crashing into the larger one and forming a single, even larger body. Their presence is all that concerns me, however, since they are directly along the path of the cargo ships heading insystem."

"We're going to jump the *Bonaventure* in right next to the cluster and a single platoon of drop-troopers are going to get out, each with rocket boosters affixed to them, along with attachment points for three Force Recon Marines to hold onto each of the Vigilante battlesuits. After the carrier jumps back out, the Marine force will conceal themselves in the debris field. When the cargo ship passes through, she will have nearly finished her braking burn, and the reduced velocity should allow the modified Vigilantes to match speed with her and board."

Another flex of his fingers on the panel and the ugly, boxy, utilitarian lines of a Tahni freighter appeared on the screen.

"The cargo ships are likely uncrewed and automated, but in the event of resistance, the Force Recon Marines will neutralize any hostiles and take over the bridge. Then they'll ride her into orbit and wait for the cargo shuttles to launch. The Recon Marines will storm the shuttles and commandeer them, then the Drop-Trooper platoon and the Force Recon Marines will ride one of the shuttles down while rigging any others that dock to explode above the ground. The cargo ship itself will be set to accelerate towards one of the orbital weapons platforms, either to distract it or ram and destroy it." He shrugged indifferently. "That would be gravy. Our main goal is simply to keep the enemy as distracted as possible. When the cargo shuttle with the Marines aboard reaches an appropriate altitude and speed, the Armored troops will drop, while the Recon Marines ride the shuttle all the way to the ground."

The view in the central display zoomed in even closer to the largest island in the largest chain, stretching out across the southern hemisphere. It was home to the center of the Tahni farming installation, the city where the workers lived, and the troops who protected them.

"The goal of the landing forces will be to disable air defenses to allow the rest of our troops to land conventionally with reduced attrition. The Drop Troopers will be tasked with taking out the SAM sites, while the Force Recon Marines will head to the ground defense laser installation and infiltrate the underground control facility and set charges to destroy it. Then both units will hold in place until the main landing force arrives."

He paused and half a dozen hissing breaths filled the silence.

"Sounds an awful lot like a suicide mission to me," Voss grumbled, and as much as I disliked her on an instinctive level, I couldn't disagree.

I'd known the general idea, but hearing it laid out like that, every part in order, it seemed the definition of a forlorn hope.

"It does," Covington said, and I blinked, staring at him. "But does it sound any more suicidal than throwing ships and troops into a meat grinder over and over?" He speared me with a dark-eyed glance. "What do you think, Sgt. Alvarez?"

Oh, shit.

"Who the hell is this guy?" Colonel Arora asked, frowning as he looked between Covington and me.

Covington smiled thinly.

"Captain Hightower keeps referring to this as my plan, but the concept is not mine. Sgt. Alvarez is one of my squad leaders under Lt. Ackley here. He received the Bronze Star for his role in the Brigantia operation as a Lance Corporal and was promoted to sergeant and attended NCO school in light of his exemplary performance in that cluster fuck. Since then, he's proven to be one of our best squad leaders. But as an enlisted man and then a junior NCO, Sgt Alvarez has a different perspective on the war than officers like us. We think of losses as the cost of doing business. We can afford to step back and keep ourselves separate, because it's what we were taught, because we can't allow ourselves to become obsessed with avoiding casualties. We record the messages to the survivors and send them off. Maybe we fight back tears or have an extra drink to drown the guilt, and then we move on, because we have to."

Covington paced in front of the holographic display, hands clasped behind his back, as if he were addressing his own troops and not a compartment full of superior officers.

"A squad leader doesn't have that sort of detachment. The men and women he leads are still close enough in rank to be his friends. He hasn't been in the service long enough to learn the lessons we're taught in OCS or the Academy. When his friends are killed, he doesn't see it as acceptable losses, doesn't see it as an unfortunate part of a necessary strategy. He sees it as a tragedy, a tragedy he feels personally responsible for."

I was having a hard time getting my breath. Covington was stripping my psyche bare in front of a room full of strangers, and I felt violated, betrayed. I wanted to run, wanted to find a hole and crawl into it. I wanted to hate him for it, but the man had not given me any reason to doubt him and I stayed still, tried to keep my face solid stone.

"Sgt. Alvarez didn't go to the Academy. He hasn't attended college. Hell, he didn't even technically graduate high school, just took an equivalency exam before he enlisted. Everything he knows about the military and its history, he has taught himself. So, when he decided there had to be a better way than throwing his friends at the Tahni and hoping enough survived to win the battle, he researched it on his own. He studied old water navy tactics, studied wars fought four and five hundred years ago, and finally, he tried to study the capabilities of our own forces but found everything was classified. Rather than accept yet another roadblock in his mission, he went to the Attack Command flight crews at the landing field on Hachiman and asked them the same technical questions." The corner of his mouth turned up. "And was promptly arrested, because why would one of our own troops care about the capabilities of his own military unless he was a security risk?"

There were a couple chuckles at that, and I thought one of them was from Cerrano. Glad *he* thought it was funny.

"I was called to come collect him from the MP station and I was prepared to be royally pissed off. But he didn't just have idle curiosity, he had a plan, or the beginnings of one. This was *his* concept and while I couldn't approve it, I could use whatever reputation I may have after a lifetime of service to try to get someone who had the authority to approve it to at least listen. And when it was finally given the green light, Lt. Ackley was the first to volunteer for the infiltration mission, because she knew Sgt. Alvarez would be going, even if he had to join another platoon to do it.

"So, let's ask Sgt. Cameron Alvarez." He cocked his head toward me. "Does it sound like a suicide mission to you?"

I stood, trying not to glare at the man openly for putting me in this position. He obviously thought it was important for me to say something, though I couldn't figure out why for the life of me. Babble threatened to come galloping out of my mouth and I had to clench my teeth to keep it under control.

"It's dangerous, sir," I said, first focused on him but then meeting the eyes of the others as well, not flinching even though I badly wanted to. "It's very dangerous, and we're not all going to live through it. But it's no more suicide than trying to hit a system as well guarded as this with the tactics we've been using. I'd say I have about an equal chance of buying it either way, and if I'm going to die, I'd rather go out with my eyes open and my guns blazing than stuck in a dropship waiting for the missile with my name on it." I shrugged. "And I'd rather do it giving the rest of my company a chance to live through this."

"Sir," I added as an afterthought, then sat back down, my ears burning.

"Ooh-rah, Sergeant," Lt. Davies, the Force Recon platoon leader said, nodding to me.

"Ooh-rah," Arora agreed. "That's good enough for me."

"Then let's stop this jabbering," Captain Hightower declared, "and get to work on a training schedule. We launch in two weeks."

"Oh, Good God, Cam," Vicky Sandoval sighed, letting her head fall back against my pillow, a thin sheen of sweat on her skin. "What in the hell have you gotten us into?"

"That's an odd thing to say right now," I told her, panting with my recent effort, rolling off of her and trying to catch my breath.

"I didn't want to kill the mood," she said, laughing quietly. "But seriously, this is fucking nuts."

As my core temperature began to cool, the bite of the chill from outside my barracks room began to penetrate even the shared body heat and I pulled the blanket over both of us. I lay on my back, only our shoulders touching.

"Everyone seemed really enthusiastic when the LT briefed us," I said, shrugging.

"Well yeah, that's because it's a kick-ass Marine wet dream. No one would dare act anything but enthusiastic about it in front of other Marines. But you get any of them alone and they'll admit to you they're scared shitless." Vicky pressed the heels of her hands against her eyes like she was trying to shut out the dim glow of the chemical strip lighting. "We're going to be alone on a planet full of Tahni. No air support, no orbital support, no reserves, no reinforcements for how long?"

"Just a half an hour," I insisted. "The rest of the strike force will be Transitioning right after we deorbit in the heavy cargo shuttles. The *Iwo Jima* is going to risk coming in closer to the planet since we'll have the defenses distracted."

"A half an hour is a fucking *eternity*," she told me. "We're all going to die."

"Lt. Ackley said the infiltration team is strictly voluntary." I felt deflated. If anyone would be jazzed about this, I figured it would be Vicky. "You can stay with the main strike force if you want."

She scowled and hit me in the shoulder, hard enough to hurt.

"You think I'd chicken out just because it's dangerous, you shithead?"

"Then what's wrong?" I asked, rubbing my sore shoulder. "Why are you upset?"

"Because no one is going to *not* volunteer," she said, rolling onto her side and glaring down at me. "Just like no one was going to act like they weren't psyched for the mission. This isn't a bunch of rear-echelon button-pushers. We're all Marines, ooh-rah?" She gave the battle cry a sarcastic edge.

"You don't think I should have told Covington what I was thinking?" I hadn't meant the question to sound so plaintive, but it did, and I winced.

"No." She sounded as if she wanted to blame me, but couldn't bring herself to do it. "No, the way it happened, there's nothing else you could have done. But damn it, Cam, we're all going to die. And I really wanted to live through this fucking war."

"You're going to," I insisted. "We have two weeks to train. We'll be ready."

I fell silent, my thoughts churning. She was right. There was nothing else I could have done, and if I died, I wouldn't regret the decision. But I couldn't put aside the things I *would* regret. And this was the last chance we were going to have to be together before the mission began.

"Vicky," I said, the words tumbling out of their own volition, freed of my control by a slip of the restraints inside my chest. "I...."

"Oh, don't...," she said, trepidation in her tone.

"I love you," I blurted.

She winced as if she'd been kicked in the gut, which wasn't quite the reaction I'd been hoping for.

"Oh, Cam," she moaned, "why did you have to go and say that?"

I thought about what Scotty had said and my shoulders sagged. We wanted different things. I'd fucked up.

"I'm sorry," I told her. "I know you just wanted things to be uncomplicated and I'm messing things up like I always do, but..."

"Shut up," she snapped, leaning down and kissing me.

The kiss caught me off guard, stole the breath out of me, and I thought I would suffocate, but I didn't dare come up for air. I thought she was trying to push it away, banish my words with the fire of passion, but she paused, pulling away from me slightly, letting her forehead touch mine, her eyes closed.

"I love you, too," she told me. "But damn it, this wasn't supposed to happen."

A tear dripped down into my face and I frowned, not understanding.

"What's wrong, Vicky?"

"I made myself a promise when all this started," she said, the words a breath in my ear. "I wanted more than anything to just serve out my enlistment and take the relocation to a nice colony and have my own place. And then I was gonna find a nice, normal civilian who'd never gone through this shit, who didn't have the same fucking nightmares I did, who never had to know what it was like to see friends die all around him. I was going to find someone normal who'd never had to kill anything but slaughter a fucking cow on a farm, someone gentle who'd had a life like we hear about in the stories. I was going to find him and fall in love and get married, and we were going to have a farm of our own and have children."

She was shuddering now, sobbing, and I pulled her closer, stroking her back, wondering just what the hell was wrong.

"And you can't do that now?" I wondered.

"No!" The word was half a moan, half a helpless laugh. "I can't do that, because I love you, Cam. And if I admit that I love you, then I'm not going to let you go. And if we live through this, I'm going to have to invite you to my farm and have your kids and we'll both have nightmares."

Something warm and soft and so totally unfamiliar filled my chest, something I hadn't felt even with Maria on Brigantia. She'd shown me compassion, human kindness and contact, but she'd been ten years older than me, with a completely alien life experience. She'd represented a hope I had never felt before, but I hadn't loved her, I'd loved the idea of the hope.

This thing with Vicky was a different sort of hope. And for the first time in my life, I didn't try to push it away.

"I think they have drugs for the nightmares," I said, grinning. "And if you think you'd like the place, I have a standing invitation to go back to Brigantia and get some prime farmland and help setting it up."

"You see?" she said, slapping me on the shoulder, sniffing back the tears and laughing softly. "You're already trying to horn in on my plans! What if I want to live on Loki instead?"

"It's cold on Loki," I pointed out. "Cold like this." I waved at the walls demonstratively. "Would that bother you? And they have those weird, furry, giant worms that burrow under the snow and hunt by vibration."

"They have *what*?" she asked, eyes going wide.

"Well, that's what I heard," I said, shrugging. "Some Force Recon lance corporal told me he used to sit out at night watching over their cattle with a rifle to try to keep the worms off them. The cattle are expensive, too. They're genetically engineered from bison and musk oxen to handle the cold."

"Jesus, suddenly you're an expert on Loki." She settled back against the pillow, her eyes clouded with consideration. "Okay, not Loki. But what if I want to live on Aphrodite? You got anything bad to say about Aphrodite?"

"I'm sure I'll think of something," I said, grinning broadly. "But I'll go anywhere you want to go, Vicky. I'll go anywhere you are."

"You say that now, city boy, but what happens when you get bored with me and a life on the farm?"

"Bored? If I live through this mission, I think I can deal with bored."

———

"This thing is pretty posh compared to the *Iwo*," Scotty said, leaning against the clear polymer of the bar in the CSS *Bonaventure*'s officer's club.

"I've never been in an officer's club before," I said, sloshing the remains of my beer around in the plastic bottle. "Are they all this small?"

"It is on the compact side," Lt. Ackley agreed, coming up behind us and gesturing to the corporal behind the bar. She didn't have to tell him what she wanted because beer was all they offered. "But let's not look a gift horse in the mouth. I mean, not only are all the NCOs and enlisted on this mission invited to the carrier's O-club for the party, but we are on one of the few ships in the Fleet that actually *have* an on-board O-club."

"It's because they're out here for so long without ever going deep into a system," Lt. Davies said. I'd seen the tall, long-faced Marine platoon leader sitting just down from Scotty and I at the bar, but I hadn't said anything to him because I was an NCO and didn't want to seem presumptuous. "These carriers usually never come far enough into a system for the crew to have shore leave except on scheduled R&R during refitting back at Inferno. They have the O-club and the NCO-club for the same reason they spin the ship for gravity when they're not in Transition Space, because otherwise, the crews would go bugnuts."

"You know a lot about the Fleet troops, sir," I said,

"I have friends from the Academy who went to Attack Command," he said.

"Do you ever wish you'd chosen Fleet, Brian?" Ackley asked him, then frowned at the beer. "You know, drinking synthaholic beer is a bit like having sex with a pleasure doll. No consequences but no emotional attachment, either."

I'd been taking a drink and nearly choked on my beer, but Davies laughed appreciatively and toasted her with his bottle.

"I can truly say," he replied, "that I have never done either... sex with a robot *or* wanting to be anything other than a Force Recon Marine."

"That's a shame," Ackley said, giving him what I could have sworn was a coy smile. "About the Force Recon thing, I meant. The other...." She shrugged. "Well, I suppose that depends on your personal tastes."

"Are you from the colonies, sir?" Scotty asked him. "I've heard most Force Recon Marines are from the colonies."

"I'm from Earth," Davies told him. "Alice Springs in Australia. My parents work on the nature preserve there."

I had a vague idea of what Australia was, but the part about the nature preserve explained it all. Davies had grown up in the outdoors, which would make him better suited for Recon.

"Ladies and gentlemen, your attention please," Top said, her voice cutting through two dozen conversations across tables and along bars in the club. It wasn't any larger than our squad bay back on Hachiman, so every eye that turned at her words could see her.

She nodded back to Captain Covington and he stepped into the center of the room, a beer in his hand.

"I wanted tonight to be an opportunity for the two platoons to meet each other," Covington said, "not as Force Recon or Drop Troopers, but simply as Marines. And I don't want to spoil the fun, but since you're all here, I did have a few things to say." His eyes scanned the compartment, touching each of ours, including mine. "You're here because you volunteered, knowing the risks you were taking, and I am damned proud of each and every one of you. I'd be leading you myself if I were allowed, but Colonel Voss denied my request to do so, said I was going to be needed for the main attack. I disagree, because your mission will be the one that decides this operation. We will all live or die based on what you do down there."

No pressure, then. I didn't say it, though, because it was the Skipper.

"Things are going to be happening fast, and you need to think even faster to stay ahead of them. The most important thing I'm going to say is something you're not going to want to hear, but you need to listen. People are going to die. There's no way around it, no miracle that will keep all of you alive. What you need to hear is that when you see your friends fall, that is not the time to give up, not the time to accept defeat. It's the time to dig down deep inside yourself and pull out the last measure and do your job."

He sniffed, as if a laugh was trying to come through but couldn't make it out.

"There was, many centuries ago, a man named Yamamoto Tsunetomo, a samurai, which was feudal Japan's warrior caste. He once said that the way of the samurai is the way of death. By that, he meant that to be a true warrior, you have to accept the fact of your death, to live each day, fight each battle not as if your survival depends on it, but as if you've already accepted death as a reality, not something to be feared. The fear of death can't keep you from doing what you have to do. Normally," he said, grinning, "that would be something I'd say to be all ooh-rah, gung-ho and badass, something to fire up the troops. But for you, this is the best advice I can give."

Covington sagged at the shoulders, a bit of the air going out of him.

"Once we drop you at the asteroid cluster, the *Bonaventure* will Transition back to the outer system to rendezvous with the *Iwo Jima* and the rest of the task force, so I won't see you again until the rest of my company touches down on Ambergris. If this is the last chance I get to speak to some of you, I want you to know it's been the proudest experience of my life to serve with men and women like you."

He raised his bottle of beer and Top did the same.

"Here's to us and those like us," he said.

"Damn few!" came the reply, and I said it as loud as anyone, raising my beer in salute.

But I wasn't looking at him. I was watching Vicky, standing beside her squad, beer raised, eyes on fire with conviction. Accepting death sounded like good advice. But I didn't think I could do it.

[19]

I didn't get claustrophobic. Tight spaces didn't bother me, and being inside the suit had always made me feel comfortable, at home. Sealing my helmet inside the bay of the dropship was one of the hardest things I'd ever done. I would be in the suit for days, be sealed inside the helmet for at least thirty hours, and that's if we had timed the freighter's course correctly. I'd be eating protein paste from a tube, drinking from another, peeing in a third, breathing recycled air until and unless we found a sealed compartment on the freighter with a breathable atmosphere. My hands shook inside the arms of the Vigilante and it was all I could do to keep the suit's hands from shaking in empathy.

"Sergeant Alvarez?" It was Dixon. She was three slots down from me in the dropship so I couldn't see her face, but her voice was quavering, her words hesitant.

"What's up, Dixon?" I asked, pulling the helmet shut, banishing my own fears to deal with hers.

"We're going to be in the suits a long time. I'm a little...." She trailed off. I wanted to laugh, not at her weakness, but at her assumption I couldn't possibly share it.

"Nervous?" I finished for her. "It's okay, none of us has ever spent this much time in a suit. Most of it, we'll be just hanging out, so don't be afraid to have the suit dose you with a tranquilizer once I give you the okay."

"Thanks, Sergeant." She sounded relieved. "I won't let you down."

"Don't say that," I snapped at her, and I could hear her gasp at the ferocity in my tone. I bit down on the anger flaring in my gut. "The one you need to worry about letting down is yourself. Don't try to live up to me, try to be the best Marine you can be."

"Yes, Sergeant," she said, quietly.

"Transition in two minutes." All crew chiefs sounded alike. It had taken me a couple of years to notice, but it was a truth of the universe. They all had a professional tone with just a hint of the irritation they felt at idiots like us taking up space on their boats and making their lives harder.

"Things will move fast once we drop out of T-space," Ackley reminded us. "The *Bonaventure* has a tight window to drop in while the system's surveillance satellites are directly in line with the system's primary, then get us to the asteroid, get the dropship back on board and jump out again. If the carrier is detected, the whole mission is a goat rope. So, drop when you're told and get off this ship."

"Transitioning."

The feeling should have been familiar by now. I'd travelled through T-space so many times in my short life, the trip through the wormhole should have been like stepping through a hatchway, but it was always the same, a wrenching not just in my gut but somewhere in my soul.

"Prep for thrust," the crew chief warned us. Like there was a damned thing we could do about it, or like any of us were out roaming around the cabin instead of locked into our drop racks. "Separation."

Maneuvering thrusters shoved us out of the docking bay and I switched the view in my HUD to the dropship's cameras. We were deep in the black, the only light coming from the distant primary star, farther away than the Sun was from the Earth, but as the dropship swung around on the bang of the steering jets, I could see the glint of that star off of the rocks.

In the Solar System, these would have been part of the Apollo cluster, asteroids hanging in the Earth-Moon system, or more generally, Trojan objects lurking in the Lagrangian Points. Their orbits weren't stable and if we came back in another few hundred thousand years, they might have been pulled away into a larger orbit around the star, but my concerns were shorter term. Like living through the next couple of days.

The fusion drive kicked us in the ass, just a brief burst, enough to get us cruising toward the rocks. They already seemed incredibly close, like I could reach out through the camera and run a finger across the rough, pitted surface.

"Ten minutes to drop."

"Thank you, Chief," Vicky murmured. "What would we do without you?"

I checked the comm board and saw with a sense of relief that she'd had me on a private channel for the comment. Not that there was anything the Chief could have done about it, but I didn't want to put Lt. Ackley in a bad place when this was all over.

"She's very informative," I agreed, loosening up now that I knew we were speaking confidentially. "I don't know who'll be happier to see us off this ship, me or her."

"Tell you what," she said, "I'd rather be us than the fucking Recon guys. They're going to have to hang on our backs in nothing but their armor, and theirs is a hell of a lot thinner than ours. One micrometeorite in the wrong place at the wrong time, they're dead before they even get the chance to drop on Ambergris. It's bad enough in the Vigilante. You couldn't pay me enough to go out there and hang on the ass end of a rock like that in light body armor."

"Recon has balls," I admitted. "I gotta give it to them, despite the fact a lot of them are dicks."

"Five minutes to drop. Dismounts move to the drop racks."

The Recon troops had been strapped into the passenger seats at the front of the dropship, but now they kicked free and floated across the compartment to the drop racks. I couldn't see their faces through the visors of their helmets, so I didn't know which of them grabbed onto my armor, latching the special D-rings onto the anchors welded into the shoulders of my armor.

"You Sgt. Alvarez?" The voice came through along with a transponder ID on the IFF feed.

"And you're Sgt. Burnett," I returned. "You one of the squad leaders?"

"Third," he confirmed. "You're First, right?"

"Yeah. Call me Cam," I added.

"Robby. You ready for this shit, man?"

"People keep asking me that. I guess I'd better be, since this was all my idea in the first place."

"Yeah, I heard that. It's why I'm hitching a ride with you. I wanted to say thanks."

"Thanks for what?" I wondered. "The best chance you'll ever have to get killed?"

"Naw, man." He hesitated a moment. "I've been on the last three drops. I've lost a lot of friends, most of them just blown out of the sky without a chance to ever pick up a gun. That's not how I wanted to go out. At least, this way, I get a chance to keep a few of them alive. And if I have to go down...." I could almost hear the shrug. "Well, at least this way, I go down swinging, right?"

"Robby," I said, smiling in the privacy of my helmet, "I couldn't have said it better myself."

"Drop! Drop! Drop!"

The external drop ports slid open and if there'd been any air in the dropship, it would have evacuated. There wasn't. The Recon Marines and us Drop-Troopers had been living off on-board air since the Transition. Another thing we didn't have for this drop was gravity. When the brackets cut loose of my suit, I didn't just fall out of the port. I had to touch a control inside the left arm of the suit to trigger a burst of the maneuvering jets strapped to the sides of my backpack. The vibration was a loud banging through the suit, a violent push downward that brought my head up against the padding at the top of my helmet.

Robby and I slid downward, clearing the metal tube of the drop gantry in less than a second, heading for the bare rock below. And I gasped for breath I couldn't catch.

I hadn't thought about this part. I hadn't thought being outside the ship would bother me, not with my suit on. My agoraphobia had faded to a background buzz in the last few months, ever since Brigantia, and it had never bothered me inside the suit, but now... It was the stars. The stars were so fucking far away, *everything* was so far away, more open than any plain on Brigantia, more desolate than any desert back home. How could I have thought I'd be able to handle this?

"Cam." My eyes were frozen on the utter blackness, the distant stars, even the arc of the asteroid beneath me, to break them loose to check the commo board, but I recognized Lt. Ackley's voice. "Cam, do you read me?"

"Yes," I rasped, my throat dry. "Yes, ma'am."

"Your heart rate just shot up. Are you okay?"

Jesus, she had time to notice that? How did officers have the time? I could barely keep track of a squad. I squeezed my eyes shut and took a deep breath, let it out slowly before I answered.

"Yes, ma'am," I said, feeling my heartbeat slowing. "Just never been out in space with nothing between me and the vacuum except a suit."

"I don't believe any of us have. Let me know if you have a problem."

"I'll be okay."

I thought I would. Somehow, just the fact she'd noticed and asked had calmed me down. I spun around with an extra burst on the steering rockets, wasting a second's worth of reaction mass just for the luxury of one last look. The rest of the platoon was sliding out in a choreographed rhythm with me, each of the Vigilante suits with a Recon Marine hooked to the back of it.

It was a slow-motion drop, leaving us all drifting slowly downward, if down had any meaning here. The dropship was already moving, its bow maneuvering thrusters firing with a flare of rockets and a puff of vapor, spinning the massive aerospacecraft end for end. It lingered there for a few seconds, probably checking on our positions, making sure no one had drifted back in line with their drive before they ignited it.

Raw plasma flared out the back of the ship, contained by a magnetic bottle, and the dropship headed back toward the carrier. The *Bonaventure* was already falling behind, far enough away that I could make out the full length of the ship. It looked like someone had taken two of the flatbread biscuits my *abuela* had used to make us and stuck them together with long, metal spokes. Except the biscuits were the habitation modules and the Transition drive units, and the spokes were the docking spars for dozens of missile cutters. They nestled there like baby scorpions riding their mother's back across the desert, waiting to be loosed.

The dropships accelerated toward their mother with desperate haste, not wanting to be left behind, and I didn't blame them. I wasn't so crazy about being left behind myself. I couldn't see below my feet with my forward cameras, but the suits had been built with that limitation in mind, and a simple switch to the video pickups facing downward from my chest plastron showed me the asteroid rushing up beneath us. The cratered rockface seemed close enough that we should have hit it in seconds, but the flight dragged on for minutes, the details of the surface growing closer and clearer, every scar which had seemed centimeters long actually growing into something a dozen meters across.

An altitude warning flashed and I squeezed the control for the space of two seconds until the display flickered green and I let off the braking thrust. We were crawling now, moving so slow I could barely detect it, and when we touched down, I wouldn't have even known if the suit's sensors hadn't told me.

I touched another unfamiliar control, added only for this mission along with the hardware for it attached to the legs of the Vigilante. Rocket-propelled anchors shot out and buried themselves in the rock of the asteroid, making sure one wrong step wouldn't send us both spinning off into space. The asteroid was small and had very little gravitational pull.

"First squad, sound off," I ordered, scanning overhead to make sure no one had experienced a malfunction.

"Graciano, down and anchored."

"Mullany, down and anchored."

"Reyfort, down and anchored."

"Linebarger, down and anchored."

"Dixon, down and anchored."

"Pickerington, down and anchored."

"Kim, down and anchored."

I switched into the platoon net.

"Scotty, First Squad is down and anchored."

"Roger that," he said, his tone clipped and taut. I hadn't really talked to him about it, but I had the sense he *really* didn't like this. "Hold tight."

Like I had other plans. The sound of my breath filled my ears, deafening in the utter silence outside. The rock was a dead place, a desert at perpetual noon, the light falling on it harsh and relentless, its shadows sharp and vertical. It was all like a sign-post from God screaming that we didn't belong here.

"Third Platoon," Lt. Ackley said, "we have at least twenty hours, and most likely thirty until the freighter comes through. Getting down here was the easy part. All that extra fuel in the tanks strapped to your armor, that's for matching velocities with the freighter. We've all gone over the procedure a thousand times by now, so don't overthink it. Follow your training, follow the guidance from your suit's on-board computer. Until then, I would urge all of you except the designated watch to have your suit inject you with a sedative and get some sleep. I'm moni-toring your vitals remotely and if I see your heart-rate or respira-tion get too high, I'll make it an order. Clear?"

There was an antiphonal chorus of, "Yes, ma'am," in reply.

"In that case, settle down and don't make any sudden move-ments. Stay anchored and keep your heads, and you'll get the chance to pull off the next impossible thing we have to do."

I tried to find the carrier, but it was just another star, barely moving...and then there was the briefest flash from the Transi-tion and it was gone.

"Our ride just took off," I told Robby, trying not to sound scared.

I *was* scared, mind you. Probably as scared as that little kid heading off through the desert alone, his father and brother lying dead behind him. As scared as that same boy stepping into the first of a series of group homes, watching the curious and indifferent and hostile eyes of strangers watching him. As scared as the teenager running through the train station, dodging a cartel hitman's bullets. As scared as the Lance Corporal falling out of the sky too high and too fast over Brigantia, his only hope a water landing that could have killed him just as dead.

"I grew up on Aphrodite," Robby said, apropos of nothing. "You ever been there?"

"I ain't never been anywhere the Marines didn't take me," I assured him, sounding, perhaps, a little impatient with the digression.

"Well, Aphrodite is a pretty nice world as colonies go. Not quite as temperate and pretty as Hermes, but it's got a whole continent about the same mean temperature and elevation as North America, so there's lots of good land. And most of it got gobbled up by the Corporate Council before my grandparents were born, so families like mine have to scratch a living where we can. And that's on the southern continent. Australius they call it. It's a nasty, dangerous place. Got its own ecosystem with a bunch of predators, not transplanted Earth fauna like some of the colonies. The best places to live are by the coast, but a lot of the mines and oil wells are inland, in the desert. That was where my family lived."

"I was born near the desert," I murmured, but I don't know if the words reached him. He seemed to be in some sort of fugue and I hoped being out here wasn't getting to him already.

"When I was young, my older brother took me out on his rover to repair one of the drillers we managed for the Corporate Council. It was pretty far out, but it needed fixing and I wanted to go along. Thought I was a big boy, all of eleven at the time."

He laughed, not a chuckle, but a deep-chest laugh, like he'd just thought of a hilarious joke.

"Then a big dust storm blew in, built up real quick, no time to get back, and we were stuck in this tiny, sheet-metal shed for three fucking days with two liters of water and a half a dozen protein bars between us. I mean, that shed was like one meter on a side and two meters tall and there was barely room for the two of us to sit down. I was about ready to go nuts after just a few hours, and my big brother Jimmy, he told me to lean back against him and go to sleep. And I slept a lot and pissed in the corner and didn't see the sun for three days, but we both got through it."

"Was that a long-winded way for you to tell me to relax and go to sleep?" I asked the Recon Marine.

"No, brother, that was a long-winded way for me to tell you that *I'm* going to relax and go to sleep." He laughed again. "Try not to wake me."

The ground shook and the glass in the windows rattled in rhythm and I clutched at my mother's arm, terrified as any four-year-old had ever been at a thunderstorm. We didn't get them often, rarely got rain at all, and my parents seemed tense. I had heard Mama talking to Papa about flooding. I thought I knew what that meant. I'd heard the story of Noah and the ark and the great flood. But God had said He wouldn't send another flood. Or at least that was the story the priest had told us. Was the priest wrong?

"Mama," I said, my voice quavering, "do we need an ark?"

She laughed, pulling me into a hug.

"No, mi Corazon, the rain is not so bad as that. We are worried about the road being washed out. The farmers need to be able to bring their produce into town so we can sell it in the market."

"Will we starve?"

Now it was Papa's turn to laugh, from his chair by the window. He was watching the rain. I was glad Anton was in his room, studying. He would have made fun of me, the way he always did.

"Things are not so bad," Papa said. "We have a closet full to the top with rice and beans. We have a solid house and the rain will not get you wet unless you run outside like a squawking chicken."

"Be nice, Fillipe," Mama chided, hugging me tighter. "He is just a little boy. Remember, Cameron," she said, caressing my cheek, "we will always be here to protect you."

"Always," Papa agreed, smiling.

"But you won't!" I cried, pulling away from Mama and standing with my hands balled into fists, glaring at them. "You won't be there! You'll be dead and I'll be alone! I won't have anyone! Why did you leave me alone?"

Mama's eyes were sad, but she showed no regret, no apology.

"Sometimes God has a plan for us, Cameron," she said. "Sometimes that plan is hard, and the road we must walk is lonely and sad, but at the end of the road is our destiny, where we were meant to be."

"We will always be proud of you, Cameron," my father said, leaning forward in his chair, regarding me with the serious, measured gaze an adult might share with someone of their own age. "Even when you had lost your way, you always kept true to the boy and the man we knew you would be."

"And when it is your time to cross over as we have done," Mama told me, "we will all be waiting for you."

They began to fade, as if the rain outside the house were sweeping them away, and when I tried to reach for them, I found I couldn't move. Something was holding me down, anchoring me in place, clasping me like the fists of a giant.

"Papa!" I yelled, fighting against the metal grip. "Mama!"

"Mama!"

I blinked awake, shaking my head and banging it against the

padding of my helmet before I realized where I was. I sucked in a breath and forced my eyes open, the HUD winking on along with my brain. Once my vision cleared, I checked the time.

"Holy shit," I muttered. I'd slept for fifteen hours.

I felt a sudden panic, realizing we'd been here for over twenty hours. Wasn't twenty hours within the possible arrival time for the freighter? But Lt. Ackley wouldn't have let me sleep through it.

Get a grip, for God's sake.

"Hey LT," I said, "you awake?"

"Always," she said, and sounded as if she needed the sleep more than I did. "You feeling okay?"

"I'm good," I said. I tried to look around using the HUD rather than moving my head, conscious of Robby still on my back, maybe still asleep. Dead space stared back at me and the roiling arose in my guts again before I let my gaze travel downward to the IFF displays. "We seeing anything yet?"

"Yep. Picked up the freighter on thermal a couple hours ago."

"Shit!" I blurted. "Why didn't you wake me up, ma'am?"

"Because it's still four hours away," she said. "Space, you know? Thermal sees a long way out here."

"Oh, yeah. When do you want me to wake up the others?"

"Give it another two hours," she decided. "That's plenty of time to get everyone in place and ready to make the jump."

"There's a lot that could go wrong with this, isn't there, ma'am?" I felt guilty asking the question. This had been my idea and I shouldn't be showing any hesitation.

"Oh, hell, yes," she agreed. "The freighter could have a crew and they could spot us and speed up. Even if they don't, someone could fuck up and head off at the wrong vector and they'd just be dead. There's no way we could go after them. And even if that doesn't happen, there's always the chance we could set off some kind of automatic alarm we don't even know about that lets the Tahni forces in orbit know we're coming and they could blow the ship to vapors. Or the cargo shuttles could have security systems we can't override and we wouldn't be able to set the charges on one of them and be left without a distraction, which would make things hard. Harder, that is." She paused. "Or something could delay the rest of the strike force, and we'd be picked off one at a time, but if we do our job, that's okay."

"Jesus Christ, ma'am," I said, trying not to moan the words. "If you thought all that could happen, why did you volunteer?"

"I don't think all that *will* happen, but all of it could. As an officer, I have to consider all those things and have a plan for them."

"And you have to keep track of all of us, too." I shook my head. "I don't know how you do it, ma'am."

"Something has to give," she told me. "We're all human and there's no magic formula that lets you be able to pay more attention than a regular person. You only have so much time. I have to think about you, so I don't have time to think about myself. I couldn't tell you for sure if I even fired my weapon on any of the last three raids."

"You did," I assured her. "I remember."

"But I don't. I use all my attention to make sure all of you are moving in the right direction, to keep the fight going according to plan. Everything else is instinct, and my instincts are nowhere near as good as yours, Alvarez."

"That sounds like it could get you killed," I said.

"Easily. Do you know what the average life expectancy is of a platoon leader in the Drop Troopers, Alvarez?"

"What?" I didn't really *want* to know, but it would have seemed rude not to ask.

"I should have been dead six months ago."

"Shit." The air went out of me. How was I supposed to respond to that? "Then why do you do it?"

"Because it has to get done. And if I don't do it, someone else will have to. Maybe someone who doesn't understand how to forget about themselves and take care of their Marines first." She sniffed, as close to a laugh as I expected to get from her under the circumstances. "And now, if you're done trying to be our resident doomsayer, I'm going to take a nap. Do me a favor and wake me up in two hours."

"Yes, ma'am."

I don't know how the hell she could sleep. If I had her responsibility, I'd never be able to sleep.

———

"Cut loose your anchors."

I passed the command down to my squad automatically, searching the menu on my control board to trigger the explosive bolts. I couldn't hear them, but I felt the vibration through the armor of the suit as the anchor units split away and bounced off the black rock of the asteroid.

"Set your suit jets to follow the vectors on your helmet computer," Lt. Ackley droned. "Sound off when you're ready."

"Sound off, First squad," I said and tried to listen to their reply.

It was hard to concentrate. The freighter distracted me. It was impossibly close, barreling down on us, flying straight on like it might have been on a collision course for the rock. On an intellectual level, I knew the ship was still hundreds of kilometers away, but I could make out the details of the cargo pods joined to its hull, the lines of the freight airlocks, the charred thrust tubes for the maneuvering thrusters.

I realized the last Marine in my squad had reported ready and I passed the word along to Scotty.

"First," Ackley said, "you're on point. Assume the freighter is occupied until we find out it isn't. The Recon troops will enter the auxiliary airlock and clear it, but if they run into trouble and call for help, you need to be ready to burn through the cargo locks and take it anyway, because this has to work. Clear?"

"Clear, ma'am!"

"Launch."

The jump-jets were muted in the vacuum, just a rattling vibration shaking me through the metal of the suit, their thrust pushing me downward, giving me the absurd feeling of standing on solid ground in the midst of open space. The asteroid sank beneath us, but I didn't take the time or concentration to watch it retreat in the downward-facing cameras. I didn't look back at the freighter, either, as much as the barreling mass of metal screamed at my peripheral vision for attention. Instead, I put all my focus into staying on the thrust vector the computer was projecting into my HUD...and a little on the IFF transponders, making sure the rest of the squad was doing the same.

I suppose it would have been easier to just take control out of the hands of the Marines altogether and let the computers do the flying, and it definitely would have been safer. But we weren't sure we'd be flying unopposed and no one wanted to be a sitting duck for a point defense turret. So we all took the option of keeping the little blue icon representing our own suit inside the bright green track on our HUD and pressing the thrust pedals down to the stops. It felt less like chasing after the freighter than racing it to a road crossing, since we'd started our burn long before it reached the asteroid. The rock had been traveling in a locked, stable position between orbits of Ambergris and her moon, while the freighter was traveling in with just enough momentum to take them past that orbit. We had to match velocities with the ship to grapple onto it. Anything more than a few meters per second difference and we'd bounce right off and not have the fuel to recover.

Alpha team was stretched out ahead of me, the closest of them a few hundred meters away, their thrusters glowing bright yellow in the darkness. And past them I could finally see Ambergris. It had been concealed by the bulk of the asteroid, but now it glowed a bright blue in the darkness, beckoning with its proximity despite the death and destruction awaiting us there.

"Oh, sweet, sweet Jesus," Robby murmured. He hadn't spoken in an hour and I'd nearly forgotten he was there. "This is some shit, Cam. I tell ya, when I signed up for Recon, the recruiters did *not* mention this as a possibility."

"Would you have chosen Armor if they had?" I asked, teasing the Straight-Leg just a bit. It was nearly automatic by this point.

"Hell, no!" he replied. "I wouldn't have let anyone implant that shit in my head! Doesn't that bother you, having those sockets? I mean, you can never get rid of them, right?"

"No," I admitted. "But I can have them repurposed once I'm out. They can optimize them for netdiving or even piloting a ship, and they'll do it free before I outprocess."

"You want to be a netdiver? Or a pilot?"

"Not really. But it's more likely I'd get some use out of them reprogrammed for that than that I'll ever operate a Vigilante again." Something caught my eyes on the HUD and I switched the laser line-of-sight transmitter to another target. "Mullany," I called. "You're drifting left. Keep your eye on the ball."

"Right. Sorry, Cam."

"How much longer we gonna be hanging our asses out here?" Robby asked.

I checked the sensor readout and almost swore. I didn't answer him, switching to the squad again.

"Five minutes until intercept. Adjust your orientation and prepare grapples."

I was surprised Ackley hadn't warned me, but she had a whole platoon to look after. She was probably watching to make sure I told everyone in time, ready to step in if I didn't. Or maybe I was just overestimating her management skills and she'd forgotten how much time was left. But I doubted it.

I hit the steering jets, turning my armor to the orientation the guidance computer suggested, facing the freighter's direction of travel...and by God, there it was. A few minutes ago, the ship had been dozens of kilometers away and now it loomed in front of me, just as the fuel reserves in my strap-on boosters zeroed out, the readouts flashing red. Perfect timing. The squad was closing in on my position on the IFF, or maybe I was closing in on theirs. Either way, we were all about to hit the same five-hundred-meter section of hull.

A warning buzzed in demand for my attention, letting me know it was time to launch the grapples and I passed the order along to the rest of the squad, even as I saw Graciano and Alpha team firing the rocket-propelled magnetic grappling hooks into the hull of the freighter. I pushed the control to trigger my own and the rocket kicked at my left side as it launched, trailing out a reel of braided BiPhase Carbide behind it. I didn't hear it strike home, but the indicator glowed green, letting me know it had a good purchase on the hull.

And if anyone happens to hear the grapples hitting or look at the feed from an external camera at the wrong time, this all goes to hell. Early. Because it's all going to hell at some point even if we do everything right.

The reel pulled us in, Robby and I, two little remoras in an ocean of nothing, attaching ourselves to a great whale and hoping it took us where we needed to go. I hadn't realized the tension I'd built up in my shoulders until we touched the hull and I felt solidity against the outside of my suit and relief washed over me. This close to the hull, I couldn't see the edge of it in any direction, just an expanse of dull, grey duralloy. Not seeing open space for the first time in two days felt indescribably good.

"We're linked in," I told Robby. "Do your thing, Straight-leg."

"Thanks for the ride, jack-head."

Robby clambered across the chest and arm of my suit, grasping the rough, pitted metal of the spaceship's hull with the magnetic gloves and boots he wore specifically for this mission. A few dozen meters away, other Recon Marines were skittering over the hull like baby spiders, awkward and seeking shelter. I checked the IFF readouts and a second wave of relief hit. Everyone in my squad was there. This was one time I wasn't at all reluctant to be the first squad in.

"First squad," I said, hearing a slight tremble in my voice, "move to the cargo lock. But be damned careful about it. Keep one hand and one foot attached to the hull at all times."

I wasn't too crazy about this part. I had a nice, stable position and they wanted me to give it up and crawl all the way down the hull another three hundred meters to the cargo airlock and wait there for Recon to do their thing. Or, if they didn't do their thing, to burn the lock open, find a place to repressurize, get out of our armor with the pulse pistol we all carried and never expected to use, and do Recon's job for them. And then what, I had no fucking idea, because the whole thing would likely be a Charlie Foxtrot.

The Vigilante had the same sort of magnetic sleeves on the hands and feet as the Recon troops did, except ours were bigger and stronger, and I put my right glove and right boot against the hull, bent over like a mountain climber, and tested the grip. It didn't come loose, so I went ahead and detached from the grapple harness, leaving the cable dangling from the hull. Someone was actually going to have to come back outside later and get rid of all of them before they could be spotted. Fortunately, that was not my problem.

I tried prying loose the magnets of one hand and foot, then moving them both over and reattaching them before letting loose with the other set, but that was painfully slow and maddeningly tedious and I gave up on it after maybe twenty meters. Instead, I began scraping the magnet across the side of the ship, leaving a double line of rough, white scrapes against the metal.

They're gonna have trouble getting their deposit back on this one. Hope they bought the extra insurance.

I kept my eyes firmly on the metal in front of me, only glancing aside once every twenty meters or so to make sure I was still heading down the curve of the freighter's superstructure toward the cargo airlock. The freighter was multipurpose, or so we'd been told. Bulk ore was carried in cargo modules, but smaller shipments, such as spare parts and replacement machinery would be accessed through the cargo airlocks, taken on board space stations, ships or shuttles. The cargo locks would be big enough to fit a Vigilante through, while the auxiliary airlocks Recon was trying to crack were only two meters on a side.

By the time I made it to the main cargo lock, Alpha team had already reached it, the four of them huddled around the metal pustule like campers around a fire. Annoyance scraped its claws against my nerves. I wanted to be next to the lock. It was an illusory comfort, but I'd take all the comfort I could get.

It didn't matter after another minute. The rest of the squad squeezed in around me, everyone crouching instinctively to get all four points of connection against the hull, as if we were all convinced the ship was going to try to shake us loose like a dog scratching at fleas.

"Good job, guys," I told them, once they were all in place. "We're almost in. Relax and keep focused."

"Oh, my God," Dixon said, strain wearing at her voice. "I'm never doing that again. I don't care if they court-martial me, throw me in the brig for the rest of the fucking war, I'm never doing that again."

"I think we're good after this one," I assured her. "We pull this off, I think they'll give us a pass for the next time."

The rest of the platoon filtered in a squad at a time and I waited until I saw Vicky pull in Fourth squad before I aimed a transmission at her.

"Have a nice trip?" I asked her, trying to sound light and flippant but not quite pulling it off.

"I blame you for this," she told me, sounding serious. "That may be the worst thing I've ever done, and I used to clean out clogged sewage pipes for extra money."

"Did everyone make it?" I asked her.

"All of my guys did. I've been too busy keeping track of them and trying to fight off panic attacks to pay attention to the rest of the platoon."

"Fair. I've barely been able to take my eyes off the side of the hull."

"Fourth Platoon," Ackley overrode our individual comms. "I'm proud of you. We just pulled off something no military unit has ever accomplished and we didn't lose anyone doing it."

"How will we know if the Recon troops get control of the ship, ma'am?" Vicky asked her. "Sorry, I mean, how will we know if they *don't?*"

"We're going to give them an hour, Sgt. Sandoval," Ackley

said. "Which should be plenty if the ship doesn't have a crew, and still just about enough if it does."

Shit. Another hour.

The suit was like a coffin now, pushing in on my chest with every breath, and I wanted nothing in life so much as to take off my helmet and take a breath from even the recycled atmosphere of a Tahni ship. I had to get out of the suit, even if it was just for a few hours.

"I want First squad at the lock," Ackley announced, "in case we have to burn through. "Alvarez," she added, "you can take point on this, personally."

"Aye, ma'am."

I wasn't sure if she was putting me up front because she was more confident in me than anyone else in the platoon or because this whole thing had been my idea and she wanted me to have the honor of getting shot first, but I was happy about it either way. The whole group of battlesuits clustered on the surface of the freighter scuttled backward like crabs on the ocean floor and I moved in.

The cargo lock could have been from any human ship I'd been on. Form followed function to some extent, as long as the builders were all bipedal humanoids. Maybe if we were fighting some sort of octopus people, their ships and airlocks and other structures would be so different, we wouldn't even recognize them, but this one was pretty basic. The lock was round, about ten meters across and surrounded by a raised rim with latches for a docking umbilical. There were no external controls that I could see, which, I supposed, made sense, since how often would someone be trying to access your cargo lock in a vacuum from the outside.

The door was thick as hell and I didn't want to think about how many shots it would take to burn through it if it came to that. I leaned against the hatch with both hands, scanning the edges of the lock, wondering where the best place to focus the plasma blasts would be...and fell right through when the damned airlock slid open without a bit of warning.

I didn't actually *fall*, of course, since there was no gravity, but I was anchored in with my feet and bending forward, so the upper torso of my suit swung in through the opening hatch and I found myself nose-to-nose with a Recon Marine.

"Hey there, Cam," Robby said, and I could just make out the grin through his visor. "Welcome aboard."

[21]

"Oh, sweet and fluffy Lord," Scotty said, sliding out of the torso of his Vigilante and floating across the cargo bay free, without even trying to guide himself anywhere in particular. "I have never been so fucking glad to be out of my armor."

"You're the platoon sergeant," I said, grinning at him. "Shouldn't you be all stoic and shit as an example for us lowly peons?"

I'd locked myself to the deck with the magnetic boots we'd brought along and was still trying to work free all the extra bullshit they'd bolted to my armor for the mission. Not that it would really get in the way in a fight, but it gave us all something productive to do besides trying to figure out how Tahni toilets worked in microgravity.

And it was a distraction from how hot and humid the fucker kept their ship. Not that I was complaining.

"I *am* setting an example," Scotty shot back, grinning at me, upside down from my orientation. "I'm setting an example of how we should all be thanking the Recon guys for getting the life support working on this heap so we could get out of the damned suits."

"Amen to that," Vicky said emphatically from across the bay.

And I couldn't argue. When the Recon troops had boarded, the ship had been un-crewed and filled with a hard vacuum, set to run on autopilot. They'd managed to find the right controls to activate the air filters and release the atmosphere from its storage tanks, though it had taken nearly an hour, and if the Tahni liked it hot, well...I could deal with hot for a few hours as long as I got to breathe.

"Hey, Cam!" Graciano called from a dozen meters away, between five or six other Vigilantes attached to the floor by their magnetic anchors. "What do you want us to do once we get the suits cleaned up?"

"Lt. Ackley wants us to gather for a briefing on the bridge," I told him. "She said she'd send word when she was ready."

There was plenty of room for us in the pressurized cargo bay...now. When we'd arrived, it had been stuffed full with machine parts, bulk food and other shit I hadn't bothered to look at too closely. We'd tossed it all out of the cargo lock to make space, with all apologies to whatever Tahni supply officer was going to lose his job. I hoped he'd invested well.

"Hey! Fourth, heads up!"

I twisted around to the hatchway leading from the cargo bay into the crew sections of the ship, an octagonal passageway lined with functionally ugly metal grating. Robby Burnett was standing in the hatchway, helmet tucked under his arm, the perpetual cocky grin I'd first seen when they'd repressurized the ship still in place on his rounded, boyish face.

"Our platoon leaders are ready for the joint briefing. Y'all had best follow me," he added, jerking a thumb over his shoulder. "This garbage scow ain't laid out like a Commonwealth ship and I wouldn't want any of y'all getting lost without your big, scary armor to show you the way."

"Fuck you, Straight-Leg," Vicky told him, but she was smiling when she said it.

Everyone was in a good mood, me included. I think we were running on a high from having made it to the ship, and I ignored the lingering fatalist still locked away in the recesses of my consciousness, warning me things were going to get much worse. He might be right, but if I'd learned anything the last couple years, it was that life was too short to dwell on the inevitability of bad things happening. I think my parents had known that better than I did.

Robby had been right, that much was sure. We would definitely have gotten lost without him. The Tahni didn't have the same sense of organizational space we did. Passageways didn't lead through things or past things, they led to one thing, which would lead to another. A corridor would dead-end in the life-support compartment and then you'd just have to go through that compartment and into the auxiliary control room and on through to what I assumed were the crew quarters—though they didn't look anything like the crew quarters on a human ship—and then through that to the bridge.

The bridge had an unfinished, raw feel to it, with bundles of superconductive cables running along the deck and strapped into the overhead and some panels hanging loose or missing entirely. The acceleration couches were ratty, their cushioning ripped and tattered and some of the flatscreen, two-D displays flickered and sparked and the whole thing had the air of a ship that went unoccupied most of the time.

It wasn't unoccupied now. The entire Recon platoon was squeezed onto the bridge and there was only room for us because of the lack of gravity. Our platoon moved upward instead of trying to fit between, and nearly a hundred Marines were crammed into the bridge across the overhead and at the tops of the rows of displays screens and hugging the backs of acceleration couches at the duty stations, a dome of humanity constructed around Lt. Ackley and Lt. Davies, who stood on either side of the command station, their magnetic boots holding them in place.

"We have twenty hours until orbital insertion," Ackley said once everyone had filtered into the compartment, "which is simultaneously far too short for the preparations we need to make and far too long for my nerves." She grinned in self-deprecation. "I just want to get this over with."

A chuckle ran through the crowd, a sound like a landslide in the mountains with so many people gathered so close together, but I didn't laugh. I thought she meant it. She was as nervous as any of us, maybe more since she was responsible for all of us.

"But since we have the time, Lt. Davies and I decided now would be a good time for a final walk-through of the Operations Order. And we're going to run through it just like they did back in Basic or Armor School, or Recon training for the Straight-Legs here." She softened the barb with a chuckle and the Recon troops responded in kind.

"Situation," she said, ticking the sections of the Op Order off on her fingers. "Under the situation, Area of Operations, first under that, terrain and weather. Let's start there. Who can give me the details of the AO?"

Vicky raised her hand and Ackley motioned toward her.

"Go ahead, Sgt. Sandoval."

"The AO is the largest island on the planet Ambergris. The terrain is flat and marshy, the weather is projected to be sunny and humid and we're supposed to hit at mid-day, local time."

"Very good. Now, next under situation, we have Enemy Forces, and under that, composition, disposition, strength, location and capabilities. Who wants it?"

This felt just like the classes in Basic or the platoon training Scotty would run during down times, and I thought that was on purpose. Ackley was trying to make this more like training, something normal.

"We don't have firm intelligence on enemy disposition," the Recon platoon sergeant, a rough-hewn older man named Schorr, took his turn. "But we know they have at least a battalion of their Shock-Troop infantry and probably a couple companies of High Guard, maybe a full battalion. They're supposed to be stationed in barracks near the spaceport, but the planet isn't anywhere near their front lines, so we have no idea how many will be deployed and on duty when we hit. There are two orbital defense platforms, but we're hoping to take one out with the freighter. They have at least a squadron of dual-environment fighters but we have no intelligence if any will be on patrol. Their main antispacecraft weapon is a ground-based laser with its own dedicated fusion reactor located between the spaceport and the city, and the city's main defense are a pair of deflector shield dishes, one on each side. The one to the east covers the spaceport as well."

"You want to take Friendly Forces as well, Gunny Schorr?" Lt. Davies invited. "Since you're on a roll?"

"For our part of the operation, the friendly forces is *us*," Schorr said, snorting without much humor. "But if we can live through our first half hour on the ground, we'll have a whole battalion of Force Recon and the rest of the battalion of Drop-Troopers coming down to support us."

"Nicely done, Gunny," Ackley took over again, the tone of her voice giving just a hint she hadn't appreciated Davies interrupting. "Now, the key to any Op-Order. Mission. What is our mission? Sgt. Alvarez, I think it's only fitting that you answer this one."

"Ma'am," I nodded, the motion sending me bobbing up and down in the microgravity. "Our mission is to disrupt enemy defenses and occupy their troops long enough to allow the main force of the strike to move into place without taking significant casualties."

I knew it as if I'd written it, because I had.

"And here's where the rubber meets the road, the part we all need to be familiar with, the how. Execution. We'll skip down to the parts that apply to us, since we aren't going to have a scheme of fire support because we have no fire support, and we don't need to discuss cas-evac because we won't have that, either, until the main force arrives. So, let's get to scheme of movement and maneuver. Anyone confident enough to take it?"

There was a long hesitation on this one. I knew it, but I didn't think she wanted me to take it. She was trying to make sure everyone knew what we were supposed to do. Scotty didn't raise his hand for the same reason.

"Dixon," I said, searching the PFC out and finding her halfway across the compartment. "You handle this one."

"Umm...." Dixon looked as if someone had smacked her between the eyes with a sledgehammer, and I thought for a moment I might have screwed up, that she wasn't up to this. But then her expression firmed up and she managed to speak. "Okay, the plan is that when the cargo shuttles arrive to dock with the freighter, the Recon troops are going to board them and take out the crews, as quietly as possible, and then the Recon troops are going to load into one and we, the Drop-Troopers, are going to take the other and launch for the spaceport. Oh, but before we launch," she said, snapping her fingers as if she'd just remembered this part, "we're going to set the controls of the freighter to accelerate at the defense platform nearest to us, and we're going to rig the cargo shuttle we're in—us Drop-Troopers —with a HypEx charge near the fuel tanks. Then, once we get to four hundred meters up, we'll drop and the charge will detonate and take out the shuttle. That should distract the enemy long enough for the Recon Marines to land and get out of their shuttle."

It was difficult not to wince at her disconnected, stream-of-consciousness answer, but I kept reminding myself that she was a private and the purpose was to give her the chance to organize her thoughts and build herself a coherent image of the plan in her head.

"And once we're down?" Ackley prompted her, a teacher trying to help a student through a test.

"Once we're down," Dixon continued, "Recon is going to head to the defense laser site, penetrate security there and sabotage the weapon, then they're going to hold up inside the facilities there and wait for reinforcement."

I envied them having the opportunity.

"And us, that is, the Drop Troops, we're going to go after the air defense turrets. There are sixteen turrets, each with a missile battery and a sensor-slaved coil gun." Her lip curled in dark amusement. "Which I think is kind of cheating, you know? I mean, their religion says that they can't have autonomous armed drones, but as long as someone actually pushes the button to fire the gun, they're happy to let the radar and lidar and thermal do the aiming for them. Hypocrites." A round of chuckles went through the crowd and Dixon smiled, tension spilling out of her shoulders. "Anyway, the emplacements are in a perimeter around the edges of the coverage of the deflector screens because...." Her eyes glazed over and I could tell she was trying to recall the exact wording she'd heard in a briefing or read on her tablet. "...because they want mutually supporting fires without their coverage arc being compromised by the deflectors."

"And that means?"

"It means they want to be able to shoot down stuff without their missiles and coil gun rounds getting diverted by their own deflectors. So, the turrets are in a big oval like ten kilometers around, that runs from the coastline back all around the edge of the city. We're going to break into two groups and First and Second squad under Lt. Ackley are heading straight south from the spaceport to the coast, then turning west, taking the route that goes by the military barracks. Third and Fourth under Gunny Hayes will turn east, towards the city to target the emplacements on that side, and we'll all meet back up again around the north side of the city, to try to put it between us and the main force of Tahni infantry, and make it harder for them to target us with air strikes. We'll try to find somewhere up north in the business districts to take shelter and wait for the other forces to drop."

"And why are we targeting the air defense turrets but not the deflectors?" Ackley asked.

"Because it would take too long for a platoon of armor to disable the projectors, ma'am. The follow-on forces will take them down and then we can get air support."

"Good job, Private Dixon."

Dixon shot me a grin and I nodded to her. She'd done well, and if nothing else, having her go through things had given everyone else a chance to get it into their heads.

"You all know the reason why it's important for everyone from me down to the lowest-ranking private here to know the plan, right?" Ackley raised an eyebrow and scanned the crowd, looking for any sign of someone who didn't. "I'm not going to bullshit you. This is real edge-of-the-knife shit we're doing. The brass didn't okay this mission because they were sure it would work, they let us do it because it's low-risk. For them, not us. Worst-case scenario, we blow the surprise and the Fleet has to come in with no prep, the way they always do, the way they had planned to begin with. Anything else happens, we provide a distraction, which can only help. For us, though..."

She shook her head, and the motion didn't send her floating away because she had a spot on the deck and the magnetic soles to keep her there.

"I could give you the odds the computers spit out about this one, if you want. Estimated casualties for this mission are one hundred percent."

The breath went out of me like I'd been kicked in the stomach and the sound of my own pulse in my ears was nearly enough to drown out the buzz of conversation washing around the compartment like a wave.

"And it doesn't matter." The statement, and the granite-solid set of Ackley's eyes silenced the chatter. "We're here to save the lives of our fellow Marines, as many of them as possible. If we fail, if those emplacements are active when the main force arrives in orbit, if that laser is functional, hundreds of Marines and Fleet crews are going to die. We might win this battle anyway, or we might come back with a bigger force in a month, or two months and try again. And the politicians and generals and admirals will cry and give speeches about how brave we all were and those of us who have families who give a shit will get folded flags and heartfelt thanks. And the war will go on, with a few hundred fewer Marines and Fleet crews. But it's *not* going to happen on my fucking watch."

The words were fierce, the expression feral and my eyes widened.

"No matter who goes down, no matter who falls, those emplacements get taken out. The laser gets taken out. If you see me, or Gunny Hayes, or Lt. Davies or one of your squad leaders go down, you step in, you step up and you Charlie Mike." That was old-style slang for Continue the Mission. I had never heard it from anyone except Top and the Skipper and I got the sense it had been old when they'd both been new recruits in the US Marine Corps. "And if you're the last Marine left standing, you fire off your last round at one of those emplacements and give our brothers and sisters a better chance at coming through this alive."

The determination in her face twisted into a smile.

"And when we all get to Valhalla, the drinks are on me. Ooh-rah?"

The reply was deafening, a hundred throats screaming at once, echoing off the bridge and hitting me like a physical force.

"Ooh-rah!"

[22]

"Ten seconds to airlock seal," Lt. Davies murmured, as if he was afraid speaking the words aloud even in the confines of his helmet would alert the Tahni crews on the other side of the cargo locks.

There were three of them, equally spaced along the upper level of the cargo bay, nearly a hundred meters apart, which was why I hadn't even noticed them when we were hanging on the outer hull waiting to get in. The Recon platoon was split between them, one squad for each and one held in reserve, guarding the store of HyPex they'd packed along with them for the operation. The boarding parties had their Gauss rifles slung at their backs, opting instead for their sidearms, 10mm slug-shooters made by a company called *Zwischenwelt Waffen Herstellung* in Earth orbit. Integrally suppressed with variable velocity, rocket-assisted ammo they could guide from their helmets. I wanted one.

And us? We waited, metal statues looming in the shadows, hiding in plain sight. If they needed us to get involved in the fight, something would have gone horribly wrong, and yet I *wanted* to be involved. I'd volunteered to grab my pulse pistol out of the cockpit and tag along with one of the raiding parties, but Davies had vetoed the idea.

"I appreciate the sentiment," he'd said, still wearing that cocky grin I wanted to resent but couldn't. "But the close-in stuff is why we're here. Not to mention, it's free-fall. Have you even had any combat training in free-fall outside a suit?"

I had to admit I hadn't, and that had been that. But I was ready to surge forward right into the cargo shuttle's freight bay with guns blazing, even if those guns would cut right through the opposite hull.

I couldn't hear the airlock hatch opening. We'd drained the air when we'd reached orbit since we didn't want the Tahni shuttle crews figuring out someone was on board their supposedly autopiloted freighter when their airlocks had to cycle before they could enter. They'd be coming out of an evacuated cargo bay into what they expected to be another evacuated cargo bay, and we were giving them just what they expected.

Right up till the second we didn't.

The airlock across from me, the first in line going from the freighter's bridge back toward the drives, slid open silently, flooding the darkened cargo bay with light, and a Tahni crewman pulled himself through, moving casually, matter-of-factly, as if he wasn't seeing what was actually in the bay but rather what he assumed would be there. Davies himself was anchored onto the rim of the lock with his magnetic boots and he reached down and yanked the vacuum-suited Tahni out of the throat of the docking umbilical, putting the muzzle of his pistol against the visor of the crewman's helmet and pulling the trigger.

No sound, no smoke, no flash, just a cloud of plastic shards and globules of red already freezing into their own tiny asteroid field. The Tahni corpse floated away, driven by the expulsion of blood and brain matter, and the rest of the squad shot through the open umbilical, not hesitating a second. I couldn't see what was happening at the other locks and resisted the urge to spy on the comm feeds from the squad leaders, but motion caught my eye on my helmet display as the Recon Marines darted into the next lock over, then the one after that.

I tensed up inside my suit, weighed down not by gravity but by helplessness and futility. Everything could go horribly wrong in a few seconds and I wouldn't arrive in time to make it right no matter how fast I acted. I hated trusting my fate to the Straight-Legs.

"Still wish you'd gone along with them, Alvarez?" Ackley asked me and I wondered if she could read my mind or was just monitoring my vitals again and noticed an elevated heart rate.

"Hell, yes, ma'am," I said, trying to sound bluff and brash. "Wanted to show these Straight-Legs that Drop-Troopers are just as good outside our armor as we are inside it."

"I don't know about you, but I'm happier inside. Besides, I think it's all over."

She must have been monitoring the Recon comms I'd neglected, because it wasn't ten seconds later that one of them stuck their head out through the airlock and gave the "all-clear" signal. I lumbered forward, laboriously detaching and reattaching each magnetic sole with a clunk I could only hear on the inside of my suit, an unnatural, echoless vibration. The docking umbilical through the cargo lock into the Tahni shuttle was cramped, narrow enough that I tried to duck instinctively, lest the suit's helmet scrape on the overhead, but it widened out on the other end into the broad, open cargo bay of the heavy lift shuttle.

The Tahni cargo birds weren't lifting bodies or any sort of airframe like ours. Instead, they went for a spherical shape to maximize interior cargo space and reentered and landed vertically. The entire cargo space was wide open, with magnetic cargo racks spaced around the interior of the sphere and fold-down gantries mounted on catwalks at intervals around the centerline of the bay to provide extra racks if needed.

The corpses of the Tahni crew were tiny against the open space, stick-figures floating aimlessly with the air currents, trailing crimson globules. Recon Marines moved in cautious, measured courses, chasing after the wayward enemy dead and corralling them toward whatever disposal they deemed expedient. I left them to it, glad for the confines of my suit for the moment if it meant I could avoid that work detail.

"Spread out along the interior hull," Ackley barked, her voice sharp enough to cut through the strangeness of the alien ship and the awe of having actually gotten this far. "Squad leaders, see to your people, get everyone locked in for reentry."

"Graciano," I said, seeing the team leader's IFF as his Vigilante squeezed through the reverse birth canal into the shuttle. "Bring Alpha over here and find everyone one of these magnetic cargo locks." I knocked the back of my suit's left hand against the magnetic ring bolted to the hull. "This lever activates it," I went on, drawing from the briefing we'd been given by the Intelligence officer back on Hachiman. "Just make sure both legs are all the way inside the ring when you pull it or you'll get the groin pull to end all groin pulls."

"Move it! Time's a'wasting, Fourth Platoon!" Scotty wasn't exactly yelling, but he was definitely emphatic. I knew why. The longer we stayed up here, the more likely it was that ground control would try to contact us, and no one left alive up here was going to be able to fake being a Tahni cargo crewman.

Caught up in the haste and furor, I scraped my magnetic soles along the deck, sliding between each of the locking rings and supervising every member of my squad as they stepped into the center of the circular magnetic platform three meters across, designed to secure the metal pallets the Tahni used for freight transport. With the flip of the oval switch, the electromagnet locked each of them in place. The suit would do the rest, locking its joints and cushioning us during reentry and I hoped someone had figured out who was going to cut us loose when it was time to drop, because you couldn't reach the damned lever once you were locked in.

I found Linebarger locking Dixon down to her spot and then manhandled him into the next one over and threw the switch myself to activate the magnets. His suit stiffened into place with a tuning-fork vibration and an electrostatic hum in the air. I checked the line; he was the last. I was the only one left in my squad, so I did a quick check of the rest of the platoon. Vicky was locking down her last trooper and I knew she'd need help throwing her own switch so I hustled over to her spot.

"I got you," I told her, gesturing to the magnet controls. "Step on in."

"Easy part's over," she said on a private channel, the electro-magnetic field pulling her into its unyielding grasp. "You know that, right?"

"The only easy day was yesterday," I quoted every drill sergeant from every basic training class ever, trying to make light of it, not wanting to think about what could happen to her.

"I'm serious," she insisted. "This might be the last time we get to talk to each other, and there's something I want to say."

"What's left to say, Vicky?" I wondered. "You know how I feel."

"I do. And that's what worries me. Down there, you can't let it affect you. If I'm in trouble and it's a choice between me or the mission, I want you to promise me you'll do your job and not try to be my white knight."

I wanted to feel outraged, wanted to be insulted that she'd think I would do something so stupid, but I couldn't. Maybe I was disciplined and dedicated enough a Marine to not let my personal feelings get in the way of the mission...and maybe I wasn't.

"All right," I said, hoping I conveyed enough gravitas this time. "I promise." Then I grinned. I just couldn't help it. "But once the mission's accomplished, I can't guarantee I won't go out in some futile blaze of glory trying to save you from hopeless odds."

That got her and she laughed, as I hoped she would. Things were too hopeless to take all this seriously.

"Fair enough. And I might have to do the same thing if your ass is on the line."

"Alvarez, get your ass into a lock now!"

I blinked, thinking for a second that it had been Vicky yelling at me before I realized it was Lt. Ackley. I clomped with clumsy, armor-plated haste over to the last unoccupied cargo ring in the line with my squad, and stepped inside the magnetic lock just as Ackley arrived at my position.

I half-expected her to lecture me about woolgathering or even caution me about my relationship with Vicky. I wouldn't have put it past her already knowing about it. But she said nothing, just flicked the oversized, oval switch next to me. The armor came to attention as if a flag officer had walked into the room, every bit of its metal surface locked into position by the force of the magnetic coils.

I was going to ask the LT who was going to flip her switch, but Lt. Davies floated across the hold and flashed her a thumbs-up, gaining purchase with his magnetic boots before he leaned in and yanked the oval switch shut.

"Everyone is secure," Davies announced on the general net, throwing himself up and out of the hold, toward the small cockpit. "Autopilot will engage in two minutes and begin programmed reentry. Charges are set for automatic detonation at one hundred meters altitude, so be off this fucking ship before then! Good luck, Jackheads."

Then he passed through the cargo lock and it slid shut behind him, leaving us alone.

"Good luck, Straight-Legs," Ackley replied, and I wondered if he heard it.

I wanted to say something inspirational to my squad, something to fill the next two minutes with anything besides the stale fear and the sound of our own breathing in our helmets, but just like with Vicky, those words had all been said and they just would have made everyone more nervous.

"Just a heads-up for the whole platoon," I said, trying to sound official, the spiel seeming to come from someone else, someone glibber and more laid back than I had ever been. "I've been notified by supply that any gear deadlined from this mission is going to have to be personally logged by each Marine, so make sure you get a written explanation from the Tahni before we leave or it might come out of your pay. Word to the wise."

The responding chuckles weren't exactly a full-throated laugh, but at least they filled the empty seconds and poked a pin in the tension.

"You *still* paying for that Vigilante you lost on Brigantia, Alvarez?" Ackley asked, laughing softly.

"Oh, God, you know it, ma'am. Supply told me I'd better hope the war lasts ten more years so I don't get out of the Marines owing the government money."

It wasn't me, I thought somewhere in the part of my brain that watched things happened and tried to rationalize actions I'd carried out instinctively, without conscious thought. I wasn't the kind of guy who could inspire people, ease their tensions, make them feel confident. I didn't deal with people at all, preferred being alone.

Yet here I was.

Something loud and insistent banged against the hull, the maneuvering rockets kicking us away from the freighter. I wished I could have seen it, wish I could have known for sure whether it did what we'd asked of it, taken its dumb and useless bulk into the orbit that would intersect the Tahni orbital defense platform. But all the hacks in the world, all the advice Mutt, our battalion armorer, had given me over the last year, wouldn't tie the comm feed from my suit into the external cameras on a Tahni freighter, so I sat in the darkness of my helmet and waited, just like everyone else.

The engine flared, pushing me towards the floor with a half a gravity of boost, just a nudge in the right direction, taking the freighter out of orbit before it cut off. I felt the pull of the planet's gravity trying to reassert itself, but the engines roared their defiance, the braking burn slowing our descent.

Any second, the Tahni could figure out what was up, could decide we weren't who our ship's ID transponder said we were and end this whole thing with a single missile. Would I even know if it happened? Would it kill us instantly or would I find myself falling again, just like Brigantia? I decided instantly would be better. Once was enough. I didn't want to have the time to think about it.

Shaking, turbulence and a stifling heat penetrating even through the armor and I couldn't keep up the fatalistic façade. I gritted my teeth and squeezed my eyes shut, wondering if I should try praying again. Was there a God listening after all? He'd allowed my parents and my brother to die, sure, but He hadn't pulled the trigger. Maybe even God couldn't save everyone. Maybe that was why He bothered with us. And maybe saving everyone wasn't the point, anyway.

If you're listening...if Anyone *is listening...I won't bother asking to live through this. There are worse things than dying.*

But if You can, if it's not against the rules or something, can You make sure my death means something?

There was a roar of rocket engines, but God wasn't in the roar.

There was a wash of heat from the friction of the reentry, but God wasn't in the heat.

There was a terrible vibration, a rattling, bone-jarring shake all the way through the hull of the shuttle, but God wasn't in the vibration.

And then, there was a still, small voice...

"Drop in thirty seconds."

The magnetic locks cut loose without a hand touching the switches, either by the hand of God or by a prearranged command linked to the altimeter, whichever was more likely. Gravity had returned and braking boost was adding to it, forcing my chin into my chest when I tried to move, but the Vigilante ignored my discomfort and the punishment of merciless physics with equal aplomb and even managed to keep me upright and balanced all the way to the cargo lock.

It opened at my presence, as if it knew I was coming. I knew this was another one of those little details the Recon guys had handled, using the computer hacks they'd been gifted by the Fleet Intelligence officers. The door opened when the altimeter hit five hundred meters and the pressure differential sucked swirling tornadoes of dust and debris out of the cargo bay, it would have taken me with it if the armor hadn't kept me in place with its massive determination.

Outside the hatch, a solid blue of cloudless day mocked me with its cheerful glow.

"Drop! Drop! Drop!"

I stepped out of the shuttle and into the hands of God.

[23]

It was odd dropping into a battle that hadn't started yet. Every time I'd dropped onto a Tahni-held world so far, people had already been trying to kill me just as hard as they could. Instead, below us, everything was placid, unsuspecting, and I felt an absurd sense of guilt for what we were about to do.

The jump-jets kicked me in the ass and jogged me out of my reverie. I tried to empty my mind of the trivial and let the data wash over me. The island wasn't as big as it had looked on the maps, though it was the biggest of the chain. Most of it was mountainous, capped by an extinct volcano that had created the whole land mass millions of years ago, but it flattened out down by the sea, and that was where the Tahni had built their base.

From four hundred meters up, the base was laid out like a child's playset, with blocky, unimaginative barracks along one side of the base, hangars and armories and warehouses and administration buildings arranged in a horseshoe shape around a central courtyard. There was some religious significance to the organization, or so the Intelligence spooks had said, but I couldn't have cared less. It was their job to understand the enemy, I just wanted to kill them.

The spaceport closed the open end of the horseshoe, fusion-form pavement glimmering in the mid-day glare, rows upon rows of shuttles, cargo haulers, dart-shaped dual-environment fighters, all lined up neatly in some pattern no human would ever have called rational. The traffic control buildings sat at the center, their sensor dishes spinning steadily near the edges of the fields, though most of the detection equipment was in orbit on board the defense platforms. Service vehicles on treads with loading cranes crept along the pavement from one landing vehicle to another and cargo trucks were lined up beside one of the freight shuttles, ready to haul out the payload one shipping container at a time.

Less than a kilometer from the edge of the landing field, the defense laser emitter hurt to look at, its focusing crystal nearly twenty meters across and shining like the eye of God, reflecting the afternoon light of the primary. It was the sword and the shields were twin deflector dishes, each a hundred meters across and wrapped with superconductive cable and ready to throw up devastating electromagnetic fields at the first sign of attack. They were a shield and also a barrier, separating the military part of the island from the civilian city, if Tahni society could be said to actually have civilians. The city wasn't anything compared to Trans-Angeles, could barely have held a candle to Tartarus, the military headquarters on Inferno. It was about the size I remembered Tijuana being when I was a kid, the occupied parts of Tijuana, not the entirety of the old city.

The civilian structures could have been constructed by an entirely different species than the military base. The base was a study in pragmatism and utility, no artifice to the place, while the city, modest as it was, at least showed the intricacies of a sentient brain. The blueprints for the buildings at the center of the town could have been copies of the MRI of a nautilus shell, tracing twists and curves no human architect would have thought possible, much less desirable. Some of the shapes were familiar, if not something I would have pictured living in or doing business from...or worshipping their version of god from. Spheres, obelisks, spirals, steppe pyramids. I couldn't have told you what style the city was built in because no human mind had envisioned it.

But a human could have designed the anti-aircraft turrets. They were ugly, and functional, and deadly as a desert scorpion, and they ringed the city and the base like a stake fence. The closest of them was just a few hundred meters down toward the beach from the spaceport and I could see it from here...so, I figured I might as well shoot at it.

"Dixon," I called, still two hundred meters off the ground, "follow my designator and launch two!"

Missiles kicked free of my backpack launchers, arcing downward like the fangs of a rattlesnake and slamming into the launcher from above, two more slicing from behind me and skimming low across the sand to strike from the base. The emplacement was mounted on tracks, like some sinister piece of construction equipment and Dixon's warheads lifted it off the packed sand just as mine pierced through to the propellant tanks of its missile battery. The concussion shook me a hundred meters in the air and I had to correct with my jets to keep from nosing in.

The spiked soles of my Vigilante's foot pads touched down on the pavement of the spaceport with a mushroom cloud climbing fifty meters into the sky as a backdrop, and I saw a groundcar speeding down the service lane past the rows of military fighters, coming towards me as if I were a trespasser who needed to be taken into custody.

"Head for the beach!" I yelled at my squad, galloping through the middle of them as they touched down on the edge of the landing field. "Hurry, we've got maybe thirty seconds!"

Out past the surf, beyond the rocks near the shore, beyond what I assumed was the local equivalent of a coral reef, structures rose out of the ocean, cylindrical, bulbous, colored a stark white in contrast to the aqua green of the seawater. The sea farms stretched for kilometers, tended by tubby barges and tugs, producing enough to feed a dozen worlds.

We were here to take that all away from them.

IFF and my eyes told me my squad had followed, and the rest of the platoon was arcing away from the spaceport on their flight down from the spherical cargo shuttle, landing down the slope to the beach, knowing what was coming next. I felt as if I should duck, as if I should find shelter, but there was none to be had. If my armor didn't shield me, nothing would.

The shuttle was huge and round and gleaming in the light from the primary, the roar of its landing rockets beating at my ear drums even through my helmet, and my heart climbed into my throat at the thought the Recon guys had fucked up, that it was going to come down directly over us. Despite the fact they were dirty Straight-Legs, though, they weren't incompetent dirty Straight-Legs, and the shuttle skated laterally as it descended until it hung in the air over the dual-environment fighters, so close it seemed the rocket exhaust would burn the paint off them.

It was exactly one hundred meters off the ground when it exploded.

We were nearly a kilometer away from ground zero, down the slope, close to the water, and it was *barely* enough. The fist of God pounded into the spaceport landing pad and the fires of hell came with it, raining from the sky like brimstone, streams of burning debris striking the beach all around us, hitting the surf and dying in sprays of steam. A few smaller pieces thumped off my armor with a ringing metallic echo.

Everyone was crouched, tensed, sure we were going to die,

and sweat was pouring down my back, the insulated padding so hot it began to adhere to my skin. But this, too, had been calculated to the last microjoule of energy, and the heat washing over the beach wasn't *quite* enough to shut down our suit systems or broil us inside the metal pressure cookers.

The debris was still falling and a cluster of the local analog for trees clinging to the last clump of dirt at the edge of the sand was burning fiercely, its leaves stripped away as if summer had abruptly turned to fall. I heard something in the distance, a sound nothing like a human alarm siren but close enough that I guessed it served the same purpose. The Tahni might not know exactly what was going on, but they knew *something* was happening. Peals of roaring thunder echoed across the beach and, behind it, the globular mass of the Recon cargo shuttle was burning its retro rockets on a descent into the grass between the base and the defense laser, banking on the confusion to get them inside.

I wished them the best of luck, but we had problems of our own.

"Fourth Platoon, you know your teams," Ackley barked. "Split up and move! First squad, you're in the lead!"

"Go Dixon!" I said. "Take point and get us out of here!"

Dixon hesitated for just a moment, and I wondered if I was going to have to replace her at point, but then she broke into a loping run, sand spraying up with each step as she headed west around the coast of the island. Alpha team fell in behind her, closing up to a staggered column, no room on the narrow beach for a standard wedge formation, then me, then Bravo.

We were down. It was real. I'd managed to convince myself it was an intellectual exercise up till this point, a what-if scenario like the ones we'd run in the simulators or out on tactical training missions. Something extra-complicated just to keep the platoon and squad leaders on their toes, to make sure everyone was paying attention. Sometimes, halfway through, they'd kill off the platoon leader and a couple squad leaders and make some buck sergeant or lance corporal take over and everything would go to hell. We'd all hate it because we knew we'd spend forever in the AAR with some candy-ass trainer who'd never been in combat explaining to us what we'd done wrong.

I'd always laughed at those scenarios, at how complicated and edge of the knife they were, at how unlikely it was that anything like that could ever get greenlit.

And it still didn't seem real. The sky was too blue, the beach too beautiful, the sand too white for it to be anything but a computer simulation. Maybe, I thought, it was better to keep telling myself that. Maybe that was the one sure way to avoid panicking.

"Ma'am, how long do you think we have before they figure out we're here?" Garrity, the Second squad leader asked. Second was behind us, a spot I wouldn't have wanted. Out front, I could take the first shot at anything we saw. Back on drag, I would have been scared shitless of taking a round to the back, getting picked off from the rear by an enemy I never saw.

"Depends on how closely they were monitoring the security cameras at the port," Ackley said with brutal honesty. "They could have figured it out already or it might take them until they realize we're attacking the next anti-aircraft turret. Good job, by the way, Alvarez," she added, "taking the initiative and opening fire from the air on the first one. Saved us some time."

"Next emplacement is in twelve hundred meters, ma'am," I said by way of reply, not bothering to thank her for the compliment. Compliments in the Marine Corps are just a prelude to giving you even harder jobs in the future.

The beach was getting narrower as we went around the horn of the island closest to the military base. I wondered idly if the Tahni used beaches for recreation like humans...well, like *rich* humans, on Earth at least. I hadn't seen any Tahni lying in the sun soaking in rays or wading out into the surf with a fishing pole, but I wondered if the military base got the short end of the stick as far as beachfront went because the high-rent civilian residences commanded the best part of the island. Whatever the reason, economic, tactical or just coincidence, our detachment went from trudging through the sand below the slope of the headland to running on dirt and in plain sight of every swinging Tahni dick at the base.

Running in formation felt ridiculously slow, and impatience gnawed at my last nerve ending, screaming at me to fly, to take the distance in long, jet-propelled hops before the enemy finally got off their asses and into their battlesuits and came after us. But we'd hashed over the idea in one meeting after another on the trip from Hachiman, and the final decision was to stay low until we were sure we'd been spotted.

The 1200 meters to the next emplacement took two minutes and I had the time to scan the sensor displays at least ten times during that time and check on Vicky's position twice and go over the plan in my head again and wonder if I should have changed my life insurance beneficiary before the mission. I'd left it all to Dak Shepherd on Brigantia, not because he needed the money but for the depressing reason that I didn't know anyone else who wasn't in the Marines and as likely to die in the war as I was. Maybe I should have left the money to Henckel's mom, though...

"There it is," Dixon said with a newbie's fondness for hearing herself talk.

But she was right. Around the curve in the shoreline it squatted in utilitarian homeliness, radar dishes spinning on either side of the emplacement, the missile launch tubes elevating and scanning back and forth across the miraculously blue sky, searching for the threats they expected. We were the threat they didn't expect, but they weren't entirely unprepared for us. The emplacements had anti-infantry weapons, KE gun turrets, one at each corner of what was essentially a giant, tracked vehicle, and even from half a kilometer away, my helmet's magnifying optics picked up the barrel of the south-facing turret traversing toward us.

"Dixon," I said, and to her credit, I didn't have to finish the command.

The plasma pulse couldn't cut through the thick armor over the turret, but it didn't have to. The KE gun's barrel melted to slag from the blast and then we were abandoning stealth for alacrity. I hit the jets and Alpha team rose with me while Bravo and Lt. Ackley laid down suppressive fire with their plasma guns. The emplacement tried to slew the missile launchers around, either to bring another of the KE turrets around or maybe even to try to depress the coil gun battery enough to deal with us, but the emplacement was huge and moved with the glacial speed of the gigantic piece of machinery that it was.

I saved my own missiles, knowing I might need them later, and let Dixon and Graciano hit this one. Four missiles seemed overkill, yet they were barely enough against the heavy armor on the skin of the emplacement. The first two battered it and the second pair ripped through the hole they'd left. It was the Tahni's own anti-aircraft missiles that did the most damage; their fuel was very energetic, as one of the Fleet techs would say. Top would have said it "blowed up real good."

Sixteen anti-aircraft emplacements, I thought as I touched down from the jet-assisted gun run. Eight for us, eight for the other detachment. Seventeen Vigilantes in each detachment, each with four missiles and shit, I sucked at math. 108 missiles? Yeah, so sixty-four of them had to go to the launchers, assuming no one missed, and that didn't leave a hell of a lot to fight the enemy with. I wished we could have carried more missiles or even had all of us issued a Boomer suit for this mission, but there was no way to strap all the extra space maneuvering shit to a Boomer, not to mention the fact they were slow as hell.

Better not miss.

"They've seen us now," Ackley decided. "No use laying low anymore. Bound by teams, stay below fifty meters and no one up for more than five seconds."

The old good news-bad news joke, but I was so happy to stop crawling and start jumping, I didn't care. They were going to figure it out at some point.

Waves of needle-nosed grass and twisted, scaly trees passed beneath my feet along with a hundred meters of ground at each jump, and in the air, I could see the military base off to our right. We were just to the south of the hangars, warehouses, and admin buildings, less than a kilometer away. Tahni males were milling about outside one of the hangars, some pointing, some raising handguns in the air and shouting. It was just about as confused and shambolic as we would be if the enemy figured out where our base was and landed troops undetected.

Down again, running at a sprint, the ground shaking, the vibration rattling my teeth and we were that much closer to the next emplacement. Just had to get this done and then we could worry about surviving. I don't know why I was looking forward to that part so much. *This* was simple, straightforward. Figuring out how to survive until the relief came was going to be a nightmare.

Behind me, Bravo team had been up and five seconds later, they were down and it was our turn again. When I was a little boy, my father showed me something his father had passed to him, down through each generation for as long as the Alvarez family had lived in Tijuana. He had a small notebook, real paper, the kind you didn't see much anymore. Someone made them on a cheap, antique fabricator deep in the old city, far from the parts still in business. Papa had drawn tiny stick figures in the corner of each page, every drawing just slightly different than the last, and when he'd flipped through the pages, the stick figures had come to life.

Tijuana was backward and abandoned, but we still had computers and datalinks. I'd seen computer animation, but this was somehow more real to me, like magic you could make with your hands and not a machine.

The view from the military base was like the flip books. Each time I hopped, I saw a slightly different picture. Where there had been a handful of looky-loos watching us, now there was most of a platoon of shock-troops, hastily dressed in their exoskeletal body armor and wielding heavy KE guns, running toward the shoreline in a poorly-organized gaggle.

"Contact right! Infantry in the open! Fire as you bear!"

I only had time for one shot from my plasma gun as I hit the top of my arc and began descending again, didn't even know if it hit. But Bravo team joined the party behind me, and even if my thermal sensors hadn't detected their weapons firing, I would have known because they dutifully announced it.

"We busted up the charge," Lt. Ackley told me as my feet touched the sandy dirt. "They're hanging back and running behind cover."

How long had we been down? Five minutes? Four? It was an eternity in combat, but each minute took us closer to the Fleet's arrival. More good news-bad news. The sooner they arrived, the sooner they could bail our asses out, but if they arrived before we took out the emplacements, the whole mission would be pointless.

"Eyes on number three," Dixon said. "And number four."

The shoreline had turned north around the horn, but the defense perimeter curved east again around the backside of the military base, to the edge of the flats where they rose steeply into mountains clad in a jaunty jungle green. The ideal place for the emplacements along the rear of the base would have been up on the mountaintop, but the air defense platforms were pre-fabbed and mass-produced and I had to assume their military was just as cheap about things like custom-built defenses as ours was. You couldn't drop a hundred-ton tracked emplacement on top of a mountain with no flat surfaces, so they'd tried to make up in numbers and overlapping fields of fire what they were giving up in tactical positioning.

The unpaved, tread-marked path along the base's perimeter had begun at the beach with one of the missile platforms every 1200 meters, but hugging the mountains at the back end of the facility, the Tahni had squeezed them in with only five or six hundred meters of separation. It was, I thought, wasteful, extravagant. On a base like this, you were only going to get so much equipment. It should have been deployed with an eye toward optimal fields of fire, not making the base commander feel better about himself. But brass was brass, whether a Tahni or a human wore it.

"Launch now, ma'am?" I asked Ackley. We were less than a kilometer away, in range of the missiles, but...

"Negative. Get us closer. The KE turrets could shoot down our missiles if we give them too much flight time. But we can't give them a free shot at us for our whole approach...cut through the base grounds."

"Aye, ma'am. Dixon!" I switched frequencies. "Graciano! Cut straight north through the Tahni base! We're trying to keep the emplacements from targeting us with their coil guns and KE turrets. Fast and hard and blast anything that moves!"

Hard right turns aren't quite as simple when you're running at over twenty-five kilometers an hour in a ton of armor, weapons and reactor. We all hit the jets, bleeding off momentum in mid-air and soaring above the four-meter wire fence around the edge of the base grounds. It was electrified, my suit's sensors told me that much, but I wasn't sure why they bothered with it. It meant less than nothing from a tactical point of view and I could only guess it was either to discourage the Tahni civilians from wandering onto the base or to keep out local wildlife. Or maybe it was just to make the commander feel better, like packing the anti-aircraft platforms in so close together.

The grounds of the base were qualitatively different than the dirt path around the outside of the fence line. Tahni were similar enough that their military was just as obsessed as ours on having neat, well-trimmed and succulent lawns. The grass wasn't really grass, but it was there and it was universal and I suppose it made sense to keep it trimmed if they weren't going to just kill all of it outright.

And if Tahni commanders were anything like human commanders, that sorry fucker was going to be *pissed* that we were trampling his grass. It sprayed up under our foot pads, pulled out in clots of sod as we landed one fire team at a time.

"Spread out!" I ordered. "Wedge formation! Keep low and don't give the defense platforms a target!"

Tahni soldiers in soft utility uniforms scattered at our rumbling approach, some firing laser carbines at us in gestures of valiant futility before they got the hell out of the way.

"Vehicle at our three o'clock!" Graciano said.

I saw it. It was an armored truck, something they probably used just to transport their shock-troops from one end of the base to the other, not good against anything more than Recon infantry, but it had a KE gun turret just behind the driver compartment and some poor, brave soul had decided they were going to be the saviors of this base and drive that dinky little truck straight at us. Dixon blew it to smoldering shreds with an almost negligent blast from her plasma gun. Another dead hero, and not the last.

We were inside their OODA loop, as Lt. Ackley liked to say. Observe, Orient, Decide Act. They were still observing and orienting and had yet to make a decision, and we were the only ones acting. They were fighting a battle on two fronts, maybe three if the Fleet cutters had already Transitioned, and they'd had no warning. It couldn't last for long, but it didn't need to.

"Contact right!" Mullany reported, his voice sharp and a bit shrill. "Armor in the open! Two of them!"

High Guard battlesuits, but only two out of what we knew might be up to a battalion. Even a ready force wouldn't be sitting in their suits all day. It took long minutes to get suits up and running; you didn't just jump in and start fighting. These two had been the first to their suits, probably already in one of the hangars, likely junior officers or NCOs, or the Tahni equivalent. A senior sergeant or a company commander would have known better, would have waited for more troops to arrive so they could attack in force. These guys were determined to be heroes, just like the driver of the armored car, running out without a thought between them.

At least they were good at their jobs. They did the right thing, hitting the jets the second they saw us, trying to get distance so their missiles would have time to arm before they fired on us, blasting their electron beamers to keep us at bay. Incandescent strands of lightning tore apart the air and I watched it pass centimeters from my head, the sort of fatalistic certainty sinking in my gut that I remembered from trying to jump the gap between rooftops back in the Underground and just knowing I'd come up short, that I'd wind up busting my ass.

The fear was bunched up inside my gut and I shoved it downward further still, isolating it from my thoughts, letting my instincts work on one level while my conscious thought operated one rung higher.

"Alpha, covering fire! Bravo, jump and flank them, don't let them get to minimum arming distance!"

Much as I admired the alien equivalent of balls on these two, I wasn't about to play fair with them, and as much as I was determined to be a good squad leader, I wasn't about to sit back and watch. Bravo was moving, so I moved with them, moved *ahead* of them, leaping into the air on shimmering jets of super-heated air, arcing in a hairpin curve to cut off the High Guard troopers before they could bypass us. Alpha put a wall of gunfire in their way and Bravo was there to cut the Tahni battle-suits off when they tried to swerve in the other direction. I was on point and I fired first, though only by a fraction of a second.

Plasma hammered into the Tahni armor, cratering chunks of it away in glowing halos of sublimating metal and both High Guard troopers tumbled out of the air, their jets cutting off either by damage or design. They were outnumbered five-to-one and at almost point-blank range, it was more of a firing squad than a battle. Except for the flashing damage indicator next to the IFF display with Dixon's name beside it.

"Status, Dixon," I said, touching down beside her.

Torn and blackened armor curled away from her left hip, but it didn't seem like the electron beam had penetrated through even to the servos of her hip or leg. Most of the damage was higher, at the bottom of her backpack. The right-hand turbine for her jump-jets was charred and if the glowing bits of metal on the ground were what I thought they were, chunks of the super-conductive magnetic coils wrapped around the inside of the Magneto Hydro Dynamic turbines...

"I'm grounded, Sergeant," the PFC told me, glumly apologetic, as if she could have dodged the electron beam. "My jets are down."

"Fuck."

I wanted to say more, wanted to unleash the full arsenal of a youth lived where people cursed in five languages and freely mixed between them, but there wasn't the time. Hulking figures were moving in the shadows of one of the hangars, and I had the feeling it was those experienced senior NCOs and officers, gathering their available troops to hit us in force like I'd have done in their place. Tahni dismounts were clotting like pools of blood, gathering in clusters with weapons, waiting for someone to give them an order. I could feel the tension of the gathering storm, the air thick with it. The eye of this hurricane was passing and the worst of it was about it hit.

"Stay in the middle with me. Chandra, you're on point. Move out!"

She wasn't just grounded. I could tell by her stride as we began trotting out of the center of the paved circle between two of the warehouses that Dixon's hip actuators were overheating.

"Ma'am," I told Ackley, "Dixon's going to slow us down."

"Understood, Alvarez." Her voice was calm and clinical and I envied her the detachment. "Recommendations?"

"Put Second squad up front," I said, hating the words even as I uttered them. "Worse comes to worst, they can finish off the mission while First holds off the hordes."

"Roger that. Garrity, get your squad on point. First is falling back."

She'd broadcast it over the general net, so my people heard it at the same time as Rich Garrity's and I watched the stoop-shouldered trolls of his squad pass through our ranks, outpacing us as we slowed to Dixon's hobbled speed.

It still wasn't so bad. Any moron could blow up an anti-aircraft emplacement, not that I was calling Garrity and his squad morons. Well, not his squad anyway. Garrity wasn't the sharpest knife in the drawer. We were still ahead of the curve. It would take them a few more minutes to get any serious opposition zeroed in on us.

"What the fuck is that?" Dixon blurted.

I was about to ask her for clarification and chew her out for being imprecise on the comms, but both proved unnecessary. We could all see it. We could *feel* it, feel the vibrations of its footsteps as it crashed out of the hangar like one of the giants of old. They'd shown us still images of these things taken by our scout drones, but I'd never expected to see one live. Or at least I'd been hoping not. It was twelve-and-a-half meters tall and bipedal, though I wouldn't call it man-shaped—more like a robot grizzly bear crossed with a praying mantis. An anti-proton reactor powered it and fifteen centimeters of molecularly-bonded armor protected its torso and the Goddamned thing had legs the size of oak trees. More of a mobile artillery piece than a tank, it packed a proton accelerator, Gauss autocannons and a lot of missiles, though I couldn't swear to whether it had a full combat load. Or needed one.

"It's a mecha," I answered Dixon's question, and I thought it was someone else's voice, because mine surely wouldn't have been so calm.

It was a Tahni mecha, and it was going to smash us into the ground like fucking bugs.

Five and a half minutes in. Damn.

[24]

"Garrity," Lt. Ackley said, "go take out those emplacements. Don't look back. Whatever happens here, those launchers have to go down."

I could barely hear her through the pounding of my pulse in my head, and it was hard to tell the rhythm of my heart from the footfalls of the mecha. It was coming out from the cover of the hangar, its rear quarter facing us, already starting to turn. In seconds, it would be clear and ready to unleash weapons meant to take out assault shuttles and hardened bunkers on us and our tiny little battlesuits.

"Yes, ma'am." It wouldn't be fair to say Garrity sounded grateful for the opportunity to run away from the thing, but I didn't feel the need to be fair and maybe I was a bit envious.

"Cam," Graciano said. His voice broke the spell and I was able to tear my eyes away from the mecha. "We have armor at our three o'clock."

The High Guard troops. There wasn't quite a platoon of them, but they were emboldened by the titan leading the charge, and they piled out of the hangar at the edge of the fence line in a loose wedge, splitting the angle between us and Garrity's squad.

The rear of Second squad's wedge was already two hundred meters away, nearly past the last line of admin buildings, and the High Guard troops hesitated for a moment in their headlong rush, as if listening to orders from their commander, whichever one of the metal gargoyles was him.

I didn't wait for Ackley to give the order. Maybe I should have, but this was *my* squad and my idea and I wasn't going to let it all fall apart now. Besides, there was only one thing to do and she knew it as well as I did.

"Graciano, you have the squad. Cut off the enemy before they can target Second."

"Cam," Graciano began, doubt in his voice. "That thing..."

"Follow your orders, Graciano," I snapped. "Go now before they... Not you, Dixon," I told the private. "You wouldn't be able to keep up, so you're going to stay here with us to kill this thing."

"Yes, Sergeant," Dixon said, her voice small and distant.

"Any orders for me, Sergeant Alvarez?" Ackley asked, her tone dry but not angry. "You ever think maybe I was going to put you in charge of fighting this thing and run away with Garrity's squad?"

"I do have an order for you, ma'am," I said, pointing at the mecha. It had cleared the edge of the hangar and was turning our way. "Help me kill that thing."

"Two of us can fly," she pointed out. "Dixon, we're going to buzz around that big, metal asshole like wasps. Use the distraction to try and stay behind him, go for the weak spots."

"I'm not sure he has any weak spots, ma'am," Dixon said.

She wasn't wrong. The cockpit of the mech was buried behind centimeters of armor, accessible only from a hatch at the bottom of the torso between the legs, and the hips and shoulders were shielded by heavy plastrons, making it impossible to disable the machine by attacking its joints.

I kept my eyes on the mecha, shuffling my Vigilante backwards, giving me just a bit more room for when the time came. The machine's proton cannon was a nautilus shell turned inside out and mounted on an arm as big around as my whole battle suit and it was swinging our way.

"Now!" I yelled and hit the jets.

I went left, staying low to the ground, less than five meters up, my jets sending up clouds of dust from the pavement. Ackley went high and right, twenty meters, over the thing's head, trying to attract its attention, and succeeding. The proton cannon hesitated in its motion and began to ponderously track upward, and Dixon used the opportunity to run like hell straight through its legs.

I fired first, though I had fuck-all notion of what exactly I should be targeting. The thing was a walking starship, all armor and power and just an obnoxious amount of weaponry. I didn't think I could reach the power and I knew I couldn't breach the armor, but maybe, I thought, I could do something about the weaponry.

The plasmoid from my main gun speared into the mecha's left arm at the elbow joint, where it transitioned from a limb into a mounted proton cannon. Metal flared and sparked and I thought maybe I'd done something meaningful before the proton cannon fired and put an end to that fantasy. I'd never been this close to a proton gun before. It was a ship's weapon, something you found on assault shuttles or missile cutters, and even then, it sometimes looked like they'd built the ship around the gun rather than the other way around, and the idea of cramming one onto an artillery piece seemed reckless and wasteful, like trying to squash a spider with a sledgehammer. Exactly the Tahni way of thinking.

The world exploded and reality tore itself to shreds around me and suddenly, it was easy to appreciate the Tahni way of thinking. I was flying through the air, out of control, tossed in a sea of turbulence from the mass of superheated air screaming in terror as it evacuated the area around the energy beam. My helmet display winked out for just a quarter of a second, plunging me into utter darkness, helpless and not even knowing which way was up and I bit down on panic and tasted blood.

I was falling and I knew it was going to hurt, even from just a few meters in the air. I was right, it did. The air went out of me and even with the gel cushioning of the interior of the battlesuit, my body felt as if I'd been worked over by one of the gangs in the Trans-Angeles Underground for a couple of hours. I didn't have the luxury of indulging in the pain, though, couldn't retreat from it into a sheltered compartment of myself the way I had when the gangs had caught me in their territory and taught me a lesson. I had to move.

The HUD revived with a red, warning flash and I hit the jets from flat on my back. The Vigilante scraped against the pavement with a sound that set my teeth on edge, coming up short against a concrete barrier set in place in front of one of the administration buildings and bouncing upward on the impact. The jets went diagonal and then vertical and I was up in the air again, but the world was different than when I'd last seen it.

Everything was burned black, from the pavement to the side of the hangar and the storage dome beside it, smoke and steam billowing in swirling roils, stirred by the jets of my Vigilante, and there was a hole the size of a swimming pool blown in the pavement where the proton blast had struck. Even the mecha, or perhaps the pilot inside it, seemed stunned by the explosion, shuffling sideways, its proton accelerator drifting away from us.

Ackley had been higher off the ground than I was, farther from the blast, and she was in the air, circling behind the huge, walking artillery battery. I was still closing in on it when she fired her plasma gun, targeting the same spot I'd struck before, near the elbow joint of the arm with the proton cannon. Honeycomb boron armor peeled away in sizzling strips and the underlying tungsten casing was laid bare like bone beneath stripped flesh.

"Dixon!" I yelled into the helmet pickup even though she would have heard me just as well with a whisper. "Shoot at the arm!"

The targeting reticle floated over the smoking, scarred section of the mecha's elbow and I touched the trigger with a fingertip on the control bar inside the suit's right arm. The Vigilante wavered in mid-flight from the recoil of the plasma gun and a flare of ionized hydrogen blasted away more of the armor. I thought I saw pitting in the tungsten through the haze of sublimated metal, but I'd spent too much time hovering in one place, and concentrated so intently on the proton cannon that I forgot the mecha had other weapons.

The missiles were useless at this range and the railgun mounted on a gimbal at the thing's left shoulder was four meters long, an artillery piece meant for long-range work, impossible to aim at targets this close. But even an artillery battery needs antipersonnel weapons to keep the infantry from swarming over it, and while the Tahni might have been brutal and ridiculously constrained by their religion, they certainly weren't stupid.

The rotary cannon at the machine's hip was fat, stubby, and primitive, equally easy to miss as to dismiss, but basic and effective for all that. I caught the barest glimpse of the flash of the propellant and then something was pounding against the chest plastron of my Vigilante with the rhythmic ferocity of a jackhammer, the sheer force blasting me backwards. Yellow warning lights flashed in my HUD and I cut my jets, dropping abruptly out of the line of fire.

I didn't *think* the rounds had penetrated my armor, but I couldn't take the time to run a diagnostic, not if I had visions of making it through this alive. I hit the ground running, sensing more than seeing the position of the other two Vigilantes. Ackley had touched down on the mecha's right side while Dixon was loping up from the left, trying to put a round into the same spot on the arm.

The mecha moved fast, faster than I would have given it credit for, its left leg sweeping across Dixon's line of advance and smashing into her side with a crash of metal on metal. She went down hard, flat on the battlesuit's squared-off backpack, firing upward reflexively, as if she'd had her finger on the trigger pad before the landing and simply squeezed it by mistake. The flare of plasma splashed against the juncture of the machine's legs, blackening the paint and melting away a hundred kilograms of armor, but not doing any significant damage.

Ackley had been trying to circle around, perhaps to get a different angle on the damaged arm, but the sweep of the machine's leg had turned it her way, bringing the cavernous emitter of the proton cannon swinging around toward her. The warning died on my lips in a thunderclap, a flash that seemed as bright as a nuclear detonation, and the only reason my HUD didn't blink out again was the bulk of the mecha twisted around, blocking me from the worst of the EMP.

Debris from the explosion of superheated pavement was a fiery hailstorm pattering against my armor, clouds of steam washing across the scene like a veil. If some beneficent deity had been trying to hide the ugliness from me, it wasn't enough. The suit's optics showed it as clear as if it had been laid out on an examination table for autopsy. It hadn't been a direct hit, but it didn't need to be, not at a range of under thirty meters. Half of Joyce Ackley's Vigilante had been burned away, melted like a wax candle, and what was left was a burnt cinder. Nothing was alive inside; nothing could have been.

I screamed and launched my suit straight at the mecha, no conscious intent in my head, only intent on revenge, as ridiculous as that was. This was war, none of it was personal, and yet it all was. I was enraged, crying, willing to trade my life for the destruction of the machine and its pilot. The thing's right arm swung toward me, a digging blade meant for the construction of field-expedient fortifications, and I dodged it with acrobatic grace born of thousands of hours in simulators, in tactical training, in real combat, and something deeper that you couldn't learn and you couldn't teach, the reason they'd chosen me for Armor to begin with.

I cut the jets and landed inside the machine's grasp, outside of the field of fire of any of its weapons and wasn't sure why I'd done it until I noticed the metal hatch dangling open between the machine's legs. It was the access hatch for the cockpit, I realized, not with a conscious series of deductions but with the instinctive grasp of the wash of data. Dixon had blasted it with her plasma gun and while she hadn't been able to burn through the armor, she'd managed to blow apart the latching mechanism. It swung on concealed hinges with the rhythm of a pendulum, and through it was the narrow tunnel straight up to the machine's cockpit.

I had an instant, a breath, the barest fraction of a second, and I fired without thought, without even seeing the targeting reticle. The plasmoid seared the edges of the access hatch on its way upward, filling the darkened tunnel with the light of an exploding sun. The machine stopped in mid-step, locked in place in mid-lunge as if it was set to begin a race. I stared at the motionless giant and wanted to shoot it again, wanted to keep hitting it until it fell down. It should fall down, I was certain of it. It wouldn't feel as if I'd avenged Lt. Ackley's death unless it toppled like the statue of some false god, brought down by the righteous indignation of a prophet like Abraham or Moses in Mama's Bible stories.

Yet I knew I could stay there for an hour firing blast after blast into that thick armor, and it would still be standing. Because life didn't care about satisfying endings, war even less so.

"Sergeant," Dixon said, and the fear and despair in her voice cut through my unreasoning rage and forced me to look around.

In the distance, out past the smoking remains of one of the air defense emplacements, a battle still raged between my squad and the High Guard platoon, and I thought it had dragged on forever until I realized our fight with the mecha had taken less than a minute.

"What are we going to do, Sergeant?" Dixon asked and, from her tone, I thought she must be repeating the question for the second time.

"You know what we're going to do, Private Dixon," I said, leading her off in a loping run out past the base perimeter. "We're going to Charlie Mike, just the way she wanted us to."

I purposefully didn't look at Lt. Ackley's remains as we ran by them, but I did let my eyes close for just a moment in silent prayer. And just in case she'd been right about the afterlife, I added a thought just for her.

Guess when we get to Valhalla, LT, I'll be buying you the first drink.

[25]

It felt like my Vigilante was weighed down with lead anchors, not being able to use the jump-jets, but I couldn't leave Dixon behind, and she was grounded for the duration. The meters crawled by, though it was mere seconds until the two of us were across the open grasslands and into the fight.

I announced my presence with a blast of plasma that took a High Guard trooper in the back of the left knee and sheared his suit's leg off in a shower of burning metal. The Tahni battlesuit collapsed and Graciano put a "go-to-hell" shot in the back of its head before the Alpha team leader turned to deal with another of the enemy troopers engaged with Corporal Chandra.

Half the enemy platoon was here, tangled up with Graciano and First squad, but the rest had gone after Second. I could see their thermal signatures heading out along the perimeter, lit up like bonfires against the backdrop of the mountains, trying to get to the squad of Drop Troopers before they could take out the next air-defense emplacement. Missiles were already arcing away from the Tahni troops and countermeasures were launching.

"Dixon, stay with Graciano."

I flew again, freed of the burden of the private and her damaged jets. Targets lit up red beneath me and I fired from nearly a kilometer away, taking one of the enemy troopers in the back of its left shoulder, blowing the arm half off the battlesuit. The High Guard suit stumbled and crashed, its wearer likely dying and in shock. The image of the Tahni inside the mangled suit flashed across my vision unbidden and I blinked it away.

"Garrity," I said, "get going, take out the rest of the air defense batteries. We'll handle these guys."

"Where's Lt. Ackley?" Garrity asked me.

I didn't answer immediately, too busy jetting down from twenty meters up to smash my shoulder into the side of a High Guard trooper, knocking him off his feet before he could blast one of Garrity's people with his electron beamer. The impact probably hurt me as much as the Tahni, but I was ready for it and stayed on my feet, slamming my suit's left fist like a hammer onto the mount for the High Guard trooper's electron beamer. Sparks flew and electricity arced between us as the power feed for the gun ruptured. I fought the instinct to put a plasma blast into the suit's chest and cut down another of the enemy troopers who'd been hitting the jets to run after Second Platoon. The plasmoid melted his suit's jets to slag and he pinwheeled downward from fifty meters up, crashing headfirst into the dirt.

There were two of the Tahni troopers left and they blasted away on their jets, heading back toward the base, probably looking to hook up with reinforcements before they tried to take us on. I let them.

"Graciano, status."

"We toasted three of them. Two dead, one damaged enough he won't be fighting in that suit again. Chandra took a bad hit, though. Her plasma gun is deadlined and she's hurting. Her suit's got her doped for the pain and she doesn't want to say anything, but we're not going to be able to count on her for anything but keeping her head down for the rest of the fight."

They were heading our way, rumbling in a steady trot through the tall grass just beyond the pavement of the base. Second was still heading straight up into the hills, jetting over the crest of the closest ridge, out of the line of the guns from the closest emplacement a few hundred meters away, and I realized I still hadn't answered Garrity's question.

"Garrity, Lt. Ackley is gone. I'm assuming command of this detachment until we hook back up with Gunny Hayes' unit. Graciano, you're acting First squad leader."

There was no response and I wondered if the signal had carried through. There shouldn't have been any jamming, not yet, and I was close enough to Graciano for the laser line-of-sight comms to work no matter what.

"Roger," Garrity said, finally, flat and emotionless, as if he was tamping his reaction down. "You're the boss, Cam." With the last, he revealed some emotion: relief. He might or might not like me being in command, but he sure as hell didn't want to be the one in charge.

"Graciano, send Linebarger and Bravo team to attract the attention of the gun crews on the next emplacement. Garrity, once they start firing at us, you hit them from above."

"How the hell are we supposed to attract their attention?" Linebarger demanded, not at all deferential despite my position of authority.

"Try shooting at them," I suggested. "I've always found it distracting as hell. Follow me."

It would have been a tough call if I'd taken the time to think about it, but I didn't. It was hard enough trying to keep track of both squads without internally debating every decision I made. I could have gone with the group striking the emplacements, and maybe I should have, to keep better command and control of the detachment, but the ones in the field of fire needed me more. I felt a sting of guilt for not staying to help cover Alpha team with Chandra injured and Dixon's jets damaged, but the mission came first, especially when the purpose of the mission was to save Marine lives.

I moved out ahead of Linebarger's team, knowing I shouldn't have been on point but was past caring. The KE gun turret on this corner of the emplacement was tracking up toward Second squad, trying to take them out before they crested the ridge and went out of its firing arc. Tufts of soil and grass flew into the air as the bursts of tantalum needles tracked toward them, coming closer with each second.

It was a long shot on the gallop, more than seven hundred meters, but I didn't have to be pinpoint accurate. The plasmoid splashed across the gun shield for the turret and the barrel slewed sideway, tantalum darts chewing up ground only twenty meters ahead of the turret as the gunner jerked it spastically. I'd fired first and it seemed to uncork the bottle. The rest of the team fired as if in a planned volley and the whole front stretch of armor at the base of the air defense battery glowed red, though I held no illusions that our guns could penetrate the centimeters-thick armor there. The KE turret swiveled toward us, but the distraction had worked for long enough.

Four missiles streaked down from the top of the ridge directly above the emplacement and drilled down through the weaker armor over the missile launch tubes. Fire consumed the huge machine and this time we were close enough that I could make out a couple of the gun crew abandoning the rig, flames licking at their backs.

"Next one, Garrity. Get to the next one."

We were running out of time.

The deflector dishes rose above the highlands past the military base, and the spires and towers of the city seemed to cluster below the edges of the dish, an optical illusion and a symbol all at once. There was only one emplacement left this side of the deflector dishes. The Tahni hadn't bothered to position any more of the batteries under the cover of the dishes, obviously, since the electromagnetic fields that would deflect missiles and proton beams and railgun rounds from above would have done the same for anything coming from below.

The last battery on our side, the end of mission if Scotty's detachment had done its job. And the first one to get off a shot with one of its missiles.

It was a desperation move, launching a spread of missiles meant to take down dropships, assault shuttles and Attack Command cutters against a squad of battlesuits. The missiles were huge and broke out from the launchers almost in slow-motion, arcing high and then coming straight down at First squad.

"Scatter!" I yelled, hitting the jets.

The weapons were designed for large spacecraft with high heat signatures, and they'd have a hard time getting a lock on us if we just got the hell out of the way. That all came to me seconds later, in mid-air, and if I'd known it when I gave the order, it had been a function of my subconscious taking control faster than I could have if I'd thought about it.

IFF signals dispersed from a tight wedge formation like a covey of quail flushed from the undergrowth only a second ahead of the rolling chain of explosions that tore apart the valley floor beneath us. The detonations spewed tons of soil into the air and the concussion erupted upward with the debris, and I wasn't sure if it was the shockwave or the solid wall of earth that hit me, but something did. I was smacked out of the air like a bug, sent tumbling dozens of meters, and I was shocked when the force pushing me down into my suit turned out to be the jump-jets firing instead of the ground slamming into me. I don't know how I'd had the mental acuity to hit the thruster control, because my brain was awash with a red haze of pain and confusion.

The only coherent thought penetrating the confusion was that I needed to get back on the ground before something shot me out of the air. If I could find ground. It seemed everywhere I tried to land was torn and cratered and I gave up on finding a flat surface and dropped into a hole two meters deep, figuring it would make good cover in case the KE gun turret was targeting us. It wasn't. The missiles had gone after us when they should have gone after Second squad, and while Garrity might not have been ambitious, he wasn't one to look a gift horse in the mouth.

The half a dozen backpack-launched missiles raining down on the air defense battery barely seemed to deserve the name compared to the four-meter long weapons the Tahni had shot at us, but they did the job. The emplacement's destruction was almost an anticlimax, a distant crump, a gout of flame escaping the edges of the huge machine, and that was it.

Eleven minutes and forty-five seconds.

It was over.

"Status report," I said, my voice a hoarse croak, the coppery tang of blood in my mouth. I found the nipple beside my mouth and took a sip of water, spitting out blood and not caring that it stained the padding beside my chin.

I didn't need to ask. The IFF signals flashing red or faded to black told the story. I just had to focus on that section of the HUD to enlarge it enough to read the names next to the icons, but my eyes didn't seem to want to focus. Or maybe I just didn't want to see.

"Second squad no casualties," Garrity said immediately, as if he wanted to get it out of the way before it sounded spiteful beside the announcements from First.

Graciano didn't answer.

Fuck.

"Umm...," Linebarger stuttered. "I, uh...Bravo Team has lost..." The man sobbed and I nearly did myself, but I had to know. "Larry...Private Kim is gone, Cam. He's just gone."

"This is Dixon." The woman's voice was almost preternaturally calm, calmer than I would have been in her place. "Corporal Graciano and Private Chandra are both KIA. It's just me and Mullany."

"Dixon, Mullany," I directed, "form up with Bravo team. Garrity, your squad has the lead. Keep moving east toward the city until we make contact with Gunny Hayes and his detachment." The words were coming from someone else, someone not inside the blubbering, helpless husk that was Cameron Isaac Alvarez.

Julio Graciano hadn't exactly been a friend. We'd never been that close. But he was a good man, a good Marine who'd never let me down, and if he'd griped it was only because he wanted to take the risks that I hogged for myself. Chandra had never complained, never shirked, always pulled her share of the load. And Larry Kim had been the funniest guy in the room in every bar we ever visited.

And they were gone just like that, with a swipe of the hand of fate, a flick of God's finger, along with Lt. Ackley. And if I sat in this hole and moped about it much longer, the Tahni forces in the military base would have time to get organized and send a coherent force after us, and all the other Marines depending on me would be dead right alongside Ackley and the others.

I hit the jets and led what was left of First squad after Garrity, leaving the dead behind us.

———

"Scotty, do you read me?"

It felt strange broadcasting the message on radio. I was sure we were going to get back-traced and have a missile ride straight up our asses, and I could only hope the Tahni might hesitate to launch on their own city. We were past the deflectors, and though it had seemed to take forever, it had only been a five-minute run at top speed. The pavement of the city streets crunched under the soles of our feet, and it seemed as if that was the only sound for kilometers around other than the persistent howling of what I assumed was the Tahni equivalent of a civil alert siren.

There were no civilians in sight, not so much as a stray dog, or the Tahni equivalent, and I had to assume the Tahni citizenry on Ambergris took emergency preparedness seriously enough to get their asses into a shelter when the sirens sounded. The city had the air of a haunted house, or a post-apocalyptic world, how I imagined parts of China and Russia must have looked after their nuclear war in the mid-Twenty-First Century. Vehicles were abandoned in the middle of the street, street-level doors hung open. I wondered if the twisted spires we passed were businesses, apartments, or government offices of some kind. Or maybe I was imposing differentiations the Tahni didn't employ and they were all three, plus other things I couldn't imagine. Form followed function, and it was easy to forget that just because the Tahni used doors and streets and cars of a sort didn't mean they thought like us.

"Damn it, Scotty," I murmured. I switched to another frequency. "Any Fourth Platoon Delta Detachment elements, this is Echo Detachment. Please respond."

"Cam, is that you?"

Oh, God. Sweet Jesus, I had never heard anything quite as welcome as that voice.

"Vicky, are you okay? What's your status?"

With her reply, my helmet comms were able to pin a location on her IFF, so I didn't have to ask her location. She was, I saw, less than three kilometers away, in what the mapping overlay told me was a manufacturing center.

"I'm good." A pause I interpreted as a shrug. "As good as any of us are. We finished the mission, but we took three KIA and two Wounded in Action with enough suit damage that they can't be moved. We're holed up inside what looks like a factory floor surrounded on three sides by concrete fifty centimeters thick. Cam, Scotty is one of the WIA. The suit has him in a medically induced coma, but I think he'll make it if we can get him up to one of the ships for treatment within the next few hours."

"Shit." I murmured. I'd really been hoping I could find Scotty and turn this whole mess over to him, go back to just worrying about my squad. "Vicky, we lost Lt. Ackley."

Her intake of breath was more than a sigh, not quite a gasp, like a sob choked off by someone strong enough to hold it inside.

"Then you're acting platoon leader," she said.

Unless you want the job. I thought it but didn't say it. It wouldn't be fair and it wouldn't be right. The chain of command had been established before the mission. Ackley, Scotty, then me, then Vicky, Nakamura and Garrity. After that, it went to team leaders and was pretty much academic. If we lost that many people, it would likely mean every Marine for themselves.

"Hold up," I ordered, and my gut twisted at the thought that it was an order. "We'll meet you there in a few."

"Cam!" It was Garrity. We'd formed a staggered column, the streets too narrow for a standard wedge, and he was up close to the front, five hundred meters ahead of me. "We got incoming bogies! Enemy aircraft!"

"Shit, I thought the shuttle blast got all their fighters!"

"Well, it missed two and they're doing a combat patrol over the city!"

I heard the roar almost before his words faded, air-breathing jets screaming a warning like some jungle cat crying in the night.

"Go!" I urged Garrity. "I shared Delta Detachment's location with your comms, get us there soonest. They have a defensible position set up and we need to be under cover now!"

Second squad rumbled forward, the accordion effect of their movement stretching us out then bunching us up before everyone could work out their intervals again, the pattern working its way through me at the center and back to what was left of First squad, just a reinforced fire team now. It all was happening too slow and those fighters were getting too close, visible on my HUD's sensor display now, a pair of pale orange darts on thermal, flying in a tight formation, shooting radar and lidar down thick enough I could have surfed into their cockpits on waves of the stuff. Hunting for us.

Why were they bothering? The main force must have Transitioned by now. Or at least I had to assume they had or this was all for nothing. But if they had, why were the fighters bothering to look for us? Revenge? Or a reasoned attempt to secure their rear before meeting the threat coming in from orbit?

"We have a missile launch!" Garrity warned, his voice breathless.

"Hug the buildings!" I yelled and took my own advice, slamming my shoulder into the concrete siding of twenty-story structure the shape of an obelisk, shaded in a burnt orange color that seemed to go with the Tahni architecture.

The others moved against the building I was taking cover against or the spires and octagons around it, barely two seconds passing before the first of the missiles hit.

I'd braced myself, physically and emotionally, expecting

something as violent and devastating as the missiles from the battery, but these were smaller, something that could fit on the hardpoints of a dual-environment fighter. Not enough to take down a building, but plenty to blow out the doors and windows of the octagonal pyramid they struck, only thirty or forty meters from where I stood.

The pavement shook and heat washed into my cockpit with tendrils of fire reaching out onto the street to devour half a dozen vehicles parked outside the pyramid. The Vigilante was made of sterner stuff and still moved when I told it to, and without its support, I would have likely collapsed. The interior of my suit was a convection oven, even the gel padding against my skin searing hot, and the stream of air across my face from the on-board air filtration system was blistering hot. I tried to take a sip of water and spit it out; it was as hot as bathwater.

"Anyone hit?" I rasped. "Any damage?"

"We're fine, boss," Linebarger told me. "A little cooked, but no one's hurt, no armor deadlined."

"Second is good," Garrity confirmed. "One suit got half-buried, but no real damage."

"Get moving, then. Before they come back around for another pass."

The street had gone from a deserted ghost town to war-torn wreckage in seconds, burning debris scattered for dozens of meters in every direction, the façade of the octagonal pyramid collapsing at street level, vehicles overturned and smoldering like a haphazard attempt at a roadblock. Irritation smoldered as well, not in the street but in my gut. The IFF transponders showed a gaggle instead of a formation, half the detachment clustered together within a few meters of each other and the rest stretched out over three hundred meters.

"Tighten that shit up, Marines," I snapped. "Staggered column, fifty-meter interval."

The detachment, which was about a squad and a half at this point, obeyed in silent embarrassment, falling into something closer to a tactical formation. The irritation wouldn't go away, and I had a suspicion it wasn't dissatisfaction with the sloppy interval discipline as it was a gut feeling I was missing something. The fighters. I couldn't see anything from them, couldn't hear the scream of their turbojets. Why would they make one missile run and give up?

We'd been staying at ground level to avoid attracting attention, but I gave up on caution and blasted up above the rooftops of the nearby buildings, drifting sideways across four intersections, scanning down the streets on optical, thermal and active radar and lidar. I was turning myself into a beacon for enemy troops, but the missile strike showed they knew where we were and if they'd given up on another airstrike...

There.

Outsized humanoid figures, throwing the buildings and vehicles around them into a false perspective, as if the whole city was a 2/3 scale playset for children. They were streaming down three parallel streets, so many of them, way too many. Someone had finally got their shit together and decided to organize that battalion's worth of High Guard troopers. And every single one of them was heading our way.

[26]

Lightning crashed and I flinched away from it, jetting twenty meters to the left as the electron beam sliced through the wall of a tawny-colored obelisk in a chain of steam explosions. I charged forward heedlessly, racing a particle accelerator to a train crossing and destined to lose.

"Second squad, cut right!"

The jets wouldn't be enough, wouldn't let me maneuver tight enough to avoid the tracking path of the beam. I slammed into the side of the building with both feet, my knees and the suit's both flexing to absorb the impact and then exploding into a leap away from the wall, leaving a pattern of spider-web cracks in its exterior layer of stucco with the bounce.

I flipped backwards, a maneuver I couldn't have taught to another Marine with three months to train them, hit the jets to stop myself in mid-air, hovering directly behind the High Guard trooper who'd been targeting me. Plasma speared through the juncture of his shoulder and neck and the battlesuit slumped, still hovering ten meters off the pavement, swaying slowly back and forth, the Tahni inside dead but the jets still triggered and firing. The suit would stay there until the turbines overheated and exploded, unless something knocked him down.

I hoped to not be here that long.

Twenty-one minutes. We'd been on planet twenty-one minutes and lost a squad's worth of troops, killed twice that many High Guard suits, a mecha and sixteen air defense emplacements and all we had to do was find a way to stay alive nine more minutes.

The High Guard troops swarmed through the cross-hatch pattern of streets, trying to cut us off before we could hook up with Vicky's force at the factory.

"I'm sending a squad out to back you up," she'd told me when I reported the incoming troops, but I'd shot the idea down instantly.

"Negative. That would just lead them back to your hiding place and they'd cut us off from reaching it. Then we'd all be screwed. Just stay there and we'll come to you."

I hadn't liked the order, hadn't liked myself for giving it. The people with me could die trying to get to Vicky's stronghold. But they had wounded and *damn it,* someone had to live through this. Maybe we could buy enough time to keep the Tahni off her until reinforcements arrived.

Another High Guard suit was on me as I touched the ground, too close for missiles but firing his electron beamer in a wide swathe, not even taking the time to aim at only ten meters distance. I threw myself to the ground and hit the jets. The crackling stream of actinic fury passed less than a meter over the Vigilante's back before the suit's left shoulder struck the Tahni trooper's legs just below the knee joints and toppled his suit off its feet.

Putting a plasma blast into the chest of the fallen trooper was an afterthought, most of my concentration spent on the big picture. The transponders weren't in a neat formation, but we'd kept together better than I thought we would, hadn't let them scatter us despite the hammer blow from multiple angles. Garrity was down. Whether dead or deadlined, I didn't know and likely wouldn't find out until this was all over, but he was out of the fight. Two more of his squad had taken hits but were still in motion, still firing. Missiles shot from somewhere, one of ours I thought, heading outward into the incoming press of High Guard suits. The Tahni couldn't use them, not as tightly packed as we were with them, but we could use what few we had left against them.

"Keep the spherical building at your backs!" I ordered, spotting the huge, rounded shape just behind the front lines of our clash with the Tahni battalion. "Keep moving, circle around it. First squad, go clockwise, Second counterclockwise. Achebe," I reminded Second squad's former Alpha team leader of his untimely promotion, "that's you. Pull the enemy into your fields of fire and support each other. Don't get caught standing in place and don't run a regular pattern."

We couldn't let the Tahni use their numbers to their full advantage, which meant using the city itself as a weapon, keeping the enemy forces divided by architectural obstacles. I hit the jets again, scooting low over the pavement and ducking behind a parked cargo truck. Electron beams converged from three different angles and ripped the vehicle apart, but I was already moving again.

It wasn't going to work. I might not have been an Academy-trained tactician, but I knew it as certainly as I knew my mother's love. We could keep them busy, whittle their numbers down some, but it wouldn't last long. Maybe with a company full of Henckels led by Covington and Top, we could take on a whole Tahni battalion, but we were a light platoon and already half ragged out.

"Dixon!" I yelled, seeing her starting to drift too far into the open. "Hug the side of the building! Keep the enemy in front of you..."

And that's when they got me, of course. What had Ackley told me? That there was only so much attention to go around, and something had to give, and it was always looking out for yourself.

I remembered the train that had killed the gang hitman back in Trans-Angeles and I imagined this was how he had to have felt. Lights flashed and a deafening bang battered my ears, and then everything went black.

Except I wasn't dead. Everything was simply black, unpowered. I still felt the gel padding around me, felt my orientation. I was on my side, which meant the suit was on its side. Not a single system was working and every touch on the controls gained me no response. The interface cables were still plugged in, but nothing was coming in nor going out.

Part of me wanted to stay right here, hope the Tahni would miss me, would assume I was dead. It would be a perfect excuse not just to live through the fight but to not have to *watch* the rest of it, not have to watch the others die. No one would think the worse of me. No one could prove I wasn't unconscious, concussed. No one but me.

I sucked in a breath and let it out in a curse, feeling around beside my right hand for the emergency ejection switch. It was an old friend, but one I'd hoped to never meet again. It still worked, powered by its own integral battery rather than the reactor in my backpack, and I nearly fell out the side of the suit's chest as the plastron swung open wide. I held on long enough to work my right arm up into the helmet and yank loose my interface cables, then tumbled out to the pavement.

I'd been in a womb of darkness and silence, and now I was born into a world of violence, heat, and thunder. Giants flew and clashed and rained incandescent energy out of the sky all around me and I wanted more than anything to get away. I ducked back into the chest of the Vigilante and pulled out a compact pulse carbine and a chest pack of reloads, then ran for the cover of what looked like some sort of public transportation, a cross between a cargo truck and a bus with an open upper deck. The driver compartment of the vehicle had been ripped away by a blast from either a plasma cannon or an electron beamer, the wound blackened like someone had attempted to cauterize it to stop the bleeding.

I was panting, gasping, and I tried to control my breathing. My actions were automatic, drilled into me time after time in escape and evasion classes. I slipped the vest on, the full magazines hanging in the pouches at the front of it weighing me down like an anchor, then buckled it across the front of my chest. The carbine was ugly, boxy, utilitarian, with a folding stock and a simple, durable optical sight and I'd fired it once in the last two years. It fired high-powered laser pulses fed by HyperExplosive cartridges and wouldn't so much as leave a nasty burn mark on a battlesuit's paint job, but it was nice as a security blanket and better than harsh language. Maybe.

I pulled the earpiece from the datalink on my belt and stuck it in place, then edged out to the corner of the bus and peeked around it. If the battle had been hard to track with IFF transponders, a mapping overlay and a HUD, it was Chaos and Old Night now. I could barely even look at it without afterimages blinding me from the discharge of energy weapons too fierce for a dismounted soldier to face.

"Achebe, do you read?" I called over my 'link. "Achebe, this is Cam, do you read?"

Nothing. She might not have heard me, or she might be dead, or she might just be too busy to answer. I tried again.

"Vicky, can you hear me?"

"Oh, my God! Cam, you're alive! I saw your transponder go dark..."

"I'm out of my suit and hiding behind a bus. Someone has to take charge of the platoon."

"Hang on," she said. "Stay there as long as you can. I'm on my way."

I wanted to argue with her, tell her she needed to worry about the platoon, not me, but I didn't want to chance another transmission. And, if I'm being brutally honest, I wanted someone to come for me. I'd been prepared to die inside my armor, expecting it, at peace with the idea. This was different, different even than Brigantia. There, I'd been out in the wilderness, alone and afraid but also away from the enemy. Here, I was a toddler wandering through a gunfight carrying a plastic toy.

A Vigilante thundered past me only five meters off the ground, its jets sweeping a hot wind across my face, as three High Guard suits trampled broken pavement and bits of debris from the surrounding buildings, chasing after the Marine Drop Trooper with steady, implacable persistence. Electron beamers discharged only twenty or thirty meters away and I jumped away from the bus I was using for cover, crying out as static electricity crackled off the metal in its body and snapped at the exposed skin on my face and neck.

I scuffled backwards against the wall of the building, nearly tripping over a jagged slab of concrete, and tried to follow the Vigilante with my eyes. The electron blasts hadn't hit it, but it was back on the ground, spinning on a heel, firing its plasma gun. I knew it was coming and I squeezed my eyes shut and even then, the raw fury of a star created purple afterimages in my retinae. I'd never heard the report of a plasma cannon outside of the suit and it was so much louder than I thought it would be, a physical blow against my chest and sinuses. More flashes and another peal of thunder and I knew an electron beamer had shot back.

When I opened my eyes, one of the High Guard suits had collapsed to the ground, half its chest armor burned away, while the Vigilante stood immobile, a blackened hole through its helmet. Claws of despair squeezed my chest as I wondered who it had been. Was it a friend? Someone I knew or just a name and a face I could barely recall? And all I could do was sit here and watch, helpless to even avenge their death.

The surviving High Guard trooper turned my way, halting in mid-step as it spotted me, and I thought maybe I wouldn't have to feel guilty about the death of my fellow Marine for very long. I stared into the glowing maw of the thing's particle accelerator for just an instant too long before I tried to run, ducking back behind the bus and heading out the other end of the vehicle.

I'm just one guy with a rifle and no armor. Maybe he won't bother firing on me.

He bothered.

I didn't remember the light or the sound or the concussion, and I was fairly certain I'd blacked out for a second, but when my senses returned, I was lying flat on my back about three meters from where I'd been a second ago and the bus was in three, separate, burning pieces across the street. I blinked away bright flashes obscuring my vision and tried to decide if I was already dead or if I should bother to try to get up. Nothing seemed broken, but my fatigues were curling smoke and I could smell burning hair. Since I didn't have much on my head, I wondered if my eyebrows were still there.

I tried to roll over onto my side, but the High Guard suit was lumbering toward me, seeming twenty meters tall instead of just four, the spiked sole of its boot looming, ready to stamp downward. Something grey and huge and moving fast slammed into the Tahni with the echoing roar of jump-jets and the High Guard suit toppled onto its back with a Vigilante atop it. The Marine battlesuit pummeled the Tahni with one left-handed punch after another, the bang-crunch of an industrial press ringing off each blow. The Vigilante straightened, raising its leg and stomping into the head of the Tahni armor until the helmet was nearly flattened, and I wasn't sure if the choice to beat the enemy pilot to death was to avoid firing an energy weapon so close to me or simply out of pure wrath.

But I knew who was inside the armor.

The chest plastron swung downward and Vicky Sandoval jumped to the pavement, rushing to my side and checking me over quickly.

"Are you okay?" she asked. "Any burn-throughs? Broken bones?"

"I'm all right," I insisted, my voice stronger than I thought it would be. My head was spinning and I thought I might have a concussion. "What the hell are you doing, Vicky? Get back in your armor! You're gonna get yourself killed!"

"There's too many of them," she said, shaking her head. She didn't seem frightened but I sure was. "They're all over the place...there's no way out of the city. Anyway, didn't I say if we pulled off the mission, I might do something stupid to save your ass?"

She grabbed me by the front of my tactical vest and pulled me into a kiss, long and lingering, and the sounds of energy weapons and explosions and carnage faded into the background with one, last opportunity for human connection. And it stayed faded. I frowned, pulling away, getting my feet underneath me.

"Wait," I said. "Do you hear that?"

"Hear what"

"Yeah, exactly." I used her shoulder to pull myself up and

realized I'd held onto my carbine somehow. I hadn't even felt it hanging from its sling around my shoulder.

No, there was something. Something above the silence, high-pitched and screaming...and coming closer with each second. Lightning crashed out of a clear blue sky and struck at something less than a kilometer away in the city, then a second bolt, a third, explosions rolling outward from where the strikes landed. Out of the mid-day sky, flying in formation, four assault shuttles emerged, sharp-edged daggers with wings. Four more on their heels, smaller and higher, but still visible.

Recon had done its job and taken down the laser.

The Fleet was here.

The deflectors would still be up, but they covered mostly the spaceport and the base, leaving most of the city open, probably on the theory that their civilians would have time to reach shelter before any attack. Which they had, but a whole battalion of their armor was in the city and it apparently hadn't escaped the notice of those assault shuttle pilots, God bless 'em.

Missiles rained down, a hailstorm to accompany the lightning, and I could actually see the cluster of warheads splitting up in mid-air, each finding its own individual target, their detonations a chain of hand-clap loud in the distance. And each Tahni battlesuit they struck would die, along with the trooper inside it.

"Dropships," Vicky breathed, pointing.

She was right. Ugly and bulbous and ungainly compared to the assault shuttles, they looked beautiful to me.

"Get back in your suit, Vicky," I told her. "Get on the comms and let the Skipper know where we are, and get our wounded a dustoff."

"You know what this means, don't you?" she asked me, grinning as she climbed back into the Vigilante through the open chest plastron. "We did it, Cam. *You* did it. All of them." She pointed upward at the dropships and shuttles. "You saved them."

I nodded, not bothering to argue with her. Then I sat down on the street and hugged my legs to myself, thinking of Graciano, Garrity, and Lt. Ackley and trying not to let myself cry because it wasn't going to end with a few tears and I just didn't have the luxury of uncontrollable sobbing right now. There was still work to do.

We'd saved them...but we hadn't saved them all.

[27]

I ran a hand over the surface of the clear tank of biotic fluid, watching the floating, insensate form of Scotty Hayes encased in it, breathing hard and deep, the oxygenated fluid filling his lungs and keeping him alive while the nanites it supported repaired his internal injuries.

"I don't know how I'm going to tell him," I admitted. "I don't know how I'm going to tell him Lt. Ackley is gone."

Vicky squeezed my arm, leaned her shoulder against mine.

"The docs said he'll be there for a few days. They'll call us when they bring him out."

I glanced around and saw the medical technicians shooting us dirty looks for taking up space in their sickbay, and decided that was Vicky's gentle way of telling me we should leave.

"What about the others?" I wondered. I nodded towards the other two occupied tanks, housing the platoon's most seriously wounded. There were other, minor injuries that had been treated immediately after we'd been shuttled back to the *Iwo Jima* thirty hours ago, but only the three of them had been seriously hurt enough to need the tanks. The Recon Marines had, ironically enough, suffered no serious casualties. Apparently, things had been so confused and hectic that the Tahni had never sent troops to check out the defense laser and the Recon element had squatted in place, waiting for an assault that never came.

"Bastian should be out in twelve hours or so," she told me. "Ekaterina a little less. Scotty had it the worst. He's lucky he made it to the sickbay. Come on," she urged me, hand still gripping my arm. "Let's get out of here and let the docs do their work."

We were back in T-space, which meant there was shipboard gravity, so we walked out instead of floating or clomping along in magnetic ship boots. I'd been in the sickbay for a couple of hours myself when we'd first arrived, just a check to make sure I hadn't sustained any major injuries, which I hadn't. Even my concussion had proven minor enough not to require microsurgery to repair the damage. I'd felt like a fraud in there next to Scotty and the others.

I let Vicky lead me to the lift banks and didn't bother to watch her work the controls. I assumed she was taking us back to the berthing compartments, since it was close to lights-out. We were sharing a compartment since there was no one around in our platoon of higher rank to give us shit about it and no one else cared.

"They didn't even lose a missile cutter on the attack," she told me. "The Tahni were so confused about the shuttle explosion at the port and the freighter destroying the orbital defense platform, they recalled all their ships and weren't in position when the Fleet Transitioned."

"Yeah," I acknowledged, not bothering to remind her she'd told me this twice already. She was trying to make me feel better about Lt. Ackley and I didn't have the heart to tell her it wasn't working. "I guess Fleet owes us one now."

"Sgt. Alvarez," Top's voice buzzed in the earpiece of my 'link. "You there?"

"Yes, Top," I said, hand going to my ear automatically. "I was just heading back to my quarters. What's up?"

"The Skipper wants to see you in his compartment before you hit the sack. Before you ask, he didn't say why and probably wouldn't want me to tell you if he had."

"Yes, Top," I said, my lip curling upward. For some reason, the more combat I saw, the more I appreciated Top's attitude. "I'll be there."

"Trouble?" Vicky asked me, an eyebrow shooting up. I wondered if she was worried Top knew about us and was going to chew me out about it.

"I don't think so. The Skipper wants to see me before lights-out. Probably wants a one-on-one debrief on the mission."

We'd had an informal AAR on the ground, just a quick info-dump so he could report to higher, but I knew Captain Covington would want a more detailed version for his official report.

Vicky glanced around, I thought making sure no one else in the lift was watching, then kissed me on the cheek.

"Don't be too long," she warned me, winking. "I'm still wiped out and I won't be able to wait up."

A laugh welled up inside me for the first time since we'd dusted off from Ambergris and I let it escape, not caring what the Fleet technicians with us in the lift car thought of it. We were just jackhead weirdos to them, anyway.

The Skipper's compartment was identical to everyone else's in the company except he didn't have to share it with anyone, and I was only able to find it because it was marked on the roster available on the ship's net via my 'link. We were on this ship so often, you'd think we'd have permanent compartments assigned, but I guess that isn't the way the military works.

"Alvarez reporting, sir," I said into the intercom beside the door.

"Come."

Covington was sitting on his bunk, tapping at the screen of a tablet with a stylus, and he didn't look up immediately, so I waited in silence. I knew the man well enough now that I figured he wouldn't keep me waiting just to be a dick. What he was working on must be important.

He tapped at it for another few seconds before he touched a control and set the tablet down, finally meeting my eyes. There was a melancholy to his expression, though perhaps it was just exhaustion. I was fairly certain he hadn't slept since before the mission.

"Have a seat, Alvarez," he told me, nodding toward a chair that folded down out of the bulkhead across from the bunk.

The chair was intensely uncomfortable, though not as uncomfortable as Covington's cool regard.

"This could have gone very badly, Alvarez. You understand that, right?"

"Yes, sir," I acknowledged. "There were times down there where I thought it *had* gone very badly."

He grunted and I wasn't sure if he was agreeing that was a good point or expressing skepticism that I actually understood.

"My point," he clarified, "is that there's a reason most military op plans are kept as simple as possible. Your plan, daring and ultimately successful as it was, was also vulnerable to single point failure. You know the term?"

I nodded.

"It means that there were points during the execution of the plan where one thing going wrong would have caused a cascade failure, bringing down every other part of the plan." I'd read the definition at NCO school and it was one of the definitions that kept cropping up in the continuing education packets I had to fill out and send in every few weeks. "But the upside of the plan," I added, "was that most of the single points of failure would have allowed us to abort without affecting the main body of the attack."

"Which is why I backed it. But I wanted to make sure you understood that we won't be trying to pull off this same tactic in system after system. I wouldn't be surprised if the Tahni have already changed their security procedures."

"Yes, sir." I shrugged. "Next time, we'll just have to come up with something better."

"Yes." He slapped the tablet gently against the palm of his hand. "Next time." He held up the tablet. "One of the unenviable tasks I have as a Company Commander is writing the next of kin. Thanks to your idea and your platoon's execution of the plan, I don't have nearly as many of those notes to write, but this one seems harder than usual."

"Lt. Ackley," I guessed.

"She was a hell of an officer," he said, nodding. "And she's going to be difficult to replace. In the short term, I'm putting my XO 1st Lt. Bradley in charge of Fourth Platoon until you get back."

I blinked, confused.

"Get back, sir?" I repeated. "Where am I going?"

"Things have changed, Alvarez," he said, and I wondered if this was part of his answer or if he was ignoring my question. "When the war began, our officer corps was filled from the ranks of Academy graduates. But the acceptance standards and graduation rates were allocated well before the war and, as you can imagine, the needs of the military have changed in the last few years." He eyed the tablet balefully. "Because our junior officers keep getting themselves killed. The Academy can't keep up with the demand, so the Space Fleet and the Marine Corps have each set up their own Officer's Candidate School back on

Inferno. You'll be gone six months, and when you return, I want you leading Fourth Platoon."

"Me?" I shook my head, perhaps in denial as much as confusion. "An officer? Why not Scotty? I mean, Gunnery Sgt. Hayes?"

"Gunnery Sgt. Hayes is a damn good Marine," he acknowledged. "But that doesn't mean he'd make a good officer. Some men and women are NCOs and some are officers and I think perhaps Hayes is as high in rank as he's ever going to get. He does his job well and has no ambition to do more, which is perfectly fine, since the Corps desperately needs good platoon sergeants."

"But Skip, I'm barely competent to be a squad leader!" I was bordering on insubordination and I knew it, but I couldn't restrain myself. I was desperate. "Lt. Ackley was talking about having me busted for that stunt at the flight line not that long ago!"

"Let's save the theatrics," Covington said, the corner of his mouth turning up as if he could see right through me, "and get down to the heart of the thing. You don't want the responsibility. You don't want to send men and women to their deaths knowing you won't always be able to follow and take the same risks."

"No, sir," I admitted readily. "I don't. Maybe after some more time as a squad leader...."

"Understandable. Particularly given what you've just been through." His expression hardened. "Unfortunately, the demands of the war and the needs of the Marine Corps outweigh our individual wants and needs. I can't order you to do this. It's volunteer only. But if it's not you, it'll wind up being someone less qualified. I'm counting on you, Cam."

And suddenly, I could see Lt. Ackley's face, her words echoing inside my head.

Because it has to get done. And if I don't do it, someone else will have to. Maybe someone who doesn't understand how to forget about themselves and take care of their Marines first.

And I stood, though tons of melancholy and regret tried to hold me down, the thought of the men and women who'd died, the thought that this would very likely mean the end of Vicky and me.

I came to attention and saluted.

"Aye aye, sir."

WHAT'S NEXT IN THE SERIES?

CONTACT FRONT
KINETIC STRIKE
DANGER CLOSE
DIRECT FIRE

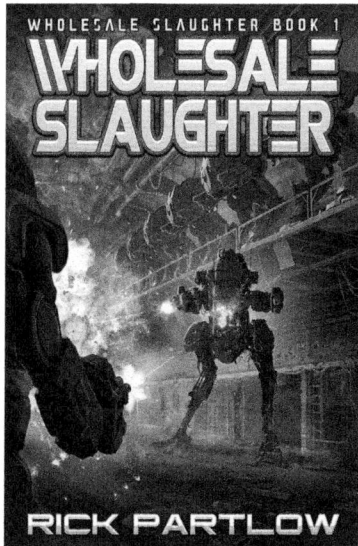

FROM THE PUBLISHER

Thank you for reading *Kinetic Strike,* book two in Drop Trooper.

We hope you enjoyed it as much as we enjoyed bringing it to you. We just wanted to take a moment to encourage you to review the book on Amazon and Goodreads. Every review helps further the author's reach and, ultimately, helps them continue writing fantastic books for us all to enjoy.

If you liked this book, check out the rest of our catalogue at www.aethonbooks.com. To sign up to receive a FREE collection from some of our best authors as well as updates regarding all new releases, visit www.aethonbooks.com/sign-up.

JOIN THE STREET TEAM! Get advanced copies of all our books, plus other free stuff and help us put out hit after hit.

SEARCH ON FACEBOOK:
AETHON STREET TEAM

RICK PARTLOW is that rarest of species, a native Floridian. Born in Tampa, he attended Florida Southern College and graduated with a degree in History and a commission in the US Army as an Infantry officer.

His lifelong love of science fiction began with Have Space Suit---Will Travel and the other Heinlein juveniles and traveled through Clifford Simak, Asimov, Clarke and on to William Gibson, Walter Jon Williams and Peter F Hamilton. And somewhere, submerged in the worlds of others, Rick began to create his own worlds.

He has written a ton of books in many different series, and his short stories have been included in seven different anthologies.

He currently lives in central Florida with his wife, two children and a willful mutt of a dog. Besides writing and reading science fiction and fantasy, he enjoys outdoor photography, hiking and camping.

www.rickpartlow.com

f

Printed in Dunstable, United Kingdom